Anna pushed the door gently. Something resisted, and she heard a soft cracking noise. She pushed harder and the door flew open. Festoons of clear tape hung from the top of the doorway like ragged bunting. Gas hissed from the fireplace; but there was no fire. Anna jumped to the window and tackled the catch and the sash. She struggled to pull the bottom half of the window up, but it wouldn't move. Then, with a great effort, she got the top half down. It stuck half-way, but it was enough. A gust of cold wind and rain blew into the room. She whirled back to the fireplace and turned off the gas-tap, her sweating fingers slipping on the pockmarked metal.

Mrs Halloran, still holding the baby and flanked by the two girls, stood gaping in the doorway.

'Get rid of your cigarette,' Anna shouted at her. 'Put it out. And get the kids out of here!'

No one moved.

'Now!' she yelled. 'Hurry!'

Anna turned back to the bed. The young man was lying on his back, fully clothed, his head turned upwards. She clenched her teeth as some atavistic horror gripped her, and felt his wrist, trying to calm herself and stop her hand shaking. His skin was cold and clammy. She backed away from the bed to the door, shouting, 'Have you got a phone?'

There was no reply. She went to the kitchen. She repeated, 'Have you got a phone?'

Mrs Halloran cleared her throat and asked in a strangled voice, 'Is he dead?'

'Yes, I'm afraid he is,' Anna said quietly.

DUPE

LIZA CODY

BANTAM BOOKS
NEW YORK · TORONTO · LONDON · SYDNEY · AUCKLAND

For Angus

DUPE

A Bantam Crime Line Book/published by arrangement with Charles
Scribner's Sons

PUBLISHING HISTORY
Scribner's edition published 1981
Bantam edition/October 1992

ISBN 0-553-29641-8

Published simultaneously in the United States and Canada

CHAPTER 1

· · · · · · · · ·

THE storm had blown itself out during the night, leaving the morning sky pale and laundered. The roofs were glistening, and Anna, looking down, could see part of the garden. She held a mug of fiercely hot and strong coffee. The grass was unkempt and speckled with weeds and fallen leaves from the plane tree by the end wall. It was an ordinary London house just north of Holland Park Avenue.

A few minutes later she took her coat and bag from the hook on the door and left the flat.

Downstairs Bea Price was also leaving for work, and while Selwyn was easing a damp *Guardian* from the letter-box she stopped and lifted two dripping milk bottles from the doorstep.

'Hello.' Selwyn turned and saw Anna waiting for the crowd in the doorway to clear.

'Another one off to hew wood and draw water.' Bea passed him the two bottles, which he clasped wetly to his chest, leaving dank marks on his grey cardigan. He still had his pyjamas on. Sometimes he wore an old hacking jacket over them, but mostly, as today, it was something knitted and faintly disreputable.

'Well, don't let me stop you,' he said, stumbling backwards as the toe of his left sock somehow caught under the heel of his right foot. Selwyn often had problems with co-ordination before breakfast.

'And what's more,' he went on, annoyed with himself, 'I want to talk to you about your blasted cat.'

'Not my blasted cat!' said Anna. Bea was still on the doorstep. There was no clear run to the road.

'Well, you encourage it. You feed it.'

'Off and on,' she admitted.

'More off than on,' Selwyn snorted. 'If its yowling round my door yesterday was anything to go by.'

'Oh, Selwyn,' his wife sighed. 'You do fuss!' She might have come out of a completely different household, so neat was she in her fawn tailored suit.

'Well, it's true,' Selwyn grumbled. 'Can't you stop it coming in?'

'You know I can't,' Anna went on, 'but you could always get on to Chaterjee about the skylight. If that were mended . . .'

'Now you're being cruel,' Selwyn interrupted. 'I'm just warning, that's all, or one of these days that moggie's going to find himself nailed by the throat to your front door.'

'Now there's cruel, if you like,' said Bea affectionately. 'Bye-bye, dear. Don't work too hard.' At last she started down the steps to the road.

'Fat chance,' murmured Anna, following.

'I heard that,' roared Selwyn, 'and don't you think I didn't.'

'I meant you to, and don't you think I didn't,' Anna called back, and Selwyn, rumpled and ready for a fight, banged the door.

The two women walked to the end of the road together.

'He doesn't mean it really,' Bea said placidly. 'It's the artistic temperament, of course,' she went on proudly, and still, after seven years of an unlikely marriage, a little surprised.

'Of course,' Anna agreed automatically, chagrined as always to find herself treating Bea more as one of her mother's generation than as someone only half a dozen years older than herself. But the gap was too great to bridge, especially on a cold Monday morning.

At Holland Park Avenue they parted, and Anna crossed Holland Park, making for Kensington High Street. Squirrels darted over her path in sharp, furtive runs through the wet leaves.

Brierly Security was housed in one of those offices few people knew existed above the raucous shops of Kensington High Street. A small black and white plate in one of the recessed doorways stated simply 'MARTIN BRIERLY'. On the third floor at the top of the stairs was a small office with a counter door. On the counter was a sign reading 'Reception', and inside was a stool and a small switchboard. This was Beryl's lair, and, later on, after morning coffee and between numerous tea breaks, this was where Beryl could be found, probably painting her fingernails.

Martin Brierly was pathologically secretive, but in so far as such a man can confide, he confided in Beryl. It was she who made out the duty rosters, passed messages and doled out expense sheets. A narrow doorway led from her office to Brierly's, and only she and Brierly had a key to it.

The office was empty now, so Anna went straight to the rec-room, taking off her coat and shivering. John Crocker was the only one there. The kettle was on, and a one-bar electric heater was fighting a losing battle with the draught.

'Morning, Johnny.' She hung up her coat and breathed warmly on her knuckles, sitting down to an unopened *Daily Mail* in front of her.

'Where is everyone? Or am I early?'

'That'll be the day.' Johnny Crocker had his back to her, and was carefully spooning powdered coffee into five mugs. 'No, Bernie's giving evidence today, so he won't be in this morning. Don't know about anyone else.'

Anna read the headlines. The kettle boiled. John filled two cups and put the kettle back on the gas to simmer. On Anna's mug was a drawing of an emaciated cockerel balanced precariously on a football. She studied it, and then added two lumps and a dash of milk to the contents.

'Look, why don't you give me the middle pages?' John said. It was his paper. 'You only read the outside, anyway; Crime and Scandal on the front, Sport at the back. You should leave the serious news to the grown-ups.'

'Sorry.' She handed him the middle pages.

A single bulb lighting the room shone on their bent heads. The small window was no more efficient at admitting light than it was at excluding the cold.

Tim Baker and Philip Maitland arrived together. Two more mugs were filled and two more papers spread on the table. It was 8.45.

Beryl came clattering in five minutes later, wreathed in Miss Dior and rabbit fur. The atmosphere immediately became both more frivolous and busy.

'One for Tim, two for Johnny, none for Phil or Anna.' She passed out the mail. 'No conference this morning, you lucky people.' She pinned the day's duty roster on the chipboard.

'What's on?' Tim asked.

Phil, who was nearest, craned his neck round and said, 'Oh shit, it's you and me for the Earls Court Road, lifting lifters. Johnny, you jammy sod, you've landed the Royal Ken, and you, young Anna, have an appointment with the Pope at ten.'

'What about?' Anna asked. 'Not another missing minor, I hope. That's all I ever get—kids and scent-counter security.'

'Well, you're not big enough for banks,' Johnny teased. 'Not cute enough for clubs and too cute for pubs.'

'Oh, don't start that again. Flipping heck. Sometimes you'd think this was a society for Victorian gents.'

'Okay, okay.' Johnny had risen and was shrugging his wide shoulders into his massive camelhair coat. 'Only you should learn to swear more potently if you want the

Equal Opportunities Board to consider you seriously for the Man's World.'

'Be good now, boys.' Beryl was a lady who bloomed most richly in all male company. Her attitude to Anna was in consequence somewhat grudging. So Anna was forced to ask again.

'Do you know what I'm wanted for?'

'Search me,' Beryl sniffed. But Anna, who had learned a thing or two in the past year, got up and made Beryl's coffee for her. Milky and with one lump. Beryl would take it back to her office, but for a moment she lingered.

'A new client, that I can say, generously passed on by one of the Commander's little friends at the club.' 'The club' meant the Metropolitan Police force. 'And since you're not on till ten'—Beryl became head prefect again—'you might give last week's expense sheets a going over. Your figures don't add up, and I can't read your writing. Oh, and do something about your hair, can't you? The Commander says you look like a polytechnic student.'

CHAPTER 2

· · · · · · · · ·

BERYL always called Martin Brierly the Commander. She was the only one who did, and although it seemed unlikely that he deserved the title Beryl stuck to it. He was a large, soft-looking man, with an almost perfectly spherical head and small, round features.

'Sit yourself down, Miss Lee.' He was looking out of the window on to the High Street. This one was double-glazed. His desk-top was bare except for a blotter and an old-fashioned silver pen-set. He pulled a long chain from his waistcoat pocket, and, choosing one of the keys at the end of it, unlocked a drawer and extracted a single brown folder. Then he relocked the drawer and resumed his position by the window.

Without referring to the contents of the folder he said, 'Mr and Mrs Jackson, Thomas and Susan, from Wiltshire. Not, shall we say, top drawer, no, definitely not top drawer, but . . . how shall I put it? Plenty of shoe leather.'

Unexpectedly he laughed, throwing his head back and making little snapping movements with his jaw.

'Motor-cars,' he went on, recovering, 'new and

second-hand, commercial vehicles, buying and selling
thereof. Large house, suburban baroque, I shouldn't wonder. Swimming pool and sauna. Some people don't know
this is England. Same old story, of course. Father comes
up the boot-strap way, children don't know they're born.
Always the same with new money. Are you following me
so far?'

'Missing minor?' asked Anna resignedly.

'Don't anticipate, young lady.' Brierly's tone was re-
proving. 'No, as a matter of fact there is no minor. The
daughter in question was twenty-two, and is not missing
but dead. As of one month ago. Late night, driving along
Cranford Lane near the airport. She went off the road and
hit a concrete post.'

'Anything unusual?'

'Police say no. But Mr Jackson has a bee in his bonnet. Insisted on an autopsy. Nothing found, of course. But
the man was making such a nuisance of himself that the
police told him to go private. Put him on to me.'

'And?'

'And we'll listen to him. Go through the motions.
See what's what. I don't know any more than I've told
you, so we'll just have to wait and see.'

He fell silent and continued to stare out of the window, leaving Anna to make the best of a hard chair and
the three Audubon prints, which were the only decoration
in a remarkably sparse office.

'I will of course conduct this initial interview.' Every
briefing Anna had attended had without fail been preceded
by a declaration of exclusive rights of some sort or another. 'Clients like to feel confident that their problems
will be handled with discretion and experience. Tact, Miss
Lee, is a virtue acquired with years. You live and learn,
Miss Lee. Live and learn.'

Anna was unsure whether Brierly's tact with clients
was a success or not, but she felt his manner with employees could do with improvement. He had not glanced
at her once since she had come into the room, and had
addressed all his remarks to the curtain-rail.

'Bit of a fly-boy, anyway, I shouldn't wonder.' Brierly's voice was again bouncing back from the double-
glazing. 'He didn't sound too enchanted with our friends
at the Met. And of course it's hard to imagine how anyone
can make the kind of pile he appears to have honestly these
days. There are a thousand shady byways in his business
for a clever man. I hear he even owns half a racehorse.'

The sneer in his voice was unmistakable now. Mr
Jackson unwittingly embodied more than one of Martin
Brierly's prejudices. This was not hard to do; Anna had
never heard him speak with unreserved approval of anyone, except perhaps Erwin Rommel.

Beryl knocked, and poked her head round the door.

'Mr and Mrs Jackson, sir,' she said in her confidential, private-secretary-to-boss voice.

'Ah, thank you, Miss Doyle.' Brierly rose and moved
round the desk. He condescended to meet clients face to
face.

The two men shook hands. Brierly was the taller, but
Jackson gave the impression of power. His muscles seemed
to be bunched and tense under his coat, and it was Brierly
who disengaged his hand with the most relief. Neither of
the women were introduced.

'A pot of tea, I think,' Brierly called as Beryl closed
the door.

'Good of you to come all this way,' began Brierly
when everyone had sat down. Anna had bobbed up and
down again like a schoolgirl at assembly.

'Well now . . .' Jackson was sitting on the edge of
his seat, his head thrust forward aggressively.

'I hope your journey was not too uncomfortable.'
Brierly did not like his flow of urbanity to be interrupted.
'Fog can be most inconvenient at this time of year, don't
you think?'

'The wife and I spent the night in town,' Mr Jackson
said abruptly.

'We wanted to be quite clear in our minds this morning,' Mrs Jackson said. Her West Country accent was
heavily restrained by elocution lessons. She was a woman
in early middle-age. Without her heavy makeup and dis-

tinctive auburned hair, she would be very plain. But she was expensively dressed and held herself upright in her chair.

'Just so,' said Brierly, glancing at her almost furtively. 'Well, I'm sure we could all do with clear minds.'

'The wife and I wanted to get this business sorted out personally, like,' Jackson started again. 'We want satisfaction, and if we can't get it from the police, we're prepared to pay for it. But we expect satisfaction.'

'Just so,' repeated Brierly. 'No stone unturned. That's what we're here for.'

Jackson's chin was jutting even further forward. 'Look, my daughter is dead, and we didn't expect to come to the police with our reasonable doubts and be treated like country bumpkins who don't know an apple from Adam. I've been around, you know. I know a bit of what's what.'

'Ah, tea,' said Brierly. 'Miss Doyle, would you pour? And after that, no interruptions.'

The tea was poured and Beryl left with heavy-footed discretion. Mr Jackson seemed to take note of Anna for the first time.

'And who's this?' he said. 'You assured me over the phone that this business would be confidential.'

'Biscuit?' offered Brierly. 'No? Ah yes, forgive me. Mr and Mrs Jackson, this is Miss Lee. Let me assure you again that your affair will be treated in the strictest confidence. All my employees are hand-picked. And I'm sure you will appreciate that an organization of this size cannot be run by one man alone. So while the, er, leg-work may be carried out by an investigator of my choosing, let me assure you that I will personally supervise and co-ordinate this case.'

'That's as may be.' Jackson was unappeased. 'But this is just a slip of a girl. And it doesn't look to me as if you're taking this too seriously, Mr Brierly.'

'We take all our cases with the utmost seriousness,' Brierly said weightily. 'Miss Lee has spent five years in the police force prior to her employment here, and subsequently has undergone the special training needed for the unique requirements of this organization.'

'Well, she looks a bit young to me,' said Jackson, unwilling to give up his objection.

'That,' said Brierly, 'I think you will agree, is in this case an advantage. But please don't doubt her ability. You have, anyway, my assurance that I will oversee every step of this enquiry.'

'I'm sure she'll do very nicely.' Mrs Jackson placed a placatory glove on her husband's arm.

Anna, who had said nothing during this exchange, recognized wryly, that, while Brierly appeared to be defending her, he was in fact vindicating Brierly Security. Privately, she knew that his opinion of her ability did not differ much from Jackson's.

'Well, since, we're all agreed.' Brierly was confident he had smothered the opposition. 'Perhaps you could tell us as much as you can about your daughter.'

Jackson began. His daughter Deirdre was the eldest of three children. There were two brothers much younger. As the first-born and only girl, he admitted, she might have been a little spoiled.

'For a long time,' his wife added, 'we thought she'd be the only one. So Tom went out of his way to give her every advantage. He doted on her.'

Mr Jackson did not disagree. She had been the apple of his eye. She had been sent to private schools. There had been music lessons and dancing classes, the best that money could buy. And in the holidays she had gone everywhere with her father. He had taken her to see clients. To the races. Even on trips abroad.

'A proper little princess,' Mrs Jackson described her.

Then, when young Deirdre was just fifteen, the first of the Jackson's two sons had been born. At first it had made no difference. But when the second son came, and the first, Jerry, was nearly three years old, it had become apparent that he was an exceptionally bright child.

'And Deirdre was never that clever,' Mrs Jackson told them. 'Not academic, anyhow. And what with little Jerry being so forward and all, well, Tom started to take more notice of him.'

'She never lacked attention,' Jackson protested.

'No,' Mrs Jackson agreed, 'but she wasn't the only pebble on the beach any more. And she changed, Mr Brierly. You wouldn't credit it.'

She had left school after a quarrel with her parents. The Jacksons had hoped she would go on with her studies. University had never been a realistic hope, but they had wanted her to be educated as they had never been.

'Accountancy, or Business Studies,' Jackson said wistfully, 'She was always good at figures. She could have been a great help to me. But she just didn't want to know.'

She had become sullen and argumentative, staying out late, not getting up in the mornings.

'The only thing she showed an interest in,' said Jackson, 'was films. Plain star-struck she was, and I think that's what caused the trouble—as if there wasn't enough of that already. She suddenly wanted to come to London and learn acting. I wasn't standing for that, of course. You don't waste good money on teaching a girl to play-act, do you? There's no future in it. Just a bit of glamour when you're young if you're lucky.'

There was a sudden silence in the room. Outside it had begun to rain.

'I wish we'd let her, now,' Mrs Jackson said, echoing Anna's thoughts. There had not been much future for Deirdre, anyway. A little glamour might have gone a long way.

Mr Jackson hurried on. 'Well, then she decided she wanted to go to a film school and learn to be a director. There were rows about that, I can tell you. In the end we compromised, and she started a photographic course at one of the local techs. She seemed to do all right there to begin with. I bought her a good camera, and she brought back some very nice snaps, I thought. But then she got herself involved with one of the teachers there in the audio-visual department, and he encouraged her silliness. So it started all over again.'

It was, Anna thought, a fairly normal description of

play in the game of Happy Families. But looking at the Jacksons, sitting there, so solid and yet so bewildered, she realized that as a family they had been divided by more than years. They had, at their own wish, brought up a middle-class daughter with middle-class dreams who could not see life as a simple matter of making the best of things and bringing home the bacon. She could not even share their own dreams of money and making good, for those had been realized, probably before she was born. What could Deirdre have done but take the money and run?

'When she'd been in London a few months,' Mrs Jackson was going on, 'I went up to see her, took her some new towels and things. But she wasn't a bit pleased to see me. She seemed sort of embarrassed. She was living in a bed-sitter then. We had some friends in Peckham who would have gladly taken her in. She had the address, but she'd never even looked them up. She didn't offer so much as a cup of tea. I wanted to take her out for a meal and shopping, but she said she had a date.'

'After that,' Mr Jackson put in, 'I told my wife not to go again. I could see how hurt she'd been. And so in the last three years we've seen her, what? Three times? No more. She seemed all right, she was always very smart and had plenty of cash. But we just couldn't tell. She'd just turn up—for Christmas or something like that—and then be gone the next day. There was never the time to talk to her properly. And if she thought we were getting too nosey, she'd clam up good and proper. We didn't even have her address. The police had to give us that.'

He stopped, humiliated in spite of his thick skin.

'So . . .' said Brierly, filling in, 'you have no idea what she'd been doing in those last years? How she made her money? Who her friends were?'

Mr Jackson shook his head. 'She said she'd been working at one of the big studios—Pinewood, was it?—as personal assistant to some director. She even told us the name of two of his films. We went to see one of them, and a load of old rubbish it was, too. But her name wasn't in the credits; we stayed till the end.'

'You think she might have been, ah, embroidering?'

'I don't know. I just don't know.' The man, suddenly stripped of his pride, seemed to be truly hurt. 'We were so close once, but now it's like talking about a stranger.'

'And the accident?' Brierly was pulling him back to solid ground, giving him a chance to recover. 'What makes you think there's something amiss?'

'No,' he said hunching his shoulders, bull-like again. 'There was no accident. Even the police could come up with no rhyme or reason for it. I taught that girl to drive myself when she was fifteen. On private roads, of course. But cars are my business. She even drove for the firm in one or two rallies. She was that good. You know, sometimes a firm like mine puts up a car in one of those cross-country events with speed stages, for publicity. Nothing big, of course, but I wouldn't have let her drive unless she'd been really good. And she was.'

'What about the car?' Brierly was about as mechanically minded as a Christmas cake.

'I went over that myself. There was nothing wrong with it, apart from where the back was bashed in. Nothing. Steering, brakes, tyres, electrics—all in good nick. She knew more about a motor than the phone number of the nearest garage. I made sure of that.'

'Hydraulics?' asked Anna.

'That too.' Jackson hardly noticed the question. 'Even the back brake-pipes—the impact was from the back, so you'd look at them—and they were intact. No. I'm telling you there was nothing.'

'And your daughter,' Brierly asked tentatively. 'Could she have been to a party?'

'She had more sense than that.' Jackson's mood had swung back to one of complete certainty. 'There was a post-mortem, naturally, and there was no trace of drink or drugs. Drugs!' He snorted and repeated, 'She had more sense than that. "Mental aberration." ' He was quoting savagely. 'That's what they said, "blackout caused by fatigue"! I never heard anything so flimsy. And what about the smell in the car?'

'What smell was that?' Brierly was tapping with his fingertips on the blotter.

'Well, the first person who came upon the crash said he smelled alcohol and some chemical smell. He thought she was drunk.'

'So there was a witness?' Brierly stopped tapping.

'No, he didn't see anything. He's quite an old boy who was just walking his dog in a bit of parkland near his house when he heard the crash. But he did say he thought there might have been another car that didn't stop.'

'Could he be sure?'

'No. He said he wouldn't swear to it.'

'So that's it, is it?' Brierly laced his fingers across his waistcoat and sat back judiciously. 'A strange smell and a possible second car?'

'There was no cause. Isn't it enough?' Jackson almost shouted. He seemed even more like a bull about to charge. 'I hope you're not going to give me the runaround like those bloody coppers. They didn't listen, wouldn't lift a finger.'

'No, no,' Brierly interrupted hastily. He had never been known to discourage a client. 'It's from small beginnings like this that we get our most interesting results.'

'What do you think happened?' Anna asked quietly.

'That's what I'm paying you to find out,' Jackson said, 'But I don't mind telling you for free, there was someone else in that car with her; someone who'd been drinking. And I wouldn't mind betting that that someone was doing the driving.'

'But Deirdre was found behind the wheel, wasn't she?' Brierly interjected.

'That's easily done. But I know it'd take more than a slippery road to trip my girl up; even if she had had a drink, which she hadn't. Or been tired; which I'd bet my last penny she wasn't. I've told you, I taught her myself. She had a lot of respect for a motor.' Jackson glared at Brierly as if daring him to find fault with his daughter's training.

'And I'll tell you something else. She was robbed. Someone stole a dead girl's money.'

'Are you sure?' Brierly asked. 'The police didn't mention that.'

'Well, they wouldn't, would they? Perhaps they thought I was hinting it was one of them, or one of the ambulance men. But when they gave her things back she only had eighty-three pence in her purse.'

'Well,' Brierly said, 'maybe that isn't very significant.'

'Not by itself, perhaps,' Jackson said darkly, 'But I gave her this special purse, see, with a concealed flap for hiding things, and four twenties to put in it. She saw the point quick enough. Her rainy-day wallet, she called it.'

'And it was this purse which was returned to you empty?' Brierly asked.

Jackson nodded. 'You ask me what I think and I'll tell you. She was giving someone a lift, someone she knew. She wouldn't pick up a stranger. And of course this someone knew about the purse and robbed her and killed her. A young girl isn't the best judge of character, but you'll find him when you know everyone she knew. There's always a rotten apple somewhere.'

'I've got this feeling, you see,' Mrs Jackson hadn't spoken for some time. 'That it's not quite right. I'd like to know, that's all.'

This was such an anti-climax that no one asked her what she would like to know, and the room fell silent for a moment.

'That's it, we want to know. Like who was responsible for this.' Anna felt that Mr Jackson was not talking about the same thing as his wife. But Mrs Jackson did not correct him. 'It wasn't an accident, so someone must be responsible.' Anna saw that Mrs Jackson was looking at her husband with an expression of incredulous sympathy which in some way mirrored her own feelings.

Brierly had no expression at all. He said, 'Well, I think we should make a few discreet enquiries, talk to her friends, her employers, that sort of thing. Feel our way in.'

'We can't help you much,' Mrs Jackson said. 'All we have is her address. We went round there to get her things. She shared a flat in Islington. There was a girl there, but she only stayed to let us in. I think we embarrassed her.'

She took a slip of paper from her bag and passed it to Brierly.

'Is there anything further?' Brierly turned to Anna for the first time.

'One thing,' she said. 'Do you have a photograph of your daughter?'

Mrs Jackson, in an automatic response, unclasped her handbag again. Mr Jackson stopped her with an interrupting gesture.

'Just a minute,' he said. 'What do you want her photo for?'

After what had gone before this seemed absurdly reticent. Was he, having failed to protect his daughter, quite literally protecting his daughter's image? 'You don't have to find her, you know. We know where she is. I only wish we didn't.'

Patiently, Anna said, 'It'd be helpful to know what she looked like. If you've no objection, I'd like to be able to present myself as a friend of the family or something like that. It'd be easier to get a sympathetic reception, easier to get people to talk to me. People resent strangers poking their noses in.'

'It's not unreasonable,' Brierly murmured, but as if reasonable ideas should be his prerogative.

'Well, I suppose there's no objection.' Jackson grudgingly lifted his restraining hand.

'I wouldn't have called her a great beauty,' Mrs Jackson muttered apologetically, extracting a plastic photocase, as if beauty might have been a saving grace, a deciding factor which Deirdre had not possessed.

'Handsome, though,' Jackson said loudly, 'presentable, you might say.'

And taking the folder from his wife he examined the photographs and extracted four. He did not pass these to Anna but placed them on the desk in front of Brierly. He turned them carefully so that Brierly, who had not asked for them, could see them, and Anna, who had, was forced to crane her neck to see them upside down. She turned again to Mr Jackson.

'Deirdre's address book would save time, if you have it.'

Mrs Jackson thought for a moment. Then she said slowly, 'There isn't one. No, I'm quite positive. There was no address book among the things the police gave us, or in what we collected from the flat. Now, that is funny.'

'Not necessarily.' Brierly roused himself. 'Things like that can be mislaid easily. But I'll check with the police station myself, and Miss Lee can ask for it when she goes to the flat. But while we're on the subject, have you had time to go through your daughter's papers yet? Bills, receipts, bank balance, that sort of thing?'

'Not yet,' said Jackson. 'But it should be easy enough. There was just the one cardboard box-file. She was pretty neat with her papers.'

'There's many a tale told in a well-kept cheque-book.' Brierly was no idiot when it came to other people's money.

'Well, we'll be back home tomorrow,' Jackson told him, 'so I'll go through it all then. I'll ring you on Wednesday morning if I find anything.' He seemed immeasurably cheered by the promise of action.

CHAPTER 3

· · · · · · · · ·

ANNA ate a solitary lunch at home. The house was quiet. Even Selwyn's stuttering typewriter was silent. Only pigeon feathers stirred on the landing, under the broken skylight witness to the cat's grisly breakfast. She spread the photographs on the table and munched joylessly through a cheese and tomato sandwich while studying them. A family group first: father and mother, each holding a small boy, and eldest daughter, squinting into the sun, framed by the porch of a mock Tudor house. Not too much help, but she could see that Deirdre was about three inches taller than her mother and a little shorter than her father. That made her about five seven, with pale skin and auburn hair. Sulky, awkward, refusing to smile, she stood slightly separated from the group.

The older three were portraits, probably taken a year or so apart, starting with a plump, smiling fourteen-year-old and ending with a discontented straight-mouthed girl of seventeen who hadn't bothered to look into the lens. If she had taken her colouring from her mother, she owed her bone structure to her father. She had a wide, square jaw, high cheek-bones and a sloping forehead. She was certainly not pretty, but she had a distinctive face. One you could pick out of a crowd. The sullen mouth was wide, and in the earlier pictures it smiled disarmingly and softly. She had good eyes too, large and dark-lashed, but the direct, guileless look of the first photo had changed, and the expression had become aggressive and veiled. The face had character, at least, and plenty of determination. Anna thought about those three painful years between fourteen and seventeen, never the easiest, even in the best of circumstances, and wondered how different the last portrait would have looked had Deirdre remained a cherished only child.

She sighed, and poured out a strong cup of tea, before reaching for the *A to Z* to look up Canonbury Terrace.

It was still raining, and the Triumph reluctantly started on a third attempt. While waiting for the demister to assert its feeble influence, Anna copied the last three figures from her milometer on to a green mileage form and filled in the destination. Employees of Brierly Security were allowed seven pence a mile if they used their own cars; a sum mean enough to rankle and to encourage inexperienced agents to try to exaggerate distances. But between them Beryl and Martin Brierly had a knowledge of London equalled only by a taxicab meter, and a fiddle had never been known to succeed.

Canonbury Terrace ran inconspicuously between two commercial roads, a dusty backwater of peeling terraced houses just south of Highbury and Islington station.

There was no reply from 23A. Anna had time to do what shopping she needed for the week and to read both evening newspapers and a third of a paperback before she saw an enormously fat girl in a scarlet leather coat open the door of the basement, and lights go on. Anna went across and knocked.

'Yes?' The girl, though huge, had small ankles and wrists. Her hair was pinky-blonde and tortured into a Monroe Windswept. She was, against all odds, extremely attractive.

'I'm sorry to bother you, but I've come about Deirdre Jackson.'

'She's dead, didn't you know?' Her voice, belying her appearance, was flat and hard, with an undisguised London accent. 'About a month ago, in a road accident.'

'Yes, I did know,' Anna said, 'But her parents sent me . . .'

'They picked up all her stuff themselves.' The girl turned her head, listening to something behind her in the flat. 'You'd better come in for a minute. I've got the kettle on.'

The kitchen was all white and yellow plastic and had the marks of neglect and confusion that shared work-areas often suffer. A bowl on the table had a rim of hardened Weetabix round the edge. A cup was half-filled with cold scummy coffee. The fat girl tutted and whisked them on to the draining board. But no further. They weren't hers, so she wouldn't wash them.

'Park yourself, why don't you?' she said. 'Fancy a cup? That naffing Northern Line proper drains you. Bleeding cattle-cars. Does nothing for your joy-de-vee, does it? I mean, when you think of all that aggro being heaved around under London.'

Anna laughed suddenly.

'It's no joke,' said the fat girl, giggling too. 'We'd probably all kill each other if we had room to move. Only if we had room to move, we wouldn't want to, would we? You can't say London Transport haven't got it all figured, can you?'

She put two cups on the table and subsided on to a loudly protesting chair, slipping her absurdly high-heeled shoes off as she did so. Her legs, thought Anna, eyeing them surreptitiously, were like up-ended Chianti bottles.

She yawned. 'I'm Tina, by the way. What's yours?'

'Anna,' said Anna.

'Your tea all right?'

'Great, thanks. Look,' Anna began, 'I'm sorry to barge in on you. But Mrs Jackson asked me to come.'

'She didn't leave nothing. I wasn't here when she came, but I checked Dee's room myself. We had to let the room again, see? No disrespect, I mean, but rent's rent, ennit?'

No disrespect, Anna felt, but not much liking either. 'You didn't find an address book, then?'

'Nothing,' Tina repeated. 'They took all her bits and pieces. And rather them than me. Not that she wasn't tidy, or anything—on the fussy side, I always thought—but I wouldn't have felt right going through her things. Are you family, then?'

'Just a friend,' Anna said carefully. 'It's not just that the book's missing, it's more, well; you know Deirdre had lost touch with her people?'

'Cut herself off, she said. Allergic to hoorays and blood sports.'

'What?'

'It's what she said. That she got wickered off with country life and Mummy's bridge parties and Daddy's gee-gees. That they wanted her to marry some Flash Harry with blue blood and no chin and a hacking jacket to go with his hacking cough and have a load of tweedy little nippers. Cods. I may be common as muck, but I've got more than two planks between me shell-likes. She may've had money up the family tree, but that was about all. Am I right?'

'Well, you're not far wrong.'

'Look, I'm sorry. I don't mean to speak ill or anything.' She did not look too sorry, and, watching her, Anna had a fleeting impression of a rare shrewdness, an ability to sum up character by provocation. Anna appreciated the technique.

'It's all right,' Anna said. 'As you've put it, she'd cut herself off for some years now. It's not me that's cut up about it.'

'Her Mum and Dad, then? I suppose they're wanting a reunion now it's too late.'

'I think you've got it in one.' Anna employed some cautious flattery.

'And this address book. Do they want to find out who her friends were, and was their one and only happy in spite of it all?'

'Well, they didn't put it like that, but if you ask me, that's what's behind it.'

Tina poured herself some more tea. Anna refused.

'It's a shame, really.' Tina's scarlet lips pouted round the rim of her cup. 'I see my mum every week. She does make-up at Thames. We're all working women in my family. Even my gran. But if anything happened to any one of us, no one'd have to go knocking on any stranger's door to find out what went wrong.'

Anna waited.

'What's more of a shame is there's only me to ask. Dee'd only been here about nine months, and, as I say, we rubbed up wrong from the kick-off. Well, there's Joyce, but she's working late tonight, and she didn't know Dee no better than I did. She was secretive in a way that was annoying. Never said where she was going or what she was doing or who she was seeing. A bit of the mystery woman, see? She only ever told you what she wanted you to know, and that like as not'd be as false as a three-pound note. Do you want a bit of toast?'

'No thanks. You mean she lived here nine months and you didn't know what her job was or who she went out with or anything like that?'

The grill smelled of burnt toast-crumbs as soon as the gas was lit. Another piece of communal equipment that no one wanted to look after.

'Sounds ridiculous, don't it? I could tell you what she told me, but I never believed half anyway.' Tina flipped the bread over. 'Like she used to race motorcars and play polo and have dinner with Jack Nicholson when he was in London and was Cecil B. DeMille's right-hand man-eater? What else?'

'Didn't she have a job, then?'

Tina mashed a huge knob of butter and a dollop of honey together on the toast. She sat down again.

'Well, she did and she didn't. Some days she didn't even go out. Other times, especially weekends, she did. But whatever it was, she never went out before lunch. She said she was working on some big production at Elstree, but that's all my eye.'

'How d'you know that?'

'Well, the hours, for a start. You ask my mum. She's been in the business I don't know how long, and you don't make films from 3 pm to 10.30. Not with the unions they've got. They can make nine to five look like overtime without even trying, so why start out with time-and-a-half and double? I work for Theatrical Costumes, and we do a bit on movies now and then. And I can tell you they're more conservative in their working hours than the bleeding town hall.'

'But she had money, didn't she? I mean she ran a car. She was well dressed and all that.'

'You're not the tax-man, are you?' Tina's wedgwood-blue eyes were bright and guileless. But she waited stubbornly. She used information as currency, Anna thought. There had to be a satisfactory trade somewhere. Deirdre and her talent for misrepresentation must have been a continual frustration to Tina's openness and curiosity.

'Funny you should say that. I work for a firm of accountants in Kensington.' Anna improvised. 'And it's odd, but you can find out more about people if you know how they spend their money than in any other way. Cherchez la pound. You can answer a lot of questions that way.'

'I thought as much.' Tina seemed quite pleased with herself. 'I suppose it's all according to your training, really. Take me, I sum people up by their clothes; and you try to judge the outcome by their income.'

'Or the other way around.' They were mates again. Tina the performer, with Anna as her appreciative audience.

'I'm not saying Dee didn't earn. She paid her rent on the dot and bought her share of the bog-paper and all that. In fact, she was a bit annoying that way. She kept a record of all our expenses in a book with a column for each of us and totalled it all up each week to make sure no one was shirking. And having the pay-phone was her idea. She was quite right, mind, but not very friendly. It was all quotas and rosters with her. She should've lived on her own, really. You always felt she resented having to share.'

'Don't you feel like that sometimes?'

'Not me, mate. I enjoy the company and always having someone to talk to. But Dee wasn't like that. She never bothered to get to know Joyce or me, and, as I say, it was bloody impossible to get to know her. Fancy a biscuit?'

Tina opened one of the cupboards under the sink, revealing momentarily a hamster's hoard of packets clumsily hidden behind the soapflakes. She sat down again and opened a box of custard creams.

'Oh, Tina, you are wicked.'

Anna, turning, had a sudden impression of being sandwiched between two dumplings. The girl who stood in the doorway was not as fat as Tina, but didn't have far to go to catch up. 'You promised,' she wailed, gazing at the custard creams with undisguised longing.

'Who pulled your chain?' Tina's voice was sharp with resentment. Then she giggled.

'You weren't supposed to be back till six. This is Joycey, our tip-top temp. She's on a diet.'

'Oh, Tina!' Joyce was gently reproachful.

'Well, only to keep you company. Look, this here's— um—Anna, isn't it? We've been talking about Dee. You know I always get hungry when I get upset,' she added virtuously.

Joyce crossed herself at Deirdre's name and sat down solemnly. With a gloomy expression she helped herself to two biscuits.

'I know what you mean,' she said sadly. 'Poor old Dee.'

They sat quietly for a minute, as if observing a ritual silence. Anna glanced from one to the other as they sat like two ruminants at either end of the table, munching neglectfully.

'We weren't that close, really, were we, Tina?'

They could have been sisters. Joyce was a faded, understated version of Tina. Her hair was fair and straight, not blonde and waved. Her clothes and makeup were less vivid. Even her voice was softer, and her eyes had none of Tina's sharp wit. Anna guessed she was the perfect foil, and that they had probably been close friends for a long time.

'Who was, then? Close to her?' Anna was beginning to feel slightly claustrophobic.

'Omar bleeding Sharif, if you listened to her,' Tina said. 'Dee never mentioned a name unless it was one you could drop.'

'Oh Tina, you do go on. She really does go on. Didn't you tell her about whatsisname? Did she tell you about that nice boy who came here?'

'I was getting to that,' Tina pouted in annoyance. 'You always disturb my rhythm, Joyce. But that just goes to show, doesn't it? When one single solitary chap does come calling for her he isn't the beautiful black-eyed hunk of Burt Reynolds we were expecting. Ever such a disappointment, it was.'

'He was nice, though, wasn't he, Tina?'

'Sweet. He had lovely manners, what I'd call a well-brought-up boy. But she was ever so embarrassed, remember, Joycey? She wasn't expecting him, and when she got in he'd been sitting here with Joyce and me for at least ten minutes, chatting. She whisked him out so fast his feet hardly touched the ground. She must've thought we'd been giving him the low-down.'

'She hated people talking behind her back,' Joyce said. 'She was a funny girl, you know. When she came back she gave us this line about him being some office boy with an urgent message from the studio. But he'd said he was taking her to the film society and he'd got tired of waiting on the corner. She was late, see.'

'Did he give a name?' Anna asked.

'She's an accountant,' Tina told Joyce. 'She likes to get to the bottom of things straight away.'

'Then you can't have been having much luck with our Tina. She likes to spin out a good story. I expect you've found that out.'

Anna grinned. 'Well, they are good stories, so I don't mind.'

'Simon, his name was,' said Tina, rewarding her. 'Simon Lester. I remember now. I had a cat called that when I was little.'

'You never.'

'I did. Not Simon. Leicester. My auntie brought him down. She was up there with some company in digs and the landlady's cat had kittens. So we called him Leicester after the town. Sweet little thing he was, till he got old enough to go out courting. Then he got smelly.'

'Oh God,' said Anna.

CHAPTER 4

. . . .

THE rain had turned to sleet by the time Anna got home. She was halfway upstairs when the Prices' door burst open, banging back against the hall wall, chipping a few more flakes of paint. A reclining bicycle shuddered and slid into a more dramatic decline.

'Is that you, Anna?' Selwyn roared at the top of his voice. 'Anna Leo. Anna the Lion. I can't see you. Why the hell don't you turn the lights on?'

'No hands, Ma.' Anna trudged slowly up a couple more steps. The hall light came on.

'There you are. What do you mean by it, coming in like a thief in the night?'

'Sorry, love, can't stop. Got to recharge this battery, and it weighs a ton.'

'Hang about. I'll open up for you.' Selwyn pounded up and edged round until he was above her.

'Keys?'

Anna waggled the little finger of her right hand, which was otherwise filled, like the left, with the Triumph's battery. Selwyn lifted the key-ring off, finished the stairs with two thunderous bounds, and opened Anna's door.

'Where?'

'Kitchen.'

Selwyn opened the kitchen door and turned the lights on.

Anna put the battery down on the work surface with some relief.

'Thanks,' she said, connecting the leads from the charger to the terminals and switching on. The needle on the meter flicked.

'Some girls would prefer a toaster.' Selwyn looked with disapproval at the charger, which had its permanent place on the surface next to the stove and conveniently near the sockets.

'Some girls,' said Anna, washing her hands, 'would prefer astronomical garage bills. Cold, isn't it?'

'Come down for a jar and a warm-up, young Leo. You got your mane wet. You can lecture me on the benefits of home mechanicking in comfort.'

She went through to the living-room and turned the gas-fire on.

'It'll be all right in here in a minute.'

Anna had taken out the door and widened the doorway between bedroom and living-room when she had first moved in. The result was much lighter and airier, having a window at both north and south ends, but was harder to heat in the winter.

'It's Bea, actually.' Selwyn had followed her in. 'She's got a couple of plugs.'

'Okay, then.' She went back to the kitchen and chose a small screwdriver from one of the cutlery trays which held her tools and went downstairs again.

'I got a new hair-dryer at the sales,' said Bea. 'And a coffee-grinder. I've always wanted one of those. Real bargains, they were.'

Anna sat cross-legged on the floor in front of the fire and set to work on the plugs. She had a sneaking suspicion that Bea could do the job just as capably but refused on principle to admit it.

'Spending all my money on electrical nonsense,' Selwyn snorted.

'Whose money?' asked Bea warningly.

Selwyn was about fifty years old, roughly fifteen years older than Bea. But it was undoubtedly he who was the child of the marriage. He had been an unashamed anarchist and Bohemian in the Fifties, a condition from which he had not yet recovered. He wrote poetry mostly, acted a little—if the parts were small enough and enough people had turned them down—and modelled for anyone who needed a large untidy middle-aged man to advertise their products.

He made enough money to keep the wolf from the door, but it was Bea's salary that kept them in the lap of the middle-class comfort he professed to despise.

'There's a shepherd's pie in the oven,' said Bea. 'And leeks if you want.'

'Of course she does,' Selwyn replied, pouring out a glass of white wine. 'She wants something to stick to those ribs. Look how thin she's become without your cauliflower cheese over Christmas.'

'Anna's not the one who needs looking after round here,' Bea said pointedly. 'Look who left a perfectly good steak and kidney pie to get dry in the oven at lunch-time.'

'I forgot, woman. I was working.'

'With a pint glass in your hand, I'll be bound.'

'See how she treats me? Anna, I need news. What's old, what's new, what's borrowed and who's blue? That's what I need, a splash from the old sordid pool. A quick dip into the sea of life—by proxy of course . . . mustn't get wet. Whose collar did you finger today?'

'Don't fuss her like that,' said Bea calmly from the kitchen, dishing up three platefuls of food in spite of having received no answer from Anna.

So Anna stayed and ate and told them something of the day's happenings.

'You'd have liked Tina,' she told Selwyn when the meal was over. 'She had a way with words. A long way, but one of her own.'

'That's lovely. I like it. Two fat girls eating crisps and

bickies and taking two hours to tell you what could be told in two minutes. And when you do get this chap's number, it's only because it's on the bloody wall by the phone.'

'Oh, I don't know,' Anna said. 'Tina's opinion of Deirdre is one foothold on shifting ground. I'll probably find I'm better off for listening to it. Besides, all sorts of things were dropped into that conversation. There's a local film society lurking in the background, for starters. That shouldn't be too hard to find. It all helps.'

'But how does she shape up as a possible candidate for a possible killing from Tina's description?'

'No better than anyone else. It was sad, though. In all Deirdre's tall stories there was no whisper of two baby brothers at home. She stayed Daddy's little princess, even though she changed the phony Tudor house to a stately home.'

'It's something everyone does, isn't it?' Selwyn yawned, and spread himself like a starfish. The button at the waistband of his trousers was missing as usual, in spite of Bea's continual efforts to spruce him up, and his gut protruded comfortably. 'Editing, I call it. I've been everything from a miner's son from the Rhondda to the love-child of a Patagonian minister. Everyone does it.'

'I don't,' said Bea, bringing in the coffee.

'You're different. You were happy with what you were and you're happy with what you've become. No illusions, see? Straight and honest, but not, thank God, straight and narrow.' He made room for her on the sofa. 'You were a good girl. Good in school, singing in the choir, selling sweets behind the counter at weekends.'

'You make it sound so boring, but I liked it.'

'You liked being approved of. If everyone else approved of what you were doing, you thought you liked it too. You never failed, see?'

'Course I did. Lots of times. But I don't see failing as any excuse for lying.'

'That's my girl. The simple moral judgement.' He put his arm round Bea and squeezed her. 'What do you think, Leo?'

'Perhaps it's freedom,' she said, 'when your past

seems like a prison, but you know you don't have to be stuck with it.'

She could remember the house in Dulwich clearly. The small rooms. The doors, always shut. The piano no one played. The collection of china ornaments. It had always been a crime to break something, but to break one of those was a sin. More than anything else, they symbolized the restrictions and repressions of that house. The feeling of walking round over-furnished rooms with your elbows clenched to your ribs. Any burst of energy, any carefree movement seemed to result in a breakage.

'Some people invent their pasts,' she went on. 'Some invent their futures, and some do both.'

'But you don't have to lie about it,' Bea persisted.

'No, you don't, but to some people it's a way of rejecting the unacceptable, if they don't have the equipment to simply invent a new life for themselves.'

'You can't invent life,' said Bea.

'Yes, you can,' said Anna, adding, 'thank God. You don't have to get stuck with anything.'

'Careful, my love.' Selwyn kissed Bea's cheek fondly. 'You're maligning all my varied professions.'

'It's different for creative people. They make things up for money.'

'Hah! You mean it's all right if you invent life for a living? Write it all down, call it a play, and it isn't a lie any more?'

'Oh, you twist everything.' Bea shook his arm off and poured more coffee into all the cups.

CHAPTER 5

· · · · · · · · ·

AT ten Anna was running in Holland Park. She ran until the blood rustled in her ears like falling leaves. Then she walked home. It was another cold day, the ground stiff with frost. Even the peacocks looked subdued.

The earlier call to the office had been routine and obligatory: name of subject, place of rendezvous and ETA. Contacting Simon Lester had been more interesting. The phone number belonged to Dalton's, a film processing laboratory near Charlotte Street. Simon Lester? Never heard of him . . . An employee? Not management? Persons working in the lab are not encouraged to accept calls of a personal nature . . . An emergency? . . . Hold the line one minute . . . I'll see what I can do . . . Putting you through now. Simon Lester, when she heard his voice, sounded anxious and embarrassed, but he would be happy to help in any way he could. He had an hour off for lunch, and would meet her at the corner of Percy Street and Charlotte Street at twelve-thirty.

With nothing to do all morning, Anna cleaned the

Triumph's spark plugs, reset the points and refitted the battery. It started at the first attempt. Damp and cold, thought Anna, and wished for the umpteenth time that she had a garage.

Simon Lester had short, curly hair, blue eyes and pale skin. He had the expression of a serious student, intelligent and eager, but a little tired. His pallor spoke more of overwork than ill health.

'I thought you'd be older,' he said as they walked to the pub where he usually had lunch. 'I thought you'd be an aunt or something like that.' He sounded relieved.

'I am an aunt,' she told him. The fact still surprised her.

'Not Dee's though? Surely?'

'Oh no.' She thought of her three-year-old nephew.

'Come to think of it, I became an uncle a few months ago.'

'Don't apologize,' Anna said. 'It can happen to anyone.'

They threaded their way through the early lunchtime crowd at the bar. He ordered half a pint of bitter and two sausage sandwiches. She had a bitter lemon and, after looking at the menu, decided to eat later.

'Well,' he said, 'what can I tell you?'

'Almost anything. The family have had practically no information for the past four years. That's what upsets her Mum and Dad as much as anything.'

'I can imagine. They must be feeling rotten.' She liked his sympathy. 'I would have gone to the funeral. But I heard about everything too late. And besides, it wouldn't have been the most tactful time to introduce myself.'

'You didn't know?'

'Not till over a week later. It was awful, because we were to have met on the night she died. But she broke the date. She had some important appointment. She said she'd phone later in the week.'

'And you didn't try to get in touch with her?'

'No.' He was looking for words, slightly embarrassed. 'If she said she'd phone me, it wasn't any use

phoning her. She would have felt crowded. The . . . er
. . . relationship was rather on her terms.'

He was obviously ill at ease. She started again,
changing direction. 'How long had you known each other?'

About a year, he told her. He had just finished three
years at film school and, having no job, was helping some
friends make a short film of their own. Amateur stuff, he
said, laughing as much at himself as at the project. Deirdre had been working in a shop that sold short lengths of
film stock to impoverished enthusiasts like himself. Celluloid Cellar it was called. They had talked about the project, and she had come out one Saturday to watch them
work.

'She didn't stay long in that job, though.' Simon
stopped and finished both his beer and the sandwich.

'Why not?' Anna prompted.

'For one thing, the money was miserly. And for another, I don't think she was meeting the kind of people
she wanted to meet. You see, she wanted to be where the
professional action was, not messing about with hopeful
amateurs like me.'

'And that's a hard door to push open, isn't it?'

More and more people had pressed into the pub, and
the air was close and stuffy. Simon took his jacket off. He
was wearing an old grey pullover under it, and Anna became aware of a curious metallic smell.

'What's that?' she asked, wrinkling her nose.

He sniffed his sleeve and laughed. 'I hardly notice it
any more. But, talking of opening doors, that's one of the
ways. You see, the industry runs an exceptionally fine
Catch-22, Hail and Farewell scheme. If you want a job,
you have to be a member of the union. But to be a member
you have to have a job. The perfect vicious circle, eh?'

'So what are you doing?'

'I'm working my ticket. There are still some jobs, if
you can stick them, which get you an unrestricted ticket
at the end of a year. Working on the baths is one of them,
and that's smelly.'

'Baths?'

'Well, it's just like processing photographs, only

much bigger. You need huge baths of developer, stopper and wash. First for the negative and then for the print. And some poor jokers have to keep the baths clean and keep the filmstock rolling through. Which is why I often smell like a chemistry set.'

'For how much longer?'

'Oh, I'm almost halfway there now. It's not pleasant, you lose a lot of illusions, but there's a lot to learn. And I suppose, if I'm honest, I've always been more interested in the technical side of things.'

'And Deirdre?' Anna brought herself back to the point. 'Was she working her ticket, too?'

Simon hesitated. He always seemed to be looking for the words that would give least offence.

'Not in the way I am,' he said in the end. 'You see, I think she was always expecting to meet someone who would open all the doors for her.'

'But she didn't, did she?'

'No, but that was why she got those dead-end jobs. Someone always flashed his connections and promised her great things in the future. For example, the chap in Celluloid Cellar fed her a line about how many famous people used his shop. And then Slinger was always boasting that he'd be a millionaire before he was forty-five, and all she had to do was tag along. It's very sad, you know. She wasted so much time.'

'Who's Slinger?'

'Frederick Slinger? That was my fault, really. Dee wanted to become a member of the film society I go to sometimes. So I took her to a member's party. He was there. He was much older than anyone else. The only one with a tie, if you know what I mean. Anyway, Dee was wearing her dynamic face, and by the end of the evening he'd offered her a job.'

'What sort of job?'

'Projectionist. He ran a projection service. That's what it boiled down to. It was so absurd.' He ran his hand through his hair. His fingers were stained brown with chemicals.

'What was?'

Again the pause, accompanied by an anxious glance.

'Well, when she found out what sort of business he was in, she told him a story about how she had taken Charlie Chaplin films round all sorts of small villages in Portugal with a vanload of stacking chairs and a generator to run the projector. She'd just seen a film called *Dirty Mary* and there's a travelling projectionist in that. The idea must have appealed to her. But I had to spend the next weekend teaching her how to use one. She had no idea! Christ!' he exploded suddenly. 'I can't believe she's dead. Not even now. She had so much more life to her than most. So many ideas and fancies. I'd never met anyone like her before. You felt she was a princess in disguise.'

Anna watched him. He seemed more angry than grieving.

'It's such a bloody waste. I keep feeling . . . I should have known. She died, and I didn't know till a week later. You should know immediately when someone you care for dies.'

Anna suddenly decided on the direct approach.

'Were you lovers?' she asked.

The question seemed to be so much a part of his private thinking that he scarcely noticed it.

'Not really. You see, it was like everything else about Dee and me. It could have gone either way. Perhaps if I'd been older or more successful or if she'd trusted me more . . . But then, she didn't trust anyone. We might have got closer. We might have drifted apart. It was too early to say. That's why I'm at such a loss. It's like having the rug pulled out from under your feet.'

He sat with his spine curved, his chin in his hand, looking at the beer mats.

'You think you've got all the time in the world,' he muttered. Anna felt he was slipping away. In a moment he would be ashamed of letting his hair down.

'Were you surprised?' she asked. 'About the way she died, I mean?' At least she could try out Tom Jackson's suspicions on him.

'I don't know,' he said dully. Then he sat up

straighter, and his eyes brightened visibly. He was indeed, she thought, someone who preferred to talk of things outside himself.

'Yes, if I think about it, I am surprised. She was very good and safe in cars. It's funny how wrong you can be. She told me, just after we'd met, that she used to drive Formula 2 racing cars, and that she had been a mechanic, and I thought it was one of her inventions. But one or two things happened to make me think there might have been something in it. She was a funny girl, you know. She had so much competence in some ways. You wouldn't think she'd need to make things up.'

'What happened?'

'It wasn't anything much. Just the way she pulled out of a bad skid on an icy road. And another time, well, it was just a blowout. It could have been quite nasty, but she made nothing of it at all. And she changed the wheel in five minutes. No fuss. You could tell she was at home with cars.'

'She was. She'd been driving since she was fifteen, and she did race a little.' Anna was glad to be able to give him some small confidence in his memories.

'Well, there you are!' he said with subdued triumph. 'I've never talked much to anyone about her. None of my friends understood her. They all thought I was wasting my time.'

Perhaps he had been, she thought, but said, 'Why didn't she get on with them?'

'I don't know. But she was impressed by success. Most of the people I know are students or trainees, you see. None of them have found their feet or a pot of gold, so maybe she made them feel inferior. She could make you feel knee-high to a caterpillar without really meaning to. It was probably her upbringing.'

They were passing the starting line again. Anna took a small notebook out of her pocket.

'Can you give me the addresses or numbers for Frederick Slinger and the film society?'

'I've got an address for him somewhere, but not on me. The film society is the Seven Sisters Film Society, and it's just off Seven Sisters Road. But it won't do you much good. They only meet on Fridays. It's a preschool playgroup in the daytime.'

He gave her the address all the same, and watched while she jotted it down.

'What exactly are you trying to do?' he asked.

'I'm trying to piece together the last four years of her life, especially the last couple of months or so.' She was glad she didn't have to lie to him about it. She felt he didn't deserve lies.

'For her parents?'

'Yes.'

He brooded about it for a while.

'You may find it rather hard, you know,' he said finally. 'Dee liked to live her life in watertight compartments. Look, I'd like to help if I can.'

'You already have.'

'No, I mean really help. Talk to people, ask questions and such. I could do with some answers myself.'

He was willing, eager, and very vulnerable. The thought of a mission had brought a pink stain to his pale face.

'No,' said Anna quickly. 'That wouldn't be a very good idea. You're too involved.'

'So are you.'

'Not like you are,' she said truthfully. 'It wouldn't do you any good. It might even hurt you. I'm doing this for her family, but even so it might turn out to be an awful liberty.'

'I see what you mean.' It was obviously all too easy to appeal to his sense of decency.

'Anyway,' he was disappointed but still helpful, 'you still want whatever I can find about Slinger, don't you?'

She did indeed. He wrote his home number in her notebook.

'Call me around six. I'll be back by then. I ought to get back to the sweatshop now.'

They stood up together. He sighed. 'I'm sorry. I feel as if I've talked more about me than about her. It must be your yellow eyes.'

'Hazel,' she corrected him, offended. 'Unless my passport deceives. And you've been a great help, don't worry.'

They edged their way out into the street.

'I've just had a thought,' he said suddenly as they approached Charlotte Street. 'I've got a couple of tickets for the National Film Theatre tonight. I don't suppose you'd like one, would you? I'm not making a pass,' he added awkwardly.

'No, I can see you're not,' she said frankly.

'They have a snack-bar upstairs, and I can give you the gen on Freddie.'

'Well, why not?' She was so pleased to see him cheerful again that she surprised herself. 'So long as it's not that bloody *Battleship Potemkin* you film buffs love so much. Thanks very much.'

He laughed. '*One-Eyed Jacks*, if you can stand it. Seven then, at the NFT?'

CHAPTER 6

· · · · · · · · · ·

ANNA walked north towards the Euston Road. In the University of London Library, with the help of a more than usually accommodating librarian, she discovered an insignificant volume called the British Federation of Film Societies Register and Handbook. The secretary of Seven Sisters Film Society was Leonard Margolin, 38 Hobbs Avenue, N4.

At King's Cross she reluctantly phoned the office with her new destination. It was a restriction she always resented.

'You're coming in after?' Beryl's voice was stretched thin. She sounded as if she was beginning a cold.

'Am I wanted?'

Beryl's sense of duty was such that she carried all her minor ailments to work. Anna had caught too many of her colds to relish being in the office at the start of yet another.

'The Commander would like a word.'

That was that. So she sighed and caught a train to Finsbury Park.

Hobbs Avenue was a double row of thin terraced

houses with pinched front gardens and short paths. It had
an air of desperate respectability common to cliques of
impoverished owner-occupiers. Anna had to walk round
an aggressively staring ginger cat to get to the front door,
which was opened by a small girl in a tartan dress and
bright red tights which emphasized the twig-like shape of
her legs. The ginger cat streaked past both of them into
the house with a raucous yell that made Anna jump.

'Is your father Mr Leonard Margolin?' she asked the
child, who was standing round-eyed and dumb in the crack
of the door.

'Mandy, did you let the cat in?' The mother's voice
had something in common with the cat's. She appeared
behind the child with it hanging supine over her arm like
a fur stole.

'She wants to talk to Daddy,' said the little girl.

'My husband isn't back yet,' she said, looking
vaguely over Anna's shoulder as if she expected him to
appear at any minute and rescue her from an unwelcome
intruder. She was a thin woman. Her skin, finely lined
around eyes and mouth, was taut across her cheekbones.
Her dark hair was like a bathing cap on her head.

'Is he still the secretary of the film society?'

'Founder, president and projectionist,' Mrs Margolin
said drily. 'I'm the secretary or general dogsbody. You'd
better come in for a moment. It's chilly on the doorstep.'

She admitted Anna and threw the cat out almost in a
single movement.

'People normally write,' she said as she led Anna
into the sitting-room. She went to the mantelpiece and
picked up a glass half-full of clear liquid that had been
tucked behind a framed photograph of Mandy. She was
not a lady who minded being caught drinking alone in the
afternoon. In fact, she seemed to be flaunting it. Anna felt
she was burning a very short fuse.

'He's a busy man. People make far too many demands on what little free time he has.' She was obviously
the self-appointed keeper of Mr Margolin's timetable, dol-
ing out his minutes with a stingy hand as if he was prof-
ligate with something that really belonged to her.

'What did you want to see him about?'

'Well, I was just enquiring about one of his members.'

'Which one?'

'It was Deirdre Jackson I wanted to ask him about.' Anna was just about to go into her routine explanation when Mrs Margolin broke in.

'That little cow! Who does she think she is? Hasn't she caused enough trouble already?' The dangling earrings she wore quivered against her long neck like leaves in a breeze.

'Does she think I was born yesterday? Getting Len off in corners, whispering behind my back. She must think I'm blind or stupid. I don't count for anything. Is that it? Married for nine years—nine bloody years—and I don't count because Miss Dee Cow-Eyes Lolita Jackson wants a turn at my husband. You're all the same. You think being young gives you licence to kill, don't you? I suppose you've come to take over where she left off. Well, I told her and I'm telling you, if I catch you trying to corrupt my husband again, I'll wipe the rotten floor with you.'

'Hold on,' said Anna, slightly stunned. 'Please, Mrs Margolin, cool down. It's not like that at all.'

'Cool!' she exploded again. 'Your great god Cool! It's uncool to protect my marriage, isn't it? It's uncool to be married in the first place, I suppose. Cool! It excuses the pygmy morals you hardly possess!'

'Please, Mrs Margolin,' Anna was almost shouting, 'no one's trying to nick your husband, and Deirdre's dead.'

That stopped her. But she was too far gone to back down.

'Serves her bloody well right,' she said, but she said it quietly.

Leonard Margolin chose this inauspicious moment to make his entrance. He looked round the door cautiously as if afraid of what he would find on the other side. His light brown eyes darted between the two women from behind thick-lensed spectacles. He wore a fawn cord jacket, slightly creased, over a polo-necked sweater. The sight of him, rather than soothing his wife, seemed to irritate her further.

'Do come in, Len, unless you want to stay outside with your ear to the keyhole. Meet this young lady who can't be bothered to tell me her name. She's just brought the happy news of Dee Jackson's death.'

Anna's first impression was that he already knew, but he came in and sat down, saying, 'How dreadful. What an awful thing. How did it happen?'

'Don't bother.' Mrs Margolin poured herself another drink. 'The young lady was just leaving.'

Without giving either of them time to respond, she herself marched out of the room and slammed the door. They faced each other across the shabby furniture, Margolin sitting with his hands dangling helplessly between his knees, Anna still standing in the centre of the room.

'It seems I kicked over an ants' nest,' she said apologetically.

'No. It's all right. She's got a bee in her bonnet about her age. That's all. Suspects every woman under thirty.' He shrugged his shoulders despondently. 'Do I look like a compulsive womanizer?'

He didn't, but Anna had met a few even less likely ones.

'She's been a trifle manic-depressive ever since Amanda was born. Never mind. That's my problem. Why did you come to me, anyway?'

'It's just that you're the head of the film society that Deirdre belonged to and I thought you might be able to help with the jigsaw puzzle. Her parents have asked me to find out about her life over the past four years. They hadn't seen much of her since she left home.'

'Oh. But how did you know where to come?'

'A friend of hers, another member . . .'

'Simon Lester? He introduced her in the first place.'

'That's right.'

'Did he mention me specifically?'

'No, I looked you up in the Register.'

'Ah, the BFFS Handbook. You're resourceful.'

'Not really. It's just there's so little to go on. Dee didn't exactly leave large footprints.'

Margolin got to his feet. He was tall, and a bit stooped.

'Well, I'm sorry I can't help you. In spite of what Sarah says I really didn't know her at all. She was just another member, and a recent one at that.'

'Is there anyone else you know who I might talk to?'

'Apart from Si Lester, I'm afraid I can't suggest anyone. And I really mustn't leave Sarah alone in this mood for too long. So if you wouldn't mind . . .'

He opened the door into the hall. From somewhere at the back of the house they could hear Sarah sobbing. Mandy sat dolefully on the stairs making an Action Man march rigidly back and forth. She didn't look up.

'Perhaps I could get in touch with you another time,' said Anna at the front door. 'At work, for instance.'

'I'm sorry. There's nothing I can add. Now I must get back to my wife.'

She passed the ginger cat on the doorstep as it shot past into the dark interior with its harsh shriek. She was just shutting the gate to the road when the front door opened again. It was Leonard Margolin, but he only tossed the cat back on to the path and closed the door again.

'You'd do better if you kept your mouth shut,' Anna told it.

CHAPTER 7

· · · · · · · · ·

CELLULOID Cellar was not even a basement. It was about ten to four when Anna found it tucked away gloomily behind Wardour Street.

Arthur Craven was plump, but had once been fat. The flesh hung round his collar in sad folds. A fine dust of dandruff adorned his shoulders, and one side of his horn-rims was held together with elastoplast.

They talked in his office, a small untidy room separated from the shop by a glass panel. He explained that he was between secretaries as he tidied a leaning tower of invoices off the second chair. A man like him was always between secretaries. Every aspect of his life looked as if it could do with a touch of organization. He remembered Deirdre Jackson well.

'I'm sorry about her accident. It must have been an awful shock. A young girl like that,' he said. 'I could do with her back here now,' he added anxiously, watching his assistant open his *Daily Mirror* before the last customer had left. 'Deirdre would never have done that. She was very good with the customers. Talked to them about their work, showed an interest. She was very efficient, too. No messy invoices for her. She kept everything neat and tidy, even this office—had a system for everything. But where do you get a girl like that these days?'

'Where *did* you get her, Mr Craven?' Anna asked.

'A friend of mine, a photographer, put her on to me. Dmitrios Bruce, his name is. She was very eager to get involved in movies, so he recommended her to come here. He knows I've always got an opening for keen youngsters. Only most of them aren't really keen at all. They expect success on a plate.'

'How did she got on with the rest of your staff?'

'There was a bit of jealousy, I'm afraid. The hard-working, ambitious ones don't seem to make too many friends. Besides, she was really a cut above the usual, so there wasn't much in common.'

'But it was different with your customers.'

One had come in, a girl in a sheepskin coat who looked like a student. She was trying to explain something to the spotty boy. He didn't seem to be listening. After a few minutes she gave up and left the shop empty-handed.

'Look at that,' said Arthur Craven helplessly. 'I'd swear that little twit is trying to lose me business. No, as I said, Deirdre was red-hot with the punters. I admit some of them are a bit vague about what they want and what they want it for. Especially the young ones who are just learning. But Deirdre tried to help. And if there was something she didn't know, she'd always ask me. She was a great one for asking questions.'

'Was there anyone who showed a special interest in her, or she in them? I mean, can you think of anyone who it'd be worth my while talking to?' Anna felt he could quite happily talk in general terms all afternoon, while Celluloid Cellar went to ruin before his very eyes.

'Well, one or two of the fellows tried it on, if that's what you mean. She wasn't exactly a dolly-bird, but quite eye-catching in a tall sort of way. Wait a minute, though. There's old whatsisname. A small-time industrials bloke. Comes in here a lot when he's working. I remember now. She went out with him once or twice on her half-day. Reggie Lottman. That's his name. You get to know them quite well if they're regulars. Maybe she had a thing about older men. He muddled along with a bit of this and that. Charity films and Bar Mitzvahs mostly.'

'I'd like to talk to him and to your friend, Mr Bruce.' Anna, aware of time passing, was beginning to be afraid of getting caught in the rush hour. She had to see Brierly before he left at six, and one of her phobias was crowded public transport.

'Just a sec.' Craven got busy with his battered card-index file. 'There you are,' he said eventually. The inadequacies of his filing system had not yet defeated him completely. 'Copy those down. You can say I sent you, if you like. A good word from a friend still counts for something, I suppose. Even these days.'

'You've been very kind, Mr Craven,' Anna said standing up.

'Half a mo. There was one other.' He stood with his hand on the door-knob. 'A young chap, very pale, with dark curly hair. She talked to him quite often. He came in a lot about a year ago but I haven't seen him since. He had very nice manners, if I remember rightly.'

'I think I already know him,' said Anna, smiling. 'But thanks very much anyway.'

Anna arrived back at the office to find Bernie Schiller writing a report on the rec-room table. He was wearing his overcoat and sitting as near the electric fire as he could without scorching his trousers.

'Hullo, love,' he said, looking up, 'you look a touch concussed.'

'Just a little too much London Town in the silly season and no lunch.'

'Now that's silly, that's very silly. Here, I'll fix you a nice cuppa.' He got up and put the kettle on. 'Never miss a meal,' he said, 'you've only got one body between you and oblivion, so take care of it.'

All his movements were slow and methodical, but he touched everything with delicacy, as though even a teaspoon was a living organism. At fifty-eight he was the oldest member of the firm, but there was no one she would prefer to rely on in a crisis.

'When you're young, you think it doesn't matter,' he continued to lecture her gently while he warmed the pot. 'You think you can live on your nerves, but you can't. Not forever, and every skipped meal brings old age that bit closer.' He filled the pot with steaming water and stood warming his hands on it.

'It's the difference between working at seventy per cent and a hundred per cent,' he went on. 'Look at you, now. If you'd had a proper lunch, you wouldn't be as whacked as you are now.'

Bernie had retired from the Force still only a sergeant. This was his choice. He had wanted to spend all his working life on the same patch, and he had turned down all the opportunities that would have taken him away from it. His local knowledge was compendious. He had a reputation for being a plodder among the younger men. But this was deceptive. His thinking was slow, deliberate and precise, like everything he did, but his motive was always human interest. It was what kept him going over the years when younger men had been promoted over him. He was a rare man, who was truly fascinated by other people. It didn't matter to him if they were bent or straight; he was never shocked or bitter. He just retained a fresh and simple curiosity about human life. Anna always felt that he was like the sailor in the *Just So Stories*, a man of 'infinite resource and sagacity'.

'Sugar? I know you don't usually, but you need the extra energy.'

'Thanks, Bernie,' she said, sipping the fierce brew gratefully. Bernie made the kind of tea a mouse could stand on.

'What are you doing back here?' he asked. 'I heard you were out chasing ghosts.'

'Reporting back to head office. Only luckily Mr B. is tied up on the blower, which gives me time to sort it out a bit.'

'Want to tell me?' Bernie had time for everything, even in the middle of writing a report of his own.

She had benefited more than once from talking things over with Bernie. So she recounted the story to him.

'Your Mr Lester sounds like a good source,' he said when she had finished.

'Do you think so?' she said dubiously. 'I get worried when I like a chap from the off.'

'Well, you make fewer mistakes than most. And he sounds as if he's on the up and up.'

They went on drinking tea in silence for a minute.

Martin Brierly, when she was at last admitted to the front office, was more than usually dismissive. 'A clear and precise verbal presentation' was what he always said he wanted, but his continual objections and interruptions didn't make it easy. When she had finished, he summed up almost contemptuously:

'We have a pathological liar enamoured of show-business. Simon Lester sees her through rose-tinted spectacles. She is a good employee to Arthur Craven. She is a good organizer, but has no talent for making friends with people her own age. Has a possible father fixation, a predilection for older men. The only one so far who might wish her harm is the neurotic wife of a film society president. I think we are probably wasting our time, Miss Lee. Still, your time is paid for until Friday at least.'

'It depends rather on what the Jacksons really think they're spending their money on,' remarked Anna. 'I thought Mrs Jackson at least would be quite happy just to know what Deirdre had been doing in the last four years.'

'You may be right,' Brierly lowered his gaze, 'but, to put it crudely if I may, Mrs Jackson is not signing the cheque. Success or failure is therefore determined by your ability to discover something a little more significant than a jealous wife in Finsbury Park. Is that clear?'

Abundantly clear, thought Anna, hurrying across the Park in the cold early night. Deirdre, who had been slowly coming alive for her as a complex, lonely figure, had been reduced to a few scathing sentences. She felt depressed.

CHAPTER 8

THE day, from its empty beginning, had telescoped round her, and she had no time to change before leaving for the National Film Theatre. Simon, on the other hand, was looking almost Byronic in a black cord suit and clean white shirt.

'Are we doomed always to meet in overcrowded bars?' Simon said cheerfully when he joined her with a couple of glasses of white wine.

'I hope not,' she replied sincerely.

But they got seats at a table overlooking the river, and the feeling of extra space soothed her considerably.

'I want to pay for my ticket,' she told him.

'It's really not necessary. But if it makes you feel better, I won't argue.' Simon was a pacifying influence, too.

'You're a prince.' She sipped some wine and began to relax. They settled up amicably.

'What do you make of the Margolins, by the way?' She felt she should start work again before she relaxed too much.

'Have you seen them already?' he asked in surprise. 'You do work quickly. Well, he teaches English at some private school in Marylebone. He's quite nice, but a bit vague. He has lousy taste in films though; shows far too many recent ones. Maybe he uses the society as a cheap way to see new movies without getting ripped off in the West End.'

'What about her?'

'Sarah? Well, she's a bit strange. I don't know it for a fact, but I was told that after her daughter was born she had a bit of a breakdown. She caught, um, what's that thing called when you don't eat?'

'Anorexia nervosa? You don't catch it.'

'That's the one. And she spent some time in hospital. I don't think she eats much even now. He's always having to persuade her. I don't think poor old Len has much of a time at home. What did they say to you?'

It was Anna's turn to pick her words carefully.

'She accused Dee of trying to corrupt her husband. But since she also accused me of the same thing, and I hadn't even met him, I didn't take it too seriously.'

'That figures. She watches him like a hawk, and she's always muscling in on his conversations, especially if they're with a woman.' But she saw regretfully that she had managed to cut a slice off his good humour.

'Does Len have that sort of reputation, though?'

'Well, there has been some gossip. But I should think that's all it is.'

'All the same,' she said slowly, 'I wouldn't mind another word with him if I could manage it without getting my eyes scratched out.'

'That's easily done.' He smiled. 'You could come to Seven Sisters as my guest on Friday. It's never crowded there, I promise. Sarah doesn't always go. And if she is there you can keep out of her way till afterwards. He almost always leaves alone to take the film down to Soho.'

'What does he do that for?'

'Well, a film is only rented for one showing, and he has to deliver it back straight away or pay extra charges.'

'I might take you up on that, then,' she said. But

Simon was looking over her shoulder with a slightly stricken expression on his face.

'Oh God,' he muttered, 'Carlo's seen me. I'm sorry.'

Carlo was very tall and very thin. His apple-green trousers looked as if they would have to be scraped off his legs when he went to bed.

'Well, well, well, if it isn't simple Simon,' he drawled in an accent that sounded as if it had been dredged up from the middle of the Atlantic. 'Guess who can't resist Brando in his prime?' He draped himself elegantly over a chair opposite Anna and next to Simon.

'Aren't you going to introduce me to your lady-friend? Simon, you're very naughty. What would the terrifying Dee Jay have to say about this?'

'Anna, this is Charles Lepinnier. And Carlo, before you put your foot where your tongue should be, Anna is Dee's cousin. And you should know that Dee was killed in an accident a month ago.'

'No! That's simply shocking!' As far as he was able, Carlo sounded genuinely disturbed. 'Poor boy, you must be absolutely heartbroken. He doted on her, you know,' he told Anna unnecessarily.

'Leave off, Carlo,' Simon warned.

'Always the stiff upper labial. What a little man you are!' Jeering seemed to be a conversational tic with him. 'Still, I always said it would end in tears. So who's comforting whom, I wonder?' His bright little eyes glittered inquisitively.

Simon was looking as if the US Cavalry had let him down at the last minute.

'Cut your teeth on Oscar Wilde, did you?' Anna said mildly. She could at least draw the enemy's fire. 'Or were you born that way?'

'Oops. She bites!' said Carlo with enthusiasm.

'The tooth is mightier than the claw.'

Carlo laughed, throwing his head back and exhibiting some yellow back teeth. He looked several degrees more human that way.

'Not bad,' he said. 'You know, you have very interesting colouring. It must be the dark eyebrows. You don't curl up and dye, do you? No, I can see you don't.'

His accent had settled on a birthplace no further west then Peckham.

'You really ought to let me cut your hair for you, though. It looks as if you do it yourself in front of the bathroom mirror. Something a little more geometric, perhaps. You've got the kind of bones that could take it.'

'Carlo works in a salon off Fulham Road,' put in Simon unwisely. Carlo's rhino eyes swivelled towards him with a menacing gleam.

'I cut Dee's for her once,' he drawled. 'She was the type who wanted to look like Katherine Ross and make a feature of her troglodyte forehead. Very aggressive round the hairline was our Dee. Only once, though. Simon here objected to me introducing her to my friends, didn't you, dear boy?'

Anna emptied her glass hurriedly. 'Could I have another glass of wine?' she asked. Simon was not reluctant to leave.

'Don't shoot.' Carlo put up his hands defensively. 'I know I shouldn't, but he's so damn earnest. All that ghastly sincerity brings out the bitch in me. Speaking of which, are you really Dee's cousin? You don't look a bit like her.'

'Strictly speaking, no. Did you know her well?'

'Who did? Answer me that. A poor man's Garbo with thorns.'

'Seriously?'

'Seriously. I saw her around with Simon now and again. She led him around by the nose. Pathetic. It was like Van Gogh and Cousin K. If that's not too recherché for you.'

'Well, Simon kept his ears intact at least.'

'Yes, but what about his balls? Sorry, sorry, but she did make him look small.'

'She must have been a profound influence on you then,' she said drily. 'You're quite a successful miniaturist yourself.'

'Ouch. That hurt.' But he received insults with a glow most people reserved for compliments. 'I'm not a good person to talk to about Dee. I didn't like her. It's no secret. And I have to admit I enjoyed taking her down a peg or three if I could. I'm not all sweetness and light, in case you hadn't noticed.'

'Which of your friends did you introduce her to? I'm trying to contact everyone who knew her.'

'Well, there was a plasterer who did some ornamental moulding for the salon. He happened to come in for a chat on the same Saturday she came in for a cut. Well, everybody knew that Dee would have sold her soul to get into movies. So I told her that Toddy was making something big at Elstree. Which was true, in a way. Only it was a volcano for a sci-fi film. So the next thing you know, Dee was fixing herself up with Toddy for a guided tour round the studios. That's all. Not very kind, I will admit. His name is Barry Todd, and he does work at Elstree. Apart from that, I don't know where you'd find him.'

Simon had somehow succeeded in penetrating the maelstrom round the bar, and was coming slowly back with three glasses. He obviously had a generous nature.

'Was there anything else?' Anna asked hurriedly. 'You mentioned friends.'

'Just artistic licence, dearie. No, there was just Toddy.'

Simon arrived with most of the wine intact.

'Ah, dear boy, one for me? What a forgiving soul you are. Well, it was nice to have met you, Cousin K. Sorry, I mean Cousin A. Slip of the tongue, no resemblance at all. Do drop around to Follicle. I mean it. I could change your whole life with a single snip.'

'I believe you, if your scissors are half as sharp as your tongue,' she said gently.

'Or half as sharp as your teeth. Look out for your ears, dear boy.'

'Affected little sod, isn't he?' said Anna as they watched him weave his way through the crowd with the pretentious grace of a model on the catwalk, wineglass held high like the Olympic Torch.

'You handled him well, though. I sometimes think he

isn't camp at all. It's just a pose he works on to aggravate people.'

'I wonder,' she said thoughtfully. 'Is his salon really called Follicle, or was he kidding?'

'No, it really is.'

'Blimey,' said Anna.

'I'd better give you this before anything else happens.' He handed her a business card. It held the address and phone number for:

F rederick S linger
 ilm   ervices

'Thanks,' she said. But the questions she had ready had to be postponed, because the bell rang for the start of *One-Eyed Jacks*. She had seen it before, and the opening scenes brought a pang of nostalgia for another place, another time and very different company. But it was an episode more comfortably forgotten, and the film was gripping enough to bury the memory quickly.

Afterwards they had coffee among the untidy pools of elderly youngsters.

'Have you got time to talk about Dee some more?' Anna asked. 'I've got a car, and I'll drive you home if you live south of Stevenage.'

He accepted the lift, but he said that since lunchtime he had been thinking about Dee, and the more he thought the more he realized that he had very few hard facts about her. He was also painfully coming to the conclusion that those he had might be untrustworthy. They had talked a lot, but mainly about films. The conversations would usually be provoked by a movie they had seen together, and invariably moved on to the movies they would make themselves. Simon said that these fantasies had become less and less satisfactory to him, but Dee had never wanted to give up the notion that films were somehow created whole, in one burst of inspiration and excitement. While he, as he grew more experienced in the technicalities, had realized that his student ventures had been mere cloud-cuckoo-land, and that real films were made painstakingly by

specialized technicians each working separately at their
own speciality. He found the techniques and specialities
fascinating. But Dee thought them boring and depressing.

'This projectionist job, how long had Dee had that?'

'About seven months, I think. Are you thinking of
going to see Mr Slinger?'

'I might give him a ring tomorrow,' she said vaguely.

'Well, good luck. Dee always said he was one of the
most paranoid characters she'd ever known. He couldn't
answer the most simple question without looking for an
ulterior motive. And she should know,' he added bitterly,
'she was like that herself. She acted as if everyone was
looking for a weapon to use against her. She wasn't easy
to get close to.'

'What did she mean by paranoia?'

'Well, apparently he never answers the phone himself
even if he's right beside it. His wife has to drop what she's
doing and answer it for him. She has a typed list of names
he won't talk to, and with anyone else she has to act as a
sort of filter system, finding out what their business is
before he'll have anything to do with it. I think Dee quite
admired him for that. And then there was the cheque he
wrote for her once. Normally, he does as much business
as he can with cash. Well, one day he had to pay her by
cheque and he gave her a long talk about how easy it was
to alter cheques and showed her a foolproof system of
writing one out so that it couldn't be altered.'

The restaurant staff were rolling down the black shut-
ters around the bar and buffet. People were drifting away
in twos and threes into the driving snow. Anna watched it
moving like mist across the river. London, with its sulphur
lighting, had taken on the colour of faded apricots. She
turned back to Simon.

'So you think he mightn't want to talk to me.'

He laughed. 'I can't think of anyone who wouldn't
want to talk to you. Look at me. I'm usually known as a
reserved type, and I've been talking the hind leg off a
donkey. No, I was just thinking, if he thought you were
from an insurance company and Dee's parents were chis-

elling for compensation or something, he'd probably slam the door in your face.'

'What on earth would her parents want compensation for? She wasn't working for him on the night she died, was she?'

'I don't think so. No, in fact, I'm sure not. If she had been, the police would have found the projector and films in the car and gone to him immediately. And if they had, the Jackson family would have known about him and you wouldn't have had to come to me for the information.'

'True,' said Anna thoughtfully. 'Have you any idea what she was doing out by the airport that night?'

'None at all.' He drank the last of his coffee. It was cold, and he made a wry face.

They were almost the last to leave. In fact, as they drove north they seemed to be the last people out in London. The bad weather had swept the streets clean of late-nighters, and the street-lights shimmering on the fresh snow illumined a clean and silent city. The Triumph's tyres hardly gripped the road surface at all; Anna had the strange sensation that she was letting the car roll home by itself. So she concentrated on driving until she was more accustomed to the car's odd, tractionless motion.

'Why do you suppose Mr Slinger is such a cautious character?' she asked eventually, gingerly taking a left-handed corner and feeling the rear of the car wagging itself like a dog's tail as she straightened out afterwards.

Simon had been watching the road in some anxiety. She noticed that his right foot was clamped to the floor of the car in a constant braking action, whereas she was hardly touching the brakes at all except on clearer patches.

'Are you sure you want to talk right now?' he asked nervously. Someone less polite might have told her to shut up and drive.

'Don't worry. I think I can get you home in one piece. You'd be more of a help if you kept talking and stopped making a dent in my floorboards.'

'Okay,' he said, making a visible attempt to unwind. 'What do you want to talk about?'

'Start by telling me about the projection business and why Mr Slinger would be such a nervous type.'

'Well, as far as I can tell, the basis of it is children's parties. He hires out projection equipment and kiddies' films. The people who work for him go to a party and show, oh, I suppose it would be Laurel and Hardy, Woody Woodpecker films, that sort of thing. Perhaps he doesn't declare half his income. That would be quite easy if he deals in cash all the time.'

'Or perhaps he has a sideline in blue movies?'

'Could be, but Dee never mentioned anything like that. Sometimes they did shows for women's clubs with Arts Council films, Mondrian or Picasso, something highbrow.'

'It couldn't sound more innocuous, could it?'

'No,' he agreed, 'but I sometimes wonder where he got the films, and if he cleared the rights, and so on.'

'Are films sort of patented, then?'

'Oh yes. There are very strict copyright protections. You aren't supposed to show films to the public unless you have the permission of the copyright holder. You can't duplicate them, either. And the world is full of collectors who want copies of their favourite film. In fact, I know all about this because one of the lab technicians I worked with got fired quite recently for duplicating a piece of Citizen Kane. He had bought the film quite legitimately but he wasn't allowed to copy it or show it publicly, you see. But a lot of private collectors like to swap and enlarge their collections with stuff their friends have, so they try to get duplicates. Sometimes they can find lab technicians who will do it on the side. It's all under the counter, of course.'

'So Freddie Slinger's Film Services might be touting illegal Abbott and Costello to minors?'

Simon laughed. 'You never know. On the other hand, they might all be films on which the rights have lapsed. In that case they'd be anyone's meat.'

Simon's flat was above a shop in Maida Vale not more than a mile and a half from where she lived. He asked her up for coffee. But it was well after midnight and she refused.

'You will keep in touch, won't you?' he asked anxiously as he was getting out of the car. 'I mean, if there's anything else I can help you with . . .'

'You'll probably be sick of the sight of me,' she said lightly. He came round to the driver's side.

'You know, you remind me of Dee in a way. It's not just that you're related, but you have some of the same qualities. You're just as cool a driver, for one thing.'

'Don't even think about it,' Anna said firmly. 'There's no similarity at all. But thanks for a very nice evening, and I will be in touch, I promise.'

She saw him wave as she drove away, and she could see him in the mirror, standing alone in the snow, watching her, until she had turned a corner.

It was one of Brierly's dictums that a person under investigation should always be unaware of the fact. But there were times, and this was one of them, when it added an extra burden to the procedure. Anna thought that if she was going to see much more of Simon she would have to come clean.

CHAPTER 9

IN spite of having got to bed so late, Anna slept uneasily and woke earlier than she had intended. There had been a partial thaw during the night, and the ground outside was fairly clear of snow. She padded quietly downstairs to collect the milk. A flock of pigeons took off into the grey sky with the sound of gloved hands clapping, but otherwise the whole street was silent. It was seven o'clock. She made coffee and took the steaming mug back to bed to wait for a more kindly time to start phoning strangers. She was reading *Portrait of a Lady*, and she picked it up to pass the time. One day, she thought, she would move to the country and spend every day peacefully. She remembered two uniquely free and happy summers in a farmhouse on Exmoor. Apart from her mother's and sister's complaints and her father's obvious boredom, they were the most carefree days she remembered of her childhood. Ones she would repeat some time. But not yet. While there was still some excitement in meeting strangers and listening to their problems, London was the place to be. She would have to be considerably more jaded and a few years older before she could leave it happily and not feel that she had left life behind too.

She rang Dmitrios Bruce at nine and got as far as an impenetrable secretary. Sorry, she said, Mr Bruce was in Nairobi, lucky old Mr Bruce, and wouldn't be back till Monday.

No, she couldn't remember anything special about Deirdre Jackson. Speak to Mr Bruce when he gets back. Thank you for calling. Thank you for nothing, thought Anna.

Reggie Lottman had not escaped the English winter. He was suffering, like everyone else in Golders Green, but he would be happy to see her whenever she chose to turn up. He thought he would be free all morning, and wasn't the weather awful?

Mrs Slinger was in the middle of some crisis when she answered the phone. 'If it's about the job,' she said, 'come at a quarter to four. Mr Slinger will see you then.' She would have to sort the muddle out later, Anna thought, but at least she had an appointment.

She didn't ring Elstree. That was too hard a nut to crack on the telephone. But she put in her routine call to the office. Beryl's cold was ripening nicely.

Reggie Lottman's house was on a street just east of Finchley Road, and within spitting distance of the crematorium. He had an air of subdued disappointment about him; greying, balding and stooped. He had welcomed her greedily, as if he had been starved of human company.

'Come in, come in, nice to meet you. Isn't it terrible outside? Worse than the winter of '46, if anything could be.'

Anna couldn't help him with that particular memory. He fussed over her and plumped up the cushions in a chair by the fire.

His office, as he called it, would have been the living-room in other circumstances. There was a desk at one end, and shelves with several small film-cans, all neatly labelled, stacked on them. A calendar hung on the wall by the desk, with a noticeboard under it. Also on the wall were two posters. One said 'WALLS HAVE EARS' and the other, 'CARELESS TALK COSTS MONEY.' The more conventional living-room furniture had been shunted down to the other end of the room, where she sat; two armchairs and a sofa in a space too small for them. Three people with long legs, Anna thought, would sit with their knees touching, like passengers in a railway carriage.

'I'm very glad you chose today to come,' Mr Lottman said, 'because I'm normally a very busy man. But what with the weather . . .' He spread his hands vaguely. His obsession with meteorology, Anna thought, seemed to indicate a rather empty life.

'It was such a shock,' he went on. 'It's not what you'd expect from a young girl like that. Death is something you're ready for at my age, but twenty-two?'

He was probably not much older than fifty-five or sixty.

'I didn't know her very well.' Deirdre was a girl no one seemed prepared to admit to knowing well. 'But she came here once or twice, and I think we understood each other even in that short time. A shared enthusiasm brings people together faster, don't you think? You're not interested in cinematography yourself by any chance?'

Anna told him it wasn't her line.

'Films, yes. Cinematography, no. Like most people these days,' he said sadly. 'What a pity. I could have taught young Deirdre a lot, you know. But there you are. It was money, of course, It always is. At her age I would have paid for the opportunity I was offering her. But young people have their priorities all wrong nowadays. What she wanted was a salary and ACTT membership. I ask you. I told her if the union knew how I operated they'd probably black me for ever. But that was just my point, don't you see? What would she learn, if all she was doing each day was loading cameras and nothing else? Working for me she'd learn to do everything. Loading, operating, lighting, recording, editing. What more could you want?'

'I suppose she had to make a living,' Anna suggested tentatively.

'A living! And what sort of a living? So what does she do? She goes to work for that gangster Freddy Slinger.'

'Do you know him, then?'

'Not him personally, no. But if you've seen one you've seen them all. Projection Services, Distributors, call them what you like. I call them gangsters. They take your work; they live on other people's efforts. And do you see a penny back?'

'Can't you protect yourself with copyrights, for instance?' Anna was thinking of what Simon had been saying the night before.

'In theory you can. It's all right for rich producers. They can pay to enforce them. But if you're independent you can't always afford to sue. I'd be a rich man if I'd got a fair percentage. If things were actually the way they're supposed to be. It's a wonder I'm not a bitter man instead.'

'I suppose it is,' she agreed doubtfully.

'It's the same with ideas, you know. Look at these.' He indicated a pile of folders on his desk. He picked one up at random and opened it. 'They're all synopses. Take this one. A documentary. A day in the life of a footballer. The whole story from breakfast to bed-time. You see, it's got it all. The national preoccupation; glamour, topicality. Does it sound familiar?'

'I think I saw something like it on TV.' Anna fed him the required line.

'There you are. I knew you were a smart girl. Ideas need funding. It takes a lot of money to make even a short documentary. So I take this little bundle along to some producer's office. "Leave it with us," they say. "We'll let you know." Two weeks later it's "Thanks, but no thanks, we'll send your script back." Nine months later it's on the box, almost word for word as it's written here.' He tapped the folder against his knee. 'Oh, they changed the title. I'll give them that. But how do you protect yourself against that sort of villainy?'

'You seem to work in a very precarious world, Mr Lottman.'

'So who's complaining?' he asked perversely. 'It's just there's too many dogs round too small a bone. But I'm not saying I haven't had my share.' He seemed to take pleasure in defending what he had just attacked.

'And Deirdre?' she prompted.

'She was a good girl; intelligent. I could have done a lot for her. But when she told me who she was going to work for that had to be it, didn't it? Kaput. Once she chose to work for one of those sharks she couldn't be trusted any more. I told her, "You pay your money and take your choice in this world, my girl. There's no going back." '

'How did she take that?'

'Oh, she said it was only temporary and that she could still work for me in her spare time. In her spare time! So I told her, "Listen, my girl, if that's your attitude you're best off where you are; find some other mug!" It was a pity, though. I was due to do a wedding in Finchley and she could have worked the Nagra. She was very bright with the equipment, picked up techniques like a flash. She'd have been an ideal assistant.'

'Did you ever see her again after that?'

'No, never. It's too late to be sorry now. But what could I do? It was as if she went over to the enemy, you see. There are some with talent in this life and some with money. And those with money, nine times out of ten, got it through some poor beggar's talent. F. Slinger, Esquire had money. See what I mean?'

Anna finally managed to crawl out of his lake of defeatism. If Deirdre had any nose for success, she thought, it was small wonder she had gone to work for the opposition. Reggie Lottman had added little to her small cache of facts. But his demands on her time and attention had been in inverse proportion to his supply of real information. He was one of those people who have never learned to protect themselves from life's rough edges, and as he grew older he had acquired only disappointment. Anna, half his age, knew for a certainty that it was not absolutely necessary to make the same mistake twice, but Lottman collected defeats and displayed them with long-suffering pride. She had found him likable in a childlike way, but, unlike a child, he had run out of time and hope, and Anna believed that talent on its own sat gracefully only on the very young. After a certain age it was what you did with it that counted, and 'fair chances' were those you engineered for yourself.

CHAPTER 10

IF there was any action going on at Elstree, it was not happening on Stage Three. It was ill-lit and deserted, like a hangar with aircraft and crew absent. What caught the eye immediately, though, was that a large area of the floor was covered with what looked like moon surface. It was pitted and cratered, with moonrocks scattered arbitrarily over the surface, and it was remarkably realistic.

'Over there, somewhere,' said her guide, waving his arm vaguely.

'Thanks a lot,' said Anna. 'I won't be long.'

'Just check with me when you leave,' he said. 'I shouldn't be doing this, by rights.'

'Whatever you say, and thanks again.' Mollified by her humble gratitude and the warm five-pound note folded close to his heart, the attendant vanished through the opening in the huge rolling doors they had entered by. It had taken a lot of sweet talk to get this far. The Bank of England couldn't have been guarded with more care. She walked slowly round the room. It was a beautiful piece of work.

Someone said, 'I bet you always thought that was made of green cheese.'

The men had made themselves a small room within a room with three screens. It was warmed by a cylinder-gas fire, and the three of them were sitting on ancient ragged armchairs. Sandwiches, thermos flasks and playing-cards were strewn domestically on a trestle table between them. She had interrupted a game of cribbage.

'It's a lovely job,' she said, gesturing behind her.

'Isn't it just?' said the fat one who had spoken first.

'You ain't seen nothing yet,' put in another. 'Wait till they crash-land on it next week. No one'll call it a lovely job then.'

'Is that what they're going to do?' she said, looking at the meticulous modeling and craftsmanship. 'What a shame. All that work.'

'We cry all the way to the bank.' The fat man laughed. It was obviously an old joke. 'What can we do you for? It isn't often we get the birds back here. They're usually more interested in the actors than the workers.'

They were all dressed alike in immaculate white overalls; one old, one fat, and one blond. She had marked the blond one as her quarry.

'I was looking for Barry Todd.' The young one blushed obligingly. He had very fair hair and a pink skin that coloured easily.

'Well, you found him then,' said the fat one disgustedly. 'Old Toddy has all the luck. One day some bit of crackling will come round looking for me.'

'The missus'd kill you, so never mind, eh?' The older man spoke for the first time.

'She would an' all,' Fatty said contentedly, 'but it'd be worth it.' He had a shiny new digital quartz watch which he looked at ostentatiously. 'Come on, Dad,' he said. 'I suppose we'd better get at it and leave Toddy to do his press-ups in peace.'

'Filthy bleeder,' Toddy called amiably after him. 'Sorry about that, but you can't take them anywhere. So what's the pitch then, sister?' He let his cigarette roll round to the corner of his mouth, and struck a Humphrey Bogart pose.

Anna explained.

'Strewth!' The cigarette was still hanging perilously from his lower lip. 'What a fucking awful shame. We weren't exactly pals, but it's a bit of a blinder, all the same. She was younger than me, even. It makes you think, doesn't it?'

She was surprised at his reaction. He looked as if the finger of death had pointed at him, too.

'I've never had anyone I know die on me before. Silly, ennit? It's not as if she was anyone close. But it's like it's one fewer to say hello to.'

She waited for him to recover. He relit his cigarette and then offered her the tobacco tin. She hadn't smoked for over a year, but she rolled a thin one now. It seemed the companionable thing to do.

'I met her at Carlo's place. But you know that, don't you?' he said. 'Did a job there once, when things were a bit thin here. He's a funny berk, is Carlo, but not half as bad as he makes out.'

'Nobody could be.'

'Yeah, he insults everyone, but the silly buggers who go there seem to lap it up. Like it's all part of the atmosphere. Anyway, the place is always up to the ceiling in trendy birds, really tasty, some of them. So I go in there every now and then for a bit of an eyeful. You never know when one of them might fancy a touch of the rough. She was there one Saturday, and Carlo was geeing her up something rotten. So he tells her where I work, only like I was one of the nobs, see, and she comes on really strong. Well, I didn't argue, did I? A trip round this place is usually good for a quick kick into the penalty area, no matter which side of the set you work. I'm sorry,' he said apologetically, 'I shouldn't be telling it like this.'

'How did she take it? When she found out.'

'Oh, very cool. Well, you know her. She didn't like to admit she'd been taken for a ride. So she pretends she knew what the game was all along. No hard feelings. She was a snotty bint in a lot of ways, but I liked her.'

'Did you see her again?'

'Not for a long time. Well, our paths wouldn't cross much, would they? Funny thing was, when I did come across her again, it wasn't anywhere flash. Perhaps she did have a taste for the rough, after all.'

'Where was that, then?'

'The Royal Oak in Wembley. It's not a regular, but I've dropped in once or twice with my cousin Pat and his mates. And blow me down if she wasn't there one evening. So we said how're y'doing and that, and I bought her and her feller a drink. She seemed really well. That was only a couple of months ago.'

'Who was she with?'

'I dunno. She didn't mention no names. Just an ordinary chap. He's on the darts team, I think, and he works at one of the labs.'

'Pale chap, was he? With dark curly hair, about five-ten and lightly built—good looking?'

'He was lightly built all right, but the rest is wrong. He was a bit tall and weedy, and he had floppy hair. Always pushing it out of his eyes. He was a Mick, an' all.'

'That's a new one on me,' Anna said. 'So that was it, was it?'

'Yeah. Not much, is it? It's too bad knowing you're not going to see her around even to say hello to.' He rolled another cigarette and lit it. 'You must think I'm a bit of a carrot going on about it like this.'

'No. I feel the same way.' She relit her stub and took a last draw on it.

'Only some of the blokes round here wouldn't understand that,' he said, glancing through the gap between the screens as if afraid he had been overheard talking in an unmanly way.

He walked with her to the big rolling doors. The fat man hooted and catcalled cheerfully from the far corner, his voice echoing weirdly round the empty stage.

'I don't suppose you're ever near the Bush,' he said as they said goodbye. 'Only there's familiar face in the Victoria almost every night if you want one.'

'It's a date,' Anna said, withdrawing her hand from his scratchy clasp. 'Cheers, and thanks for talking to me.'

CHAPTER 11

· · · · · · · · · · ·

WITH Bernie's advice fresh in her mind she sat in her car and ate a packet of cod and chips. The fish was fresh and hot, the chips were not, so she left most of them in a waste-bin attached to a nearby lamp-post. Frederick Slinger lived deep in the dreary labyrinth that was Harrow. She checked his street in the *A to Z* and then, because there were nearly two hours to spare before her appointment there, she drove out to London Airport. She found Cranford Lane in a no-man's-land between the airport and the M4. It ran straight between two desolate pieces of waste-land and was bordered on one side by a sturdy wire fence attached to concrete stanchions. There were street-lights on the other side, and then a long expanse of untended earth. In the distance Anna could see Heathrow's industrial ring. She drove slowly up and down the lane until she found a concrete post which bore the marks of an impact. Then she pulled up and got out. An icy wind lashed in from the north, making her ears and teeth ache. From about a quarter of a mile away she could see a hunched figure plodding slowly towards her. She

pulled up the collar of her coat and snuggled her chin into
the polo-neck of her sweater. It was a bleak and unpro-
tected spot. A faint roar of traffic came to her from either
side, and heavy-bellied aircraft regularly cut through the
low cloud overhead. The maelstrom of human activity
seemed to orbit on this empty axis. The snow added to
the sense of desolation.

Anna crossed the road and stood looking back at the
marked post, trying to imagine Deirdre's car crumpled
against it, not a hard exercise in that monochromatic land-
scape. She crossed back to the post and scraped some of
the snow away from the base. She uncovered a few thin
shards of glass, but any evidence of skidding had been
eroded in the intervening month.

'The end of the bloody world,' she murmured to herself, squatting on her heels, gazing like an archeologist at
the glass arrowheads in her gloved hand.

'There was an accident there.'

She stood up and faced the speaker, who turned out
to be the plodding figure she had noticed earlier.

'I know,' she said. 'I was just having a look-see.'

With his beaky nose emerging from his balaclava, a
soft hat, and no chin visible under a multiplicity of woolly
scarves and collars, he looked like an ancient tortoise
peering shyly from under his shell. A dog of no identifi-
able breed appeared from behind the Triumph. It also was
wearing a thick wool coat. It waddled over to her and sat
with its grizzled muzzle raised between her and the old
man.

'She won't see much now, will she, old girl?' The
old man addressed the dog affectionately. It grimaced at
him toothlessly. 'She should have been here when it happened, like we were, eh?'

'You were the first one here, then?' Anna asked him.

'That's right,' he said simply. 'And the only ones,
weren't we, old girl? Are you from the insurance company?' he added sharply.

'No. The parents of the girl who died here asked me
to find out as much about the crash as I can.'

'I thought you looked a bit young for insurance.' He

squinted at her and sighed. 'But, you know, even policemen and soldiers look like schoolboys these days. We're
getting on a bit now, aren't we, old dear?'

'Would you like to sit in the car out of the wind for
a while?' she said. 'I'd like to ask one or two questions if
you don't mind.'

'Now that's a kind thought. Shall we do that, sweetheart, shall we?'

She opened the car door for him, and the dog nipped
stiff-legged in ahead of him and sat on the back seat. The
old man crawled in slowly, arranging his sartorial bulk as
comfortably as he could. Anna got in from the other side.

'Perhaps she'll take us somewhere sunny. You'd like
that, wouldn't you?' he said. 'I wouldn't touch her, if I
were you, her temper's a little uncertain nowadays.'

Anna laughed. 'I'm not quite sure who you're talking
to,' she said, 'but I promise you my temper's all right.'

'It's a habit I got into when the wife died, talking to
the dog. It drives my daughter-in-law wild,' he added with
some satisfaction. 'She thinks I'm in my dotage. Well, if
they treat you like a child, I think you end up acting like
one. Now, where were we?'

'Well, would you tell me about the crash? Where you
were, and what you saw?'

'Certainly,' he said with dignity. 'We were over
there,' he pointed to the copse, which was opposite the
houses some distance away, 'having a bit of a stroll. We
don't sleep as well as we used to. And the old girl's blad-
der isn't as efficient as it should be. If you'll pardon my
mentioning it. We heard a crash and glass breaking, and
I thought "Oh, oh, someone's come to grief." '

'About what time was that?'

'Ten past two,' he said precisely. 'So we came over
here. And there was this Cortina rammed up backwards
against that post.' He turned his body and aligned it with
the car he remembered, looking down his hand as if it
were the barrel of a gun. Then he turned back to Anna
and held the hand out to her.

'I'm Alastair Driver, by the way. You must excuse my

getting into your motorcar without introducing myself. My manners must be getting as bad as everyone else's.'

Anna shook his hand belatedly and murmured her own name.

'That's better,' he said. 'I thought there was something missing. Now, where was I? Oh yes, so there was the car with all its lights on and the engine still running. So I opened the door to see if the driver was hurt, and to turn the engine off. You're supposed to do that, you know. I heard it on the wireless. In case of an explosion, I believe.

'Anyway, she just toppled out of the car like a doll. She wasn't wearing the safety-belt, you see. It might have saved her life if she had.'

Anna said, 'That must have been nasty for you.'

'Oh, I've seen dead bodies before, in both wars. Women and children, too. But, you're right, it was very sad and rather shocking. She had lovely hair, you know, all long and spread out on the ground like one of those pictures of Ophelia drowned.'

She broke into his grave silence. 'What did you do then?'

'Oh, I turned off the motor. And then I checked her pulse. But she was gone. We don't walk very fast, of course, so it was several minutes before we got here, and you know it may be my imagination, but she seemed quite cold. So I covered her up. She had a rug in the back of her car like you do. Her handbag had fallen out, too, and it had spilled all around her. I covered that, too. It didn't seem quite decent, somehow. My wife used to be very private about what she kept in her handbag, and it didn't look right all open and everything strewn around. Then I went back home to phone the police.'

'Didn't anyone else hear the accident?'

'Well, they wouldn't would they? It's all the double-glazing they've got to keep the aircraft noise out. Sometimes you feel as if you've got cotton-wool in your ears when you're indoors.'

'No other passers-by?'

'None. Well, as you can see, not many people use this road.'

'I wonder why she did. Someone said you smelled alcohol and something else when you first got here.'

'There's nothing wrong with our noses, is there, old girl? Yes, when I opened the door, I smelled whisky. That's not a smell you forget. And something else. I thought at first it was petrol leaking, but it wasn't that. No, it was more like corroded metal. I told the police, but as it had gone by the time they got here, they weren't very interested.'

'And someone also said you thought there might have been two cars.'

'Ah, well, I couldn't be sure about that. There's noise from the main road all the time.'

'Was it icy?'

'Yes, it was fairly icy,' he remembered with his eyes shut.

'You've recalled it all very vividly.' Anna looked at the slightly glaucous eyes which belied his beak-like nose.

'And why shouldn't I?' he said snappishly. 'It's a common misapprehension among the young that the elderly lose their memories. Speaking for myself, I remember things better now than I used to when I was busy all day. I might forget where I put my spectacles now and then, but an incident as dramatic as that stands out like a sore thumb in the tedium of my life now.'

'Then can you remember any details? For instance, what had spilled out of the handbag?'

Mr Driver closed his eyes again. Then he started to count off on his fingers: 'A cheque book, a paying-in book, a wallet, a powder compact, a lipstick; other make-up things, I don't recognise them all; dark glasses, cigarettes, paper handkerchiefs, two biros, some loose change, a square lighter, a pair of scissors.' He opened his eyes. 'I can't think of anything else.'

'Good grief!' Anna was amazed. 'How do you recall all that?'

'I don't know,' he said simply, 'but it's like a picture

that's stayed in my mind, her lying there with all her things around her. It happens sometimes, when I get a shock.'

'Do you remember seeing any notebook, diary or address book?'

'No, but they might have stayed in the bag. Not everything came out, you know.'

'Was there anything at all, when you first arrived, that might have led you to think it wasn't an accident?'

'Foul play, you mean?' he asked calmly. 'No, nothing at all. Except it is a very silly place for an accident, if there was no other car to avoid.'

'Well, Mr Driver,' Anna said, 'you've been a great help.'

'Not at all, not at all. It's been a pleasure talking to you. I wish we met more fresh faces.' He shook her hand again. 'What was she like, the girl who died?'

'I never met her,' she said, glad to be truthful about it for once. 'But from all reports, intelligent, ambitious, energetic, organized and a bit mysterious. Can I drop you back at your house?'

'No, no,' he said, feeling for the handle, 'we've had our warm-up, thank you very much, and we mustn't let ourselves get stiff. We must keep moving, you see, or I'm afraid we'll stop altogether.'

CHAPTER 12

· · · · · · · · · ·

ANNA, lost in a maze of similar houses, still managed to be twenty minutes early. The Slingers lived at the end of a cul-de-sac of semi-detached houses, all mock-gabled and pebble-dashed, front doors painted in fresh primary colours, all net-curtained, front-gardened and gated. The cul-de-sac, like a blunt instrument, intruded on a school playing-field behind. The turning-space at the end was lined with cars.

Anna unlatched the gate and slowly walked to the front door. She rang the bell. A young man with long greasy hair and chilblained hands opened the door.

'Yes?'

'I've an appointment with Mr Slinger.'

'Well, you'd better come in then, but you'll have to wait.'

In the early winter dark of the hallway no one had thought to turn on the light. Several people were moving equipment from the back of the house and piling it by the front door. She stood out of the way, half-hidden by a row of hanging coats, and saw that what had appeared to be a semi-detached house had in fact been knocked into something larger by the simple device of an archway in the wall through to the house next door.

They were an oddly assorted crew, from the young chap who had let her in to a middle-aged man with a strawberry nose. Each of them working for himself, tripping over each other's piles and knocking into each other in the confined space. A tall, porcine man came in from the back.

'Get a bleeding move on, will you?' he said. 'What's got into you? You're like a bunch of old women.'

A girl emerged from an open door on the left. He pounced on her.

'What the fuck're you doing in there?'

'Looking for another take-up spool, Mr Slinger.'

'Look, Maureen, you know the form. You don't take equipment without you get my okay, and you don't go in there.'

'Come with me. You should know by now it's all in the garage.'

He went through the house with the girl trailing disconsolately behind him, shouting over his shoulder, 'Just get your bums on the road, you lot.'

Someone muttered, 'Fascist bastard,' but overcoats were put on hastily and they began moving the piles of gear out into the freezing afternoon.

A woman in a red woollen dress came down the stairs; a patch of bright colour in the gloom. She turned on the hall light and discovered Anna in the corner.

'Hello. Who are you?'

'I phoned earlier today. Someone let me in.'

'That's right,' the woman said. She was tall and big-boned, but carefully dressed and made up. 'You're early. Why don't you come in here and have a cup of coffee while you wait?'

She led the way through the arch into the next-door house, which by contrast was quiet and empty. The living-room was dominated by a huge television set and a lot of new electronic apparatus. The furniture all looked new, too: a white plastic-covered chesterfield with matching armchairs, low hard-edged coffee-tables and white melamine-coated shelf units. There were no books or pictures, but a large backlit aquarium added a modicum of colour and life to the stark production-line look of the room.

'That's nice,' said Anna of the fish.

'Isn't it?' But the woman was obviously referring to the whole room, which she surveyed with mysterious satisfaction, running her hand lovingly over the plastic surface of a chair. In spite of her height and blonde shop-window appearance, she had a worn, slightly intimidated air.

'I won't be long,' she said and left Anna alone with the fish. She could hear the noise of the departing work-force dimly as if from another world. She moved over to the door, which had been left slightly open.

'Now, bugger off, Maureen,' she heard Mr Slinger say, 'or you'll be late.'

A door banged. Someone said, 'Look at this projector, Mr Slinger, it's just junk. It's all clapped out. Can't I have a newer one for a change?'

'All in good time. If you treated the gear a bit more carefully . . . you've got hands like a ferkin' blacksmith . . . why don't you just piss off and stop whining.'

The door slammed twice more. Then he said, 'You all set, Bill?'

An older voice, 'Just off. You know, he's not wrong, Freddy. Some of this stuff is falling to bits.'

'I know, I know. But I've got some new ones coming in next week. Two of them, brand new, and dead cheap. I had a bit of luck with a fresh driver.'

'How do you do it, Freddy?'

'Don't ask, old son, don't even ask. Who's the coffee for, Audrey?'

'The girl who rang this morning. She's in there.'

'Oh, all right. I'll be in in a sec. Make one for me, too, will you?'

Anna moved smoothly away from the door, and when Audrey Slinger came in with the coffee she was at the window overlooking the garden and playing-field.

'My husband won't be a minute,' Mrs Slinger said as she handed over the cup. There were two lumps of sugar in the saucer.

She left the room as if someone were shooing her. Anna drifted back to her previous vantage point in time to hear Slinger say ' . . . no bleedin' luck at all with them.'

'Know what you mean, sport.'

'Either they're too mousey and thick as a gravedigger's boot or they're smart . . .'

'Which gets us . . .'

'Right, Bill. Up to here in the cactus.'

'Well, I'll leave you to it, then, and be on my bike . . .'

Anna left the rest unheard and retreated to the window. Ever since she had entered the house, she had been glad that her misunderstanding with Mrs Slinger on the phone that morning had given her an alternative approach. That Frederick Slinger was bent was beyond question. But that was merely an instant character evaluation. To her, bentness was only a potential. It could indicate anything from minor dishonesty to full-scale villainy. She could see it in young children just as clearly as in practiced criminals. Slinger had that potential. Whether it added up to any more than picking up projectors from the back of a lorry, she didn't know and did not want to guess. But her instinct was to back off and observe him and his business from a position where her own aims could be protected. She wished she knew more about the film business in general and projectors in particular. Especially, she hoped that Slinger would give her a job.

When he came in, he was brisk and businesslike. His voice was unlike the one she had heard in the hall, suaver, more toned-down.

'Ah, good afternoon, Miss . . . ?'

'Lee, Anna Lee.'

'Well, do sit down, Miss Lee.'

Anna perched cautiously on the edge of a white chair. It looked as if it would sigh rudely if she plumped herself down in it comfortably.

'I understand you're looking for a job.' He smiled and sat down too. He had an infectious smile which pushed his plump cheeks up till they nearly hid his careful brown eyes.

Anna's favourite device for drawing people out was one that Selwyn had once called the Narcissus Ploy. Quietly responsive, she would become a mirror to the person she was talking to, who gained confidence in the presence of someone so like himself and often revealed more than was wise. It demanded time and patience, though. When the technique foundered, it was because the target was waiting to take his cue from her. With some dismay she saw that Slinger was balanced like a chameleon deciding what colour to change to. He would bully the weak, be a chum to the strong and take an intelligent interest in the intelligent. Narcissus was not a game that two could play.

'What made you think that I could help you?' Slinger asked.

'A friend of mine took her four-year-old to a party where your films were being shown,' she said slowly, feeling her way. 'She thought it was such a good idea that she asked for one of your cards. Her child's birthday is coming up in a couple of months. She talked to the projectionist about what sort of arrangements had to be made, and he happened to mention that it would be wise to book early because it was the busy season and you were slightly understaffed at the moment. She knew that I was looking for part-time work and she thought it might suit me.'

'Are you familiar with projectors and 16mm film?'

'Yes,' said Anna, mentally crossing her fingers.

Mercifully, the phone rang. Mrs Slinger answered, and Slinger took the call in his office.

'How come you're in need of a part-time job?' he asked when he came back.

'A project I'm working on at present has run over schedule,' Anna said, donnishly fussy. 'We're all right for materials, of course, but personally I'm getting a little low on living expenses. You know how it is. If you had a position you could offer me, I know the hours would fit perfectly and I'd eat more regularly.'

'What sort of project would that be?' He was friendly, curious and unshakably non-committal.

'I don't know how familiar you are with Actias selene?' she said, dipping into some half-remembered natural history.

'Not at all,' he admitted cheerfully, but not stopping
her, as she had hoped her would.

'One of the lovelier long-tailed moths from Southeast
Asia.' Anna wished she had a pair of spectacles to polish.
'We are attempting to film the entire life cycle. It sounds
simple enough, but we have run into a few snags.'

'For instance?'

'Er, for instance, well, I expect you're aware that heat
and light speed up the, ah, metabolic rate? Well, in attempting to light the, ah, subject in order to film it, we
find that we are seriously disturbing its bio-rhythm, even
so much as to cause desiccation in the pupae.'

'Yeah? Well, what can you do about that?' His attention was beginning to flag, but he was smiling broadly.
He seemed to find her amusing.

'Glass and water sandwich in the end,' she said confidingly, beginning to enjoy herself. 'And then you wouldn't
believe the trouble we've had keeping a fresh supply of
walnut leaves. Actias selene larvae won't touch anything
else. They're such choosy little beggars. We can get them
on mail-order from Japan, but how do you keep twenty-
five pounds of walnut leaves fresh?' she appealed to Mrs
Slinger.

'Very tricky, I expect,' Mrs Slinger said, blinking
rapidly.

'Quite!' Anna agreed. 'Of course, one can always
keep the imago quite happy on twelve-to-one sugar and
water solution. That's simple. But we've yet to produce a
perfect imago under our working conditions. So, you can
see the problem, can't you? No breeding-fit, mint-
condition moth, no film.'

'I see,' said Slinger. But she saw, quite happily, that
this was untrue.

'If I was able to find some work for you here,' he
went on, 'would it only be a temporary arrangement?'

It was time to show the necessary Achilles heel, so
she ducked her head and looked up at him.

'Well, as a matter of fact,' she said reluctantly, 'this is not the first time I've found myself financially embarrassed right in the middle of something.'

'Financially embarrassed!' He slapped the arm of his chair. 'That's good.'

'So, what with one thing and another, it would be very useful to have a small income independent of grants or producers, and of course, if it could be arranged, independent of Inland Revenue and National Insurance, too.'

'Inland Revenue!' He looked at his wife and laughed. 'You're a bit of a card all round, aren't you? So you wouldn't mind doing the tax-man out of a few bob, "if it could be arranged?" '

'Well,' she said huffily, 'the boot is usually firmly on the other foot, isn't it?'

'You can say that again! If I decide to take you, when could you start?'

'Almost immediately.' She tried to inject the correct degree of eagerness. 'I can easily sort it out with my colleagues. We work in shifts anyway. One has to keep a twenty-four-hour watch in case one of the little beggars chooses four in the morning to turn in the performance of a lifetime. Lepidopterae are far, far more inconsistent than actors.'

He was amused with her, and more than a little superior, which was to Anna a very satisfactory state of affairs.

'Well, maybe I can help you after all.' His tone was nicely patronizing. 'It just happens that I do have a very hectic weekend coming up, so how would Saturday suit?'

'Wonderful!' cried Anna, jumping up. 'Absolutely marvellous. Thank you so much!'

He laughed. 'Calm down. It's just a trial. Then, if you work out all right, we'll see how we go from there. Okay?'

They talked about money and transport for a while, Anna preserving her unworldly, grateful pose. Then he said: 'Right, Saturday morning then. Be here at ten-thirty sharp. You have to be in Stanmore at eleven-fifteen. It's a wedding, and you have to keep the kids happy for an hour while everyone else shovels down the champagne. You can handle kids, I suppose?'

'Oh yes.'

'Then you should manage fine. I don't see why we shouldn't get on very satisfactorily,' he went on more expansively, as he showed her out, 'I can always find a place in my organization for a bright girl. You scratch my back and I'll scratch yours. Do you know that ten years ago we were in the East End? Now look at us.'

'I've always admired people with an acute business sense,' she said admiringly. 'I've never had much luck with money.'

'It's not a question of luck,' he said, shaking her hand. 'It's having a good idea and knowing how to exploit it. Timing's the key. Good timing in business is everything.'

Anna drove away with a smile and a nagging sense of self-contempt. She smiled because she had enjoyed the pantomime. The self-contempt was for the same reason. She went directly to the Royal Oak in Wembley.

The barman was sitting on his stool with his arms folded on the counter, reading the *Evening Standard*. A few old men scattered at the tables nursed their pints and chatted fitfully. The floor was swept, the ashtrays were clean and the beer-mats still dry. It was only in this early-evening hiatus that Anna found pubs tolerable. She asked for a shandy and talked quietly to the barman, telling him in a leisurely, undramatic way who she was looking for. Without seeming too inquisitive, she learned that his name was Francis Neary and that he was a laboratory worker at Colour Cine Services. The barman told her where his lodgings were and his landlady's name. She was often found in the Oak, too.

'I don't know how a pub gets Irish,' he said, 'but this one's on the brink. Don't get me wrong. I like 'em, but it takes all sorts to make the world go round. And I'm a bloke who likes all sorts. So, if this place goes all the way shamrock, I'm off somewhere else. An Irish pub is an Irish pub, if you see what I mean.'

He refilled her glass and turned away to serve some new customers. Anna waited more impatiently now. The public bar was filling up and, if Francis didn't come soon, she would have to find another opportunity to talk to him.

'You run a darts team here, don't you?' she said when the barman came back. 'Is it any good?'

'Not bad,' he told her. 'Your boyo used to be one of the leading lights. But his game's gone off lately. Perhaps he's been too long on the graveyard shift. You often find the odd hours affect a man's eye.'

She hardly needed the barman's confirmation when Francis Neary came in twenty minutes later. He was about six foot two, very thin and round-shouldered. A palm-like frond of oily brown hair seemed to be irresistibly attracted towards his nose. He had a small chin and an active Adam's apple, which bobbed excitedly when she offered him a drink and asked to talk to him for a few minutes.

'Don't know what we'd be talking about,' he said, looking about him to see if anyone was watching. 'We haven't met, have we?'

He was very self-conscious. Walking to a table and sitting down was achieved in stiff jerky movements, and the thin film of grease which had made his nose shine spread across his entire face.

'I don't know no girls,' he said when she asked him about Deirdre. 'I don't know what you're talking about. I come in here to drink with my mates. I don't go talking to no girls.'

He wiped the palms of his hands on his thighs, leaving a dark stain on the faded denim.

'Someone who knew Deirdre said he saw you both in here about two months ago,' Anna persisted.

'Who said?' He looked all around him. His eyes turned down at the corners.

'He bought you a drink,' she went on patiently. 'A fair chap. Don't you remember?'

'Look, I don't know who you mean. Well, maybe I do buy a girl a drink now and again. What's the harm in that? I can't remember them all. What's it to you?'

She showed him the photo of Deirdre.

'You'd remember her, surely?'

He looked down at the picture on the table between

them. She couldn't see his eyes, but his lower lip was moist and slack. He pushed the photo away.

'I don't remember her or him or anyone else,' he said slowly. 'Look, why don't you stop bothering me. You can stuff your drink.'

Anna shrugged and stood up. She said, 'She's dead now and I wanted to find anyone who might have talked to her.'

He looked up at her.

'What difference does that make?' he asked.

'You tell me,' said Anna, because she felt tired and disgusted and wanted the last word for a change.

He got up suddenly. 'What's that supposed to mean?'

'Nothing at all,' she said, wearily turning to leave. But he grabbed her arm.

'Look, you,' he hissed at her, 'why don't you mind your own bloody business and I'll mind mine.'

She pulled her arm free and went out. She knew she would have to talk to Francis Neary again and she did not relish the prospect. The evening had turned sour, and she wanted to go home to a meal and a hot bath. Francis Neary could wait.

CHAPTER 13

THE phone was ringing as she let herself into her flat. 'Where have you been?' Beryl's voice was nasal and peremptory. 'Mr Brierly especially wanted a word before he left. It's too late now, but there are one or two things he wants you to know. You really should ring in more regularly. It's most inconsiderate of you. I'm phoning from my home now, and I don't like to bring work home.'

'Nor do I,' Anna muttered. Then, louder and more wisely, she added, 'Sorry, Beryl, but things sort of stacked up on me.'

'It's a civilized country, you know. It's not as if you're a hundred miles from the nearest phone.' It was no use apologizing to Beryl. Apologies only fed her grievances and did nothing to soothe them.

'Mr Jackson phoned this morning.' Beryl got to the point eventually. 'He went through Deirdre's papers as was suggested. He says she had been drawing unemployment benefit for the last seven months or so and depositing that exact sum weekly in her current account. He is not happy about that. In the main, withdrawals correspond with receipts she kept.' She sounded as if she were reading from shorthand notes.

'Deirdre had a deposit account which was £1263 in credit. Apparently most of that was a gift from her father for her nineteenth birthday, at a time when he thought she might be persuaded to come home. The rest is accumulated interest. She never touched the capital. He isn't happy about that, either. There were no building society accounts or any investments. The rest of her papers surprised him only because they were completely impersonal. You asked for all this, didn't you?'

'Yes.'

'Well, I hope it's helpful, then. The next thing is, Mr Jackson is coming to London on Friday. The Commander tried to put him off but he insisted—a bit hysterical, if you ask me. So get something on paper, will you? An interim report will do, but please make it readable for once. We may have to make copies. Anna?'

'Mmm?'

'Did you hear me? A report. Not amended casenotes!'

'Yes, I heard. Beryl? Will you get the doctor's report? Cause of death and all that.'

'If you really think it's necessary. Mr Brierly did say he thought you were taking this too seriously.'

'I just want to be thorough. He can't complain about that. And, Beryl, can you find something out for me? Frederick Slinger.' Anna described him and gave his address. 'I need to know if he has a yellow sheet. And Francis Neary . . . N-E-A-R-Y. They're both wasps in the marmalade at first glance.'

'You don't ask for much, do you?' Beryl sounded insulted.

'I know, but you do have the connections. That chap in Central Records eats out of your hand. You know that. If anyone can, it's you.'

'Well, I'll try,' Beryl said, mollified. 'But I'll have to go through the Commander. If he says no, it's no.'

'Thanks, Beryl. Is that everything?'

'It's all for now. Jackson's appointment is Friday, two p.m. Got that?'

'Got it. And a report. Good night, Beryl.'

Anna lit the gas-fire. Then she took a deep breath and dialled Simon's number.

'How are you?' he said, sounding pleased. 'I'm glad you rang. I was afraid I made a bad impression last night, and then it occurred to me that I didn't know how to get in touch with you.'

'Well, here I am. Look, can I see you tomorrow evening?'

'Sure,' he said, 'but why not now?'

'There isn't time now. When do you get off work?'

'Five-thirty. I get back here usually about six. What's it all about?'

'Can you show me how to use a 16mm projector?'

'Christ!' he said. 'What have you done?'

'I got Dee's old job. But that's not all. There's quite a lot I have to tell you. And then, if you still want to help, I'd be only too grateful. Can you hang on a minute? There's someone at the door.'

She let Selwyn in and went back to the phone.

'Si? Are you still there?'

'Yeah . . . sorry, I was a bit surprised. What on earth are you doing, Anna? This amateur sleuthing could get you into trouble.'

She laughed. 'I'll explain it all tomorrow. Sixish, then?'

'Okay, but take care.'

'You too.' He rang off.

'Do I see bags under your eyes?' Selwyn said, turning away from a reproduction of one of Hockney's sunny Californian swimming pools. 'Or are they social circles?'

'Wotcha, Selwyn,' Anna said, moving purposefully towards the bathroom, shedding coat, scarf and bag as she went.

'Bea says have you got an orange she can borrow for the crumble?' he shouted over the noise of running water.

'In the kitchen.'

'Where?'

Anna passed him, standing perplexed at the kitchen door. The fruit dish was conspicuous on the table, but Selwyn was not one to notice the obvious. She handed him an orange.

'Ta. Are you coming down? Bea said to say there's a mountain of stew going begging. More a volcano I should say, all red hot and bubbling like molten lava, it is, and threatening to deluge Pompeii if you don't come and help us with it.'

Her introduction to the Prices, only a couple of days after she had moved into the flat, had been typical of their subsequent relationship. Selwyn, thinking he had blown the fuses of the entire house by poking an electric fire with a wire coat-hanger, had stormed around in the dark unable to find the fuse-boxes. He had lived there for nine years. Anna, drawn unwillingly into the panic, had spent half an hour convincing him that there was a power cut, and that it was impossible for his carelessness to have deprived most of London of its power supply. She had then supplied two torches and a dozen candles, and Bea had cooked bacon and eggs on a Primus stove. They made numerous demands on her, but their hospitality was generous in proportion. As neighbours they did most of the running, but Anna enjoyed their company and was very willing to be carried along in their slipstream. Sometimes, when she was tired and anxious, she would have preferred to share a house with xenophobes, but mainly it was a situation, with more benefits than disadvantages.

'Not tonight, thanks,' she said on her way back to the bathroom. 'I've got too much to do.'

'We're poised to win the Ashes,' he said seductively. 'I thought you might want to watch,' and spoiled it all by adding, 'And the chain's come off again.'

Selwyn's bicycle was a constant source of harassment to him, its simple engineering being quite beyond his comprehension. Anna prayed fervently that he would never forsake his principles and own a car.

'Honest, Selwyn.' She had turned off the taps, and on an impulse was thumbing through the A to D telephone directory. 'I've been on the road all day and now I've got to write a report. I'll do your bike in the morning. I promise.'

'Have you no soul, girl? How often will you see England win the Ashes? It's something to tell your grandchildren. Where were you, Granny, when England were fighting for their honour in Australia? What's up?'

Anna had stopped leafing through the directory, and was sitting immobile on the edge of the bed—having just seen that Colour Cine Services' laboratory was situated on the south perimeter road of Heathrow Airport.

'Nothing,' she said. 'Well, maybe nothing. On the other hand it could be a dirty great something.'

Suddenly, she was no longer tired and discouraged, so after her bath she went downstairs to hot stew and cricket.

CHAPTER 14

· · · · · · · · · ·

THE cat woke Anna at eight, wailing outside her door like a neutered donkey. She let him in, and he galloped into the kitchen. She danced around opening a can of food for him, trying to avoid the touch of his cold wet fur as he wound himself round her bed-warm ankles. She hadn't seen him for over a week, so she stroked him while he ate. He would never let her touch him when he was satisfied, but permitted minor intimacies when he was hungry. As soon as he had eaten he wanted to leave, so she let him out of the front door and collected the milk at the same time.

At nine o'clock she telephoned Colour Cine Services and asked for the personnel manager. Her call was re-routed and mislaid. After listening to the characteristic singing noise of an empty line for a couple of minutes, she started again. This time she found the personnel manager's personal assistant. Mr Smythe wasn't in yet. He must have been delayed. No, we don't know when he will be available. Leave your number and he'll contact you some time during the day. Sorry, that's the best we can do. Anyway we are not permitted to reveal personal details of personnel to unauthorized persons over the telephone. Redirect this call to the works manager? I'll try. She tried and failed. Anna dialled CCS's number again and talked to the works manager. He had just come in. The late shift had clocked off twenty minutes ago. No, he didn't know who they were, he just had to cope with the mess they left behind.

Anna cleaned her teeth. It didn't help, but it made her feel fresher. She selected some tools from the cutlery tray and went down to attend to Selwyn's bicycle. As she slipped the chain over the sprocket wheel and retightened it, Selwyn appeared at his doorway dishevelled and still in his pyjamas. He had his coffee cup in his hand. His hair was like a heron's nest and he complained of a headache. Anna refused more coffee, but brought him two aspirins from the bathroom.

'It's going to be a bad day, I know it,' he prophesied, swilling the tablets down with his cold coffee. 'It's still dark out there. The sun will never rise. I won't be able to work. My muse will never come calling on a day like this.'

'That's right,' said Anna, trying to edge past him to the front door, 'blame it on a woman.'

'You don't understand what it's like waiting here with only four walls for company, dredging my poor soul till it's empty.'

'You should join a union. Ask for better conditions and incentive bonuses.'

'You're right.' Selwyn cheered up slightly. 'Think of the headlines, ''Panic Buying as Poets Threaten Strike Action.'' We'd have the nation on its knees in no time.'

'There you go.' She had achieved the doorstep by now. 'Get Ted Hughes as your General Secretary. He's got the right sort of name and I'm told he expresses himself rather well.'

'Disloyal! That's what you are,' Selwyn yelled, slamming the door behind her.

Anna drove to Wembley in the freezing rain. Car wheels ploughed furrows in the drenched roads and threw up dirty spray which blurred her windscreen. The wipers beat their metronomic rhythm attempting to clear it.

The barman at the Oak had named the street Francis Neary lived in, but he didn't know the number. She parked near the corner and went into a newsagent's to enquire.

Number fifty-one was a tawdry building backing onto a railway line. The front door had once been dark green, but now was cracked and dirty. The bell did not work, so she hammered on the door with the heel of her hand. Somewhere inside a baby was crying. A tiny woman opened up after a long wait. She could not have been taller than four foot ten. The two little girls clinging to her skirt looked large and round by comparison, as if they had sapped the life out of her as they grew, leaving her shrunken and wrinkled. Strangely, she looked both too old and too young to have children of that age. Her coppery hair was cut straight just below her earlobes like a school-girl's, but she had a cigarette glued to her lower lip.

'What is it?' she said through the smoke. 'I've a baby crying back there.'

'Mrs Halloran?' Anna asked, and when the woman nodded, went on, 'Is Francis Neary back from work yet?'

'He never went out,' Mrs. Halloran said. 'You'd better come in or go away. That wee article's going to burst hisself.'

Indeed, the tone of the baby's crying had changed to a hysterical scream. She followed the little woman along the dark passage, an obstacle-course strewn with broken push-chairs and toys, into the kitchen. The baby was sitting on the floor in a pool of urine, his scarlet face swollen with rage. Mrs Halloran picked the baby up, and he quietened miraculously. 'It's his teeth.' She dribbled smoke into the baby's face, but he didn't seem to mind this any more than she minded clasping his sodden body to the front of her dressing-gown. They were all in their night-clothes. Piles of dirty dishes were stacked in and around the sink, and dirty clothes were left where they had been dropped.

'Francis didn't go to work last night,' the little woman said, looking anxiously round for an empty chair to sit on.

'He came back drunk last night. I told him he should be away to his job, but he shut the door in my face.'

'Is he still in, then?' Anna asked, breathing shallowly through her mouth. The smell of the kitchen made her stomach tighten.

'For all I know.' Mrs Halloran lit a fresh cigarette from the butt of the old one. 'I didn't hear him go out, but I've got too much to do without keeping an eye on that one.'

'I'd like a word with him if I may.'

'Suit yourself. But you can tell him from me, he'll be looking for another room if he doesn't stop this carry-on. I told him he should've gone home for Christmas. He's been proper down in the mouth for weeks.'

'Where's his room?' Anna asked, impatient to leave. 'I'll go up and see if he's in.'

'He's not upstairs. I gave him the front room, the one on the left.' She went to the door to see that Anna got the right one.

She knocked, but there was no answer.

'Sleeping it off, most like,' the little woman said. 'You can go in. There's no key.'

Anna pushed the door gently. Something resisted, and she heard a soft cracking noise. She pushed harder and the door flew open. Festoons of clear tape hung from the top of the doorway liked ragged bunting. Francis had sellotaped himself in. Gas hissed from the fireplace; but there was no fire. Anna jumped to the window and tackled the catch and the sash. He had sealed the window with sellotape too. She struggled to pull the bottom half of the window up, but it wouldn't move. Then, with a great effort, she got the top half down. It stuck half-way, but it was enough. A gust of cold wind and rain blew into the room. She whirled back to the fireplace and turned off the gas-tap, her sweating fingers slipping on the pockmarked metal.

Mrs Halloran, still holding the baby and flanked by the two girls, stood gaping in the doorway.

'Get rid of your fag,' Anna shouted at her. 'Put it out. And get the kids out of here!'

No one moved.

'Now!' she yelled. 'Hurry!'

Mrs Halloran tore herself away from the room and vanished into the darkness of the passage.

She turned back to the bed. Francis Neary was lying on his back, fully clothed. His head was turned upwards, and his mouth was full of white and brown vomit. It covered the lower part of his face and spread over the front of his shirt and collar on to the pillow. Anna locked her throat to stop herself from retching. She could not bring herself to look for a pulse in his neck, for the putrid mess was everywhere, even in his hair. She clenched her teeth as some atavistic horror gripped her, and felt his wrist, trying to calm herself and stop her hand shaking. It was like touching cheese, so cold and clammy was his skin. Anna had an obsessive urge to wash. She backed away from the bed to the door, shouting, 'Have you got a phone?'

There was no reply. She went to the kitchen. They had formed a tight little group. Mrs Halloran at the centre was sitting stiffly upright on the edge of her chair. But for the livid spots of colour high on her cheekbones she looked almost as pale as Francis Neary.

'I said, have you got a phone?'

They stared at her as if she was speaking a foreign language, their mouths as wide open as their eyes. Anna repressed a desire to slap the woman's face, and forced herself to speak more gently.

'Someone must phone for the ambulance and the police. Now, is there a phone in the house?'

Mrs Halloran cleared her throat, but her voice was still strangled. 'Is he dead?'

'Yes, I'm afraid he is,' Anna said quietly. 'Please tell me where I can find a phone.'

'He shouldn't have done it here. This is a Catholic house.'

'I know, it's awful for you,' Anna said demonically, anger beginning to clutch at her like the hand of sanity. 'But, please, could you tell me if there's a telephone in this house?'

'They've got one next door.' The woman stood up. 'We're not stopping in this house with him.'

'Where are you going?' Anna asked despairingly.

'Next door.' The woman picked up a child's blanket to wrap round the baby, and they went to the back door like a refugee family.

'Will you phone the police, then?'

'I have to get hold of the Father. He'll know what should be done.'

'Ring 999 first, please. Get the police. It's important.'

'You shouldn't have come here!' Mrs Halloran turned on her in anger. 'Bringing your bad luck.'

Anna went back to the bedroom. Her temper had cleared her head a little, and she was able to look around more calmly. It was a poor room. Faded brown linoleum covered the floor, and dust-balls had collected under the bed and chest of drawers. Apart from the wardrobe and a small chair, the only other piece of furniture was a bedside cabinet. A white plastic crucifix hung over the head of the bed and on the opposite wall over the gas-fire was a picture of a green girl, nude to the waist with her arms stretched above her head.

Avoiding the bed, she examined the cabinet. A piece of white paper was folded crookedly and lay on top of an untidy pile of Marvel comics. She unfolded it.

'Dear Mother,' it read.

> I am sorry. I could not help it. If you only knew what I have been going through, you will forgive me.
>
> Your loving son,
> Fran.

The words were blotched and sprawling. Francis had no envelope to put it in, nor a stamp to send it with. She wondered if Mrs Neary would ever read her son's letter. She folded it and put it back gently. There were some letters still in their torn envelopes, each bearing a Northern Ireland postmark, in the drawer underneath. She didn't touch them. Next to them lay a prayer book and a rosary.

Both of these had dust on them. Further back was a single unopened packet of contraceptives. It was dusty, too.

Turning away, she kicked an empty whisky bottle under the bed. The unexpected sound made her jump. In the grey-rimmed wash-basin she found a tumbler, cracked when it had dropped into the bowl, four or five white tablets, half-dissolved in the damp, and a small brown bottle. She picked it up, mechanically putting her fingers inside the neck to do so. It had contained a hundred non-soluble aspirin. Now it was empty. She put it back. The glass shelf above the basin held a toothbrush, a screwed-up tube of toothpaste, a dirty comb and a preparation to prevent premature balding. Anna caught sight of herself in the mirror behind them. The whites of her eyes were showing.

She opened the drawers of the chest; nothing in the bottom two but some shirts and sweaters and dirty laundry. In the top drawer, nestling among the socks and vests, were a black and silver transistor radio and a similar cassette tape recorder. Both looked new and expensive.

The cheap suitcase on top of the wardrobe was empty. Two suits were hanging in the cupboard. One was threadbare and shiny. The other looked unworn, and was a charcoal grey worsted made to measure. It had a waistcoat, and was the sort of suit footballers wear to inspect the pitch at Wembley. A green silk tie hung on another hanger with a white drip-dry shirt which still had celluloid under the collar. A pair of zip-up black boots were lined up neatly under the suit.

His raincoat hung on a hook behind the door. The pockets held sweet-papers, seven toffees, a packet of ten No. 6, a box of Swans, a latch-key, a bundle of pools coupons, a dirty handkerchief and about thirty-five pence in small change. His wallet was probably in the jacket he had on. She was prevented from looking by a hammering on the front door. As she went to open it she wondered vaguely if she had left searching the body till last in just that hope of being interrupted.

There were two uniformed policemen on the doorstep. The younger one stared at her in disbelief and said, 'Are you the lady who called in?'

'Course not,' said the older one. 'This is Halloran's dump. I came here two years ago. His missus was beating him up.'

'Domestics!' the young one sneered knowingly. He looked like a probationer to Anna; fair, pink and slightly spotty.

'Well now, Miss, what's going on here?' The older one was looking her over carefully.

'There's a chap in there who seems to have killed himself.'

'Has he, indeed!' he said soothingly. She thought she must have sounded more jittery than she intended.

'Well, let's just go and have a look, shall we?' She showed them the bedroom.

'Have you been in here?' asked the young one.

'Yes.'

'Why?'

'To turn the gas off and open the window,' Anna sighed. The window was still open, and her wet footprints were obvious on the rain-soaked floor under it.

The older one was looking at the sellotape hanging in ribbons from the door-frame.

'Gas, eh?' the younger one said, stepping boldly over to the bed, and looked at Francis. He made a throttled gagging sound and covered his mouth and nose with his handkerchief.

'Why don't you take a look round the rest of the house, Bisgood?' his partner said evenly, without turning round.

Bisgood left quickly. Anna heard him blowing his nose raspingly in the passage.

The older man progressed slowly round the room. He stopped at the wash-basin and picked up the aspirin bottle, holding it on the end of a propelling pencil.

'It looks like laddie here was a belt-and-braces man,' he said.

Anna said, 'It's natural gas, so he might have needed the braces.'

He knelt down by the fire, turned the gas-tap on for a second and sniffed.

'Poor stupid bastard,' he muttered. 'Who is he, do you know?'

'Francis Neary. He lodged here.'

'And where's Mrs Halloran gone?'

'She went next door with the children. There's a phone there. She was pretty shocked.'

'I see.' He had got to the note now. He read it and put it back.

'Well, let's get out of here for now. There's a doctor and the ambulance coming shortly.' He was having a last slow look round. 'I expect you could do with a cup of tea.'

But he seemed to drop the idea when he saw the kitchen, and didn't mention it again.

'She wouldn't exactly win any Housewife of the Year awards, would she?' Bisgood had recovered. 'The rest of the house is just as bad, Collin; you should look at the bathroom.'

Ignoring him, Collin took out his notebook and jotted something in it.

'Perhaps I should have your name and address now, Miss,' he said.

Anna told him and he wrote it down.

'Not what I'd call a neighbour, then,' he said, watching her. 'Want a smoke? It's quite safe now.'

She shook her head.

'Do you want to tell us what you were doing here, then?'

'I came to talk to Mr Neary.' She drew a deep breath, and wished she hadn't. The atmosphere in the kitchen had not improved.

'Knew him well, did you, Miss?'

'I met him for the first time last night.'

'Last night, eh? And you came round to talk to him again this morning, but he was dead. That's a shame.'

She took her identification card out of her bag and handed it to him.

'One of the midnight cowgirls!' said Bisgood, looking over his shoulder. 'What were you doing to him? Debt collecting?'

'No.'

'Well, would you like to tell us what you were do-ing?' Collin handed the card back. 'This doesn't mean a thing.'

'I know,' Anna sighed. It was true enough. She could have had all sorts of identity cards printed any time she wanted. 'But at least it shows I'm not hiding anything. And if someone rings this number and talks to my boss, he can vouch for me and confirm what the position is.'

'If you decide to tell us what that is.' But he took the card back, looked at it again and handed it to his partner. 'Phone these details through, will you, Bisgood? It might save time.'

'What a cock-up!' he said happily as he went out. 'I thought she was a social worker.'

'So what is the position?' Collin said when he had gone.

'I don't understand it myself,' she told him. 'I saw him in the pub last night in connection with a job I'm working on. It seemed quite straightforward at the time. I'm looking for contacts of a girl who died in an accident last month. He had been seen talking to her. But when I asked him about it he denied knowing her.'

'And you didn't believe him.'

'That's right. So I thought I'd try again this morning when he'd got back from work. Give him a chance to cool down.'

'He was on the night shift, then?'

'Yes, but his landlady says he didn't go to work last night. She said he'd been drinking heavily and shut him-self in his room.'

They were interrupted by the arrival of the doctor and the ambulancemen. Collin showed them into the bedroom while Anna stayed in the kitchen. He came back with Bis-good.

'Someone isn't happy,' Bisgood was saying, 'not happy at all.'

'A policeman's lot,' murmured Anna.

'What's that?' Bisgood said, flushing. 'Maybe you

should watch your lip. You're in dead schtook as it is. We've had instructions to bring you in with us.'

'Gilbert and Sullivan,' Collin said wearily. 'Leave it be.'

They left the house. Anna turned her face up to the wind and rain, luxuriating in the icy wetness.

'Where do you think you're going?' Bisgood caught her arm as she started up the street.

'My car. It's up there opposite the newsagent.'

'You're supposed to come with us.'

'Oh, shove it!' Anna exploded suddenly. 'I can follow you in my own car. You aren't taking me in. I'm coming in!'

'Take it easy,' Collin said to no one in particular. 'It's all right if she takes her own car. You aren't arresting her, you know. Do you know the way?'

'I'll follow you.'

They drove processionally to the police station.

CHAPTER 15

· · · · · · · · · ·

ANNA waited under the steady gaze of a desk sergeant who seemed to have nothing better to do. She sat on a hard wooden bench, her eyes half-closed against the flickering of faulty strip-lighting. A dried-up rubber plant was dying protractedly in the corner. She wished she had not given up smoking. Sometimes she shared her bench, but mostly she had it to herself. Patience was supposed to be an English virtue, and it was ruthlessly exploited by most English institutions.

After an hour or so Collin came down the steps. He exchanged nods with the desk sergeant and sat down beside her.

'We've been in touch with your governor,' he said, 'and it seems he's like that with the Chief Super.' He crossed his fingers.

'I'm not surprised,' Anna said tiredly. 'He's like that with the brass everywhere. I don't know how he does it.'

'And I've been on to AD District and they've confirmed they handed Jackson on to your mob. So you're in the clear as far as that goes.'

He found a crumpled packet of cigarettes in his pocket and lit one for her.

'Look, Sarge,' he turned to the man at the desk, 'we're just going down to the canteen for a spot of brew, if anyone asks.'

They went down a flight of stairs and along a corridor to the canteen.

'Were you ever in the cops?' he asked as they went.

'Yes, for five long years.'

'I thought so. You mustn't mind Bisgood. He's young. But some people in your line of work are very fly indeed. And some of the worst were cops once.'

'I know,' she said, 'but my boss runs a completely legitimate firm as far as I can see.'

'Okay, but you do admit it's not always the case. Do you want something to eat?'

She watched the canteen assistant pile sausage, egg and chips on to his plate and shook her head.

'Feeling a bit off-colour, are you? You must have seen that sort of thing before.'

'I have, but it doesn't help.'

'You were right about the natural gas, you know. Silly thing is, the doc says he doesn't think there were enough pills in the bottle to do the trick. But what with the booze and gas and everything the poor bugger passed out and inhaled his own vomit. That's what killed him.'

He put a huge forkful of chips into his mouth and munched slowly. Anna looked away.

'What made you leave the force?' he said with his mouth full.

'I don't know really. I just didn't seem to be getting anywhere.'

'I suppose it can be a bit of a dead end for women,' he said thoughtfully. 'Especially if they don't know how to type.'

'Especially if they do,' she corrected him. He smiled for the first time since she'd seen him.

He finished his food in silence and wiped his plate with a folded slice of bread and butter. Then he started on the rice pudding and custard. Anna went to the counter for a fresh cup of tea and didn't go back till he had finished.

'Well now,' he pushed his chair back, 'your boss says it's his company's policy to co-operate with the police. And my boss would like a little co-operation. Is that all right by you?'

'It's fine by me,' she told him, 'only I don't really know what to tell you. Everything seemed fairly kosher till this morning.'

'Only your Mr Brierly told us you asked his secretary if two of your subjects had records. Why did you do that?'

'Just that they both seemed a bit dodgy to me. It's a quick way of knowing which way the land lies.'

'Is this just nose or have you any hard evidence that a crime has been committed?'

'None at all, and what's more, should there be any, Mr Brierly would turn it in. He always does.'

'Okay. I'll take your word for that. So why do you think Neary chose this moment to turn up his toes?'

'I don't know. There's nothing to make me think it's connected with what I'm working on, but it's a nasty co-incidence.'

'But if he had something on his conscience, something big, and he thought you were on to it, he might do something then.'

'He might have, but I hope not. It would have been easier for him to do a bunk.'

'What exactly did you say to him last night?'

'I asked him if he knew Deirdre Jackson and he said no. I told him he had been seen with her. He said he couldn't remember all the girls he'd had drinks with. I showed him her picture and he said he didn't know her and he'd never seen her.'

'And you didn't believe him. What else did you say?'

'I told him she was dead and I was getting in touch with all her known contacts. I think that was about all.'

'How did you get on to him in the first place?'

'A friend of Deirdre's saw her with him in the Oak. He described Neary. The barman told me his name.'

'So there could have been a mistake?'

'There could have been, but I don't think so. I think Neary knew her.'

'Nose again. Can I have a look at that picture?'

Anna gave him the picture. He studied it, then looked back at her with his lips pursed.

'I know,' she said unhappily, 'if Deirdre was out drinking with Neary, it wasn't for the pleasure of his company.'

'Well, cheer up. It might be something completely different. Debts, love-life, VD, you name it. Can I keep this photo? I thought I might show it to the landlord and see if he recognizes her.'

'Yes, I was going to do that too. Will you let me know what he says?'

'I might. If you keep me informed about what you're doing. There might be something in this for both of us,' he said with a wink. 'I've been waiting for a commander's certificate for years.'

Anna gave him a card with her home number on it.

'I'll do what I can,' she said.

'By the by,' he said as they left the canteen, 'your governor said to see him when you finish here. I nearly forgot.'

'Got a cold, too?' said Tim as they passed each other at the entrance. 'You're looking a little on the plain side.'

'Thanks a lot,' Anna said. 'How are things on the top floor today?'

'Rock bottom, as per usual.'

She went slowly up the stairs. Beryl was playing arpeggios on the IBM. She paused to sneeze into a pink tissue, and saw Anna.

'It's no good you sneaking past like that. You're well on the carpet this time.'

'Hello to you, too, Beryl.'

'It's no use taking it out on me, dear. I didn't set off five phone calls in half an hour. Anyway, you're in luck for the time being. The Commander's in conference. How's the report coming?'

'Getting longer by the minute.'

'Well, you've got lots of time now. By the way, that accident report you requested has come through. Next time fill in a proper requisition slip like everyone else.'

She handed Anna a typed sheet.

'Thank you very much,' Anna said. 'I suppose you haven't got those record sheets too?'

'Mr Brierly's handling that personally now. Well, what did you expect after this morning's flap?'

The rec-room was dark and empty. She switched on the light and the fire. Then she filled the kettle and methodically made a cup of tea, and drank it holding the mug in both hands for warmth. She read the medical report twice. Then she picked up the phone and asked for an outside line.

Dr Michaelson sounded young and exhausted.

'I'm on Casualty Intake,' he said. 'I'd like to help, but I haven't got much time.'

'I'll try not to take too much of it then,' Anna said. 'You did the autopsy report on a girl called Deirdre Jackson who died in an accident on the eighth of December last year.'

'Remind me, can you?'

'Her car spun off an icy road and hit a post, rear on. Cause of death, if I've got it right, dislocation of atlanto/occipital joint caused by neck extension.'

'Oh yes, got you. That was a hell of a week. First bad ice of the year, if I remember rightly. What's the problem?'

'You said there were contusions on the face into which blood hadn't flowed.'

'Yes, but that is consistent with this type of injury.'

'And you also said that the body temperature was very low.'

'Right. When it was found, the body had fallen out of the car, and the air temperature was below freezing.'

'Okay, but you mentioned slight bruising on both upper arms near the shoulder.'

'That's right. Look, just what is it you want to know?'

'Well, I know that all the injuries look perfectly consistent with the position of the car and the weather and so

on, but is it even remotely possible that Deirdre could have
sustained the same injuries in a struggle about half an hour
prior to the accident?'

'Oh, I see what you mean. Well, given all the facts
as they are, yes, it is theoretically possible. But it's sup-
posing a hell of a lot. For instance, someone would have
had to fake a remarkably realistic crash and further, whoever did that did not have much time, settling of the blood
pigment being what it was. It's all a little too clever for
me.'

'I see,' Anna said thoughtfully. 'What about the
bruises on the upper arms?'

'Yes, they were recent, but they were very faint. Of
course, it's horses for courses with contusions. Some people bruise very easily,' Dr Michaelson added scientifically,
'she could have got those kissing her boyfriend goodnight.'

'But if it turned out she did get herself killed in some
sort of fracas, you wouldn't throw up your hands in medical disbelief?'

'No, I suppose I wouldn't. But don't bring me into it
if you can possibly help it. I'm up to *my* neck with broken
ones. Road conditions haven't changed much in the last
month.'

'Well, thanks very much for talking to me, Dr Michaelson,' she said. 'I must say, you're very open-minded
for a doctor.'

'Give me time.' She could hear the humour in his
voice. 'I'm not rich and successful yet!'

He rang off.

'You've been making waves, Miss Lee.' Brierly leant forward with his arms resting on the desk in front of him,
his fingers linked and his thumbs rotating. 'I don't like
waves. The consequence of your actions is that I have been
compelled to spend the best part of this afternoon convincing the powers that be at Q District that we are not a
firm of thugs who get pleasure out of driving innocent
civilians to suicide.'

Anna was quite literally on the carpet. She had not been offered a chair.

'No, let me finish,' he held up his hand. 'I agree you had no option but to inform the police. But things should not have been allowed to get to the state where such a situation was necessary. When you saw that that fool was too hard for you to handle you should have withdrawn and handed him over to someone more suited to the task.'

'Are you saying, then, that you think Francis Neary's suicide is linked to this enquiry?' He wanted it both ways, Anna thought.

'I didn't say that. If you would attend more closely, I am merely pointing out that you should have dealt with him more tactfully or left him alone. As it is, you have put the reputation of this office in jeopardy with the authorities, and I'm not happy about it at all. I spend a lot of time and trouble fostering good relations.'

Too bloody much, she thought, but murmured yet another apology instead.

'Well, we'll leave it at that for now. But when the Jacksons arrive tomorrow, I want a concise and well-ordered presentation. Is that clear? I want to finish this case up quickly before you cause any more nonsense.'

She left the room in a subdued rage.

'Never mind,' Beryl said smugly from her cubbyhole. 'It'll all come out in the wash.' She had left the intercom on and had overhead the entire interview.

'Perfect!' Anna muttered going downstairs. 'Bloody perfect.'

CHAPTER 16

· · · · · · · · · ·

ANNA ate a toasted cheese and mushroom sandwich in front of the fire. The room warmed up slowly and Billie Holiday sang 'Gloomy Sunday' from the record player on the shelf.

She sat on the rug with her notebook in front of her and started writing her report. She had bathed and washed her hair as soon as she had got home, and now, warm for the first time since she had left the flat that morning, she felt the tension draining away like dirty water out of the bath.

It was five-forty-five when she woke up with a feeling of dislocation. The telephone was ringing, and it was dark outside.

'He thinks he saw her,' the strange voice on the phone said.

'Sorry? What was that?'

'What's the matter with you? You asleep or something? I'll start again. This is Collinwood, Wembley station. Are you with me now?'

'Yes. Go on, Mr Collinwood,' she said, identifying him as 'Collin'.

'That's better.' He was chewing gum, and sounded indistinct. 'I took that picture of yours back to the Oak. Hinkly, that's the landlord, is seventy-five per cent sure she's the girl Neary was seen with two months ago. He remembered because Neary never had any success with the ladies and everyone ribbed him about it afterwards. It seems Neary lost his rag then and got thoroughly pissed. So it looks like the ball's in your court.'

'What about last night?'

'Same thing. He got stinking and he wrote a letter.'

'A letter?'

'That's what I said. Seems he bought an envelope and a stamp off Hinkly.'

'Who to?'

'Ah-ha, you have woken up at last. The note he left was to his old mum, wasn't it? I won't ask you whether you looked at it or not! Hinkly didn't see who to. He took it with him when he left. Just thought I'd warn you.'

'Yes, thanks. Thanks a lot.'

'Did you say who you were when you talked to him?'

'I told him my name, but nothing else.'

'Well, it's probably nothing anyway. Have you got anything for me?'

'Not yet, unless you want some of the bollocking I got from my boss this afternoon.'

'Don't bother, I get enough of my own. But keep in touch.'

She hung up, grabbed her coat and bag and ran for the car.

Simon opened the door draped in a towel and dripping water all over the carpet.

'I thought you'd changed your mind,' he said by way of greeting, grappling with the towel and trying to walk straight at the same time. 'Give me a minute. There should be some beer somewhere.'

She looked around the sitting-room. It was a riot of technical journals, home-made stereo systems, newspapers, and over-spilling ashtrays. Someone was studying electronics. A circuit-board lay on top of a pile of books. There were three ancient televisions, one on top of the other, each facing a different armchair, and a hopeless tangle of aerials growing like modern sculpture from the top of the pile. Anna started to laugh.

'They're all tuned to different stations,' Simon said when he came back. 'Actually, not one of the sets will get all stations. It saves argument. Would you like a beer?'

A huge table of elements was taped to the wall. Beside it, hanging on nails, were three squash rackets. Someone was mending an antique brass microscope. It was lying at one end of a table, the rest of which was taken up by a handsome old mains radio, also in bits. Simon sipped his beer and looked round as if seeing the chaos for the first time.

'Dee didn't come here very often. I can see why, I suppose. It is a tip, and she was very orderly, fastidious almost. Well, you knew her.'

'That's what I wanted to talk to you about. Can we sit down? I've got a lot of explaining to do.'

He cleared books and papers off two chairs.

'Fire away then.'

'The truth is,' she said, 'I never knew Dee at all. She was not a relative or a friend, and before Monday I had never met her parents, or even knew the family existed. I work for a firm of private enquiry agents, and Dee's father employed us because he doesn't think her death is quite the accident it appears to be.'

'Does he think she was murdered, or something?' He drank some more beer and choked.

'Hold on! I don't know what he thinks really. He just can't believe that his daughter could have died in a sordid little accident in some lonely road. He wants someone to be responsible. That's all. It's not unusual.'

'And what do you think? Could she have been murdered?' He looked stunned.

'I don't think anything yet. You mustn't think that because there's an investigator involved it necessarily means there's been a killing.' She shrugged. 'I'm telling you this now because this is the third day running I've had to pick your brains, and it didn't seem fair to go on doing so under false pretences.'

Simon got up and walked rapidly over to the window and back.

'I don't know,' he said at last. 'All those things I told you about Dee and me, I don't know if I would have told you if I'd known you were a private detective. I thought you were grieving about her like I was.'

'I know. I know,' Anna said sadly. 'That's what I mean. It isn't fair. It's unforgivable, in fact. But I didn't know, when I first met you, that you would be the only one I'd find who knew Dee well and who cared enough about her to help me.'

'How do I know you are who you say you are now?' He was looking at her now with a mixed expression of disillusion and interest.

She gave him her identity card. It was getting more fresh air than usual today. He looked at it carefully.

'The name's the same,' he said. 'You didn't make that up, at least.'

'I could have.' She might as well let him have it all. 'Anyone can have a card like that printed up. Look at it. It's just a common or garden printed card with a cheap passport photo on it. Can you see an official stamp? Metropolitan Police? Home Office?'

'No.' He looked at the card again.

'Well, my boss has one of these done for all his employees. He uses a printer in Earls Court. It takes twenty-four hours. You could have one yourself if you wanted it. All it does is lend respectability. I don't even have to have one, and what's more I don't have to show it to you. There are no official regulations for private investigators other than the laws everyone has to abide by. We don't have to have qualifications or licences. Anyone can set himself up as one if he wants to.'

'But that's ridiculous.' Simon handed back the card as if it was waste paper.

'Yes, it is. And worse than that, it's bloody stupid. There isn't even a central register.'

'But the firm you work for would be fairly respectable, wouldn't it?'

'It is, but you've only my word for it.'

'Shit, Anna.' He rumpled his hair nervously. 'This gets worse and worse. Do you carry a gun or something?' He eyed her shoulder-bag suspiciously.

'God, no!' she laughed. 'I hate guns. I've never touched one outside of a practice range. If I can't talk my way out of a tricky situation, I run like the clappers.'

He smiled uncertainly. 'Look, why are you telling me all this? It's almost as if you want me to think you're untrustworthy.'

'No, I don't. That's the last thing I want. I want you to go on helping me. But I want to give you enough information so that you can make the choice for yourself with your eyes open.'

'What about the things I've told you? Who knows about that?'

'I make out a report for Dee's parents. That's what they're paying for. You are in it, and all the factual things you've told me, but anything private and personal, your feelings, for instance, are just between you and me.'

'Okay. Well, I'll have to think about that. Now, what about getting Dee's old job? What made you do a thing like that?'

'I think Freddie Slinger is crooked.' Anna told him about the afternoon in Harrow. 'I just want another chance to see if I can get a line on what he's up to,' She finished up, 'If anything happened to Dee that isn't quite hunky-dory, it could have started there. I've got an idea that Slinger is in some way connected to a lab called CCS.'

'Colour Cine Services,' he interrupted, 'out by Heathrow?'

'That's the one. It's about ten minutes away from the spot where Dee's car was found. There's a connection between Dee and CCS, another between Dee and Slinger, and if there's one between Slinger and CCS, I'd like to find it before Slinger knows I'm looking, see?'

'Well,' he said breathing deeply, 'you've got a lot of

cheek, I will say that for you. Do you want some more beer?'

He was a long time getting it, and when he came back he sat in silence for a while, turning the glass slowly in his hands. Then he got up and hauled a large case out from under the table.

'One 16mm film projector and a can of rubbishy home movie to thread it with,' he said. 'I suppose I'd better show you how it works, or you'll have egg on your face come Saturday.'

He stood in front of her chair, looking sheepish.

'I don't mind helping you pull one over on Slinger. But I object to you pulling one over on me. Not very consistent, am I?' he said. 'The only problem now is that I can't find the bloody screen. Any suggestions?'

'What about looking under the bed?' Anna said, relieved.

'Good idea.' He set off for the bedroom, but turned and said, 'You didn't have to tell me at all, so thanks for that.'

It was well after midnight when she got home. A folded piece of paper addressed to Leo was pinned to the door of her flat. She took it inside to read.

'Dear D. Fector,' it said,

> Ashes to England, Aussies to dust, if the telly don't get you the radio must. Bea says I'm overtired as a skunk and have to go to bed and could you look at the whatsit under the sink in the morning?
>
> (signed) Sal E. Brater.

By the look of his handwriting, Anna reckoned that Selwyn had been celebrating long before starting the note. She had not missed the cricket. Simon's flatmates had returned especially to see it, bearing carrier bags loaded with take-away curry, and they had all watched the cricket eating with spoons from the aluminium foil boxes. In spite of this interlude, Anna was now an adept projectionist.

CHAPTER 17

· · · · · · · · · ·

IN the dark Francis Neary raised his dead arms and pulled her down on him to embrace her. She shrieked as her face inexorably approached his. His mouth was still filled with blood-flecked vomit. She woke up biting the pillow and sweating coldly. She washed and changed into a fresh pair of pyjamas. They had been left behind months ago, and were far too big. As she drank warm milk by the fire she felt the aching loneliness of the dark small hours. Unwilling to return to bed, she collected the quilt and pillow and settled down on the rug with the heat and flame of the gas-fire for company. She had not intended to stay there long, but when the ringing phone woke her at seven-thirty, she got up with a headache, stiff from having slept on the floor for three hours.

"Ullo, this is Tina here. Remember me?' The cheerful voice at the end of the line sounded as if its owner had enjoyed eight hours' uninterrupted slumber. 'The postman's just been, and there's a letter for Dee. Do you want it? You said to let you know if anything turned up.'

'Yes. Thanks for ringing. What sort of letter is it?'

'Oh, nothing much. It looks like a catalogue for thermal underwear. Yes, the firm's name is on the envelope.'

'Well, I wouldn't bother sending it on then, if that's all it is,' Anna said, wondering why Tina had troubled at all.

'Only the letter wasn't sent here first.' Tina's voice was full of sly enjoyment. 'It was forwarded, see?'

'Oh, well,' Anna said with awakened interest, 'if you'll just read the previous address on it . . .'

'Only it's been crossed out,' Tina interrupted contentedly, 'and it's a bit difficult to make out.'

It was like squeezing the last half inch out of a tube of toothpaste, but Anna finally got the address of a flat near Stamford Bridge out of her.

'I suppose you'll want the PS, too.' Milking the call for every last drop of amusement she could muster.

'If it's not too much bother.'

'Just trying to help. It says on the back, "Where are you, stranger?" That's in the same writing as this address. So it looks as if Dee had one friend at least,' Tina added maliciously.

'Yes, it does.' She thanked Tina appropriately and hung up.

She bathed and dressed quickly, and was filtering some coffee when Bea tapped at the door.

'Want some coffee, Bea? I was coming down after. I gather you've got a blocked drain.'

'No. I can't stop. Ta. But that's what I wanted to tell you. It's not blocked. There was a bit of cellophane from the biscuit packet caught in the plug-hole and Selwyn emptied the teapot over it. That's all. He got a bit overexcited last night, what with the cricket and everything. Funny, isn't it? He's no good at sports himself. Couldn't catch a cold, even. Well, you know what men are like.'

Anna heard her tiptapping carefully downstairs on her black patent shoes and turned her attention back to the coffee pot. She still had to write the report. That had to be done before she saw the Jacksons, and done well too, if past experience was anything to go by. Whether she had a good case or not, she knew she could lose it just by presenting it badly. This one was still almost as ambiguous as it had been on Monday. And, after yesterday's fiasco, she knew that Brierly was within an inch of advising the Jacksons to give it up altogether. This was what she wanted to avoid. That the case was coming to feel like her own property was a feeling she mistrusted but was familiar with. The illusory nature of the possession did not, however, soften the fierce stab of frustration when a case was closed before she felt it was finished. So she sat down to write, ordering her notes and her thoughts with care. In the end it wouldn't matter how much of the report was fact and how much guesswork as long as grammar and spelling were correct, and most important, so long as she wrote it with authority.

It took several hours and another pot of coffee. When it was finished, the bin under the desk was full of crumpled balls of paper and a headache was battering a steady rhythm on the back of her skull. She took a couple of tablets to quieten it and then changed her clothes; the report was not the only thing she would have to present with authority. She put on her best boots for height and a cream silk shirt with coral cufflinks for weight. Then a soft green skirt and sleeveless jacket for colour. It made a change, anyway. The image in the mirror was quite classy. But the face still looked as if it had had a bad night, pale, and a little woebegone. So she made up her eyes and added a little lightener to hide the dark smudges under them.

'The things you do for public relations,' she said, sneering at herself. She turned her back on the mirror and went out in disgust.

'It looks neat enough,' Beryl said grudgingly as she fed the report page by page through the Xerox, collecting four copies of each from the tray underneath. 'I wish you'd brought it in earlier, though. I won't have time to go out for lunch now. Why don't you go down and bring me up a couple of hamburgers from McDonald's, if you want to do something useful.'

Anna went down the stairs to the High Street.

'With cheese!' Beryl's afterthought floated behind her.

The service was paid back when copies of the report,

neatly trimmed and stapled into smart blue folders, were handed to Mr and Mrs Jackson in Brierly's office three quarters of an hour later.

'This all looks very professional,' Mr Jackson said, beginning to read, and missing the offended glare Brierly directed at him.

Mrs Jackson was a slow reader. They all sat politely silent while she finished.

'Well,' she said when she looked up at last. 'What a to-do! You have done well, though,' turning to Anna, 'after all, we gave you nothing to go on. Absolutely nothing.'

'Miss Lee is a professional, as I said,' Brierly interjected sourly. 'This proves nothing, you understand.'

'Doesn't it, though!' Jackson's shoulders bunched themselves aggressively. 'Miss Lee only has to talk to this Neary fellow about my daughter and he turns his face to the wall! It's as plain as the nose on your face. He killed my daughter and, when it looked as if he was going to have to answer for it, he killed himself!'

Anna winced.

'There's absolutely no proof of any connection whatsoever,' Brierly said firmly, 'and if you'll notice, Miss Lee herself has provided none.'

'Give her time. It only happened yesterday . . .'

'And what's more, the police are now involved with that side of the affair. They will investigate Neary's background, and I've no doubt they will turn up other more convincing reasons for his suicide. What we have so far is purely circumstantial.'

'The police,' Jackson said contemptuously, 'are only interested because of what Miss Lee has told them so far. They can't see further than the nearest hot dinner. It seems to me that you've told them everything and they've told you nothing. I ask you, just where are all the ideas coming from? Not them, anyway.'

'I suppose they are sometimes found to be lacking in imagination,' Brierly muttered, always susceptible to flattery. 'But I was going to suggest that we leave this part of the investigation in their capable hands. One of their top men at Wembley has indicated to me personally that they would prefer it that way.'

'I'm not sure as how I'm very interested in what they'd prefer,' Jackson said. 'What I want is results. As a matter of fact, I see here,' he stabbed the report with a finger like a well-filled pork sausage, 'that Miss Lee wants to know if this Neary had a police record. I'd like to know that, too.'

'Ah, yes. The result of that enquiry only came through this morning. That is why it's not included in this report. The answer is that he had a suspended sentence and fine for being involved in an affray after a football match at Arsenal Football Club. Youthful high spirits, I suppose.'

'History of violence, more like,' Jackson said, 'and what about this Frederick Slinger my daughter was working for?'

'There are no convictions against him. Although it seems that about twelve years ago the chaps at Stepney showed an interest.'

'Why was that, Mr Brierly?' Anna asked.

'It seems that his name cropped up after the robbery of a jeweller's in Bond Street.' He was talking to her as he rarely did, as someone with a common interest. 'Not that he was involved directly. They caught all the actual perpetrators very soon after the crime, but he was a known associate and, among others, was kept under observation for a while. A small proportion of the stolen goods had not been recovered, you see. There was never any evidence against him. It was just a wait and see operation.'

'And now he's living the life of Riley in a big house in Harrow,' Mr Jackson said loudly, breaking the spell. 'It smells fishy to me.'

'Let's not jump to conclusions . . .'

'That's right,' Mrs Jackson interrupted, 'You mustn't forget, Thomas, that we started from nothing ourselves. How would you feel if someone started making accusations like that about us?'

'I'm not making accusations, and we've never associated with any criminals.'

'How do you know?' she asked with unaccustomed spirit. 'There's many a time in the beginning when we did a deal and asked no questions. We were just that thankful for the business.'

'This is different,' her husband said angrily.

Brierly coughed tactfully. 'Shall we get back to the business in hand?' he said. 'I don't think any link between Slinger and a robbery twelve years ago can possibly interest us now.'

'A leopard don't change his spots all that easily.' Jackson glanced sideways at his wife, but she had given up the challenge.

'The way I see it is that Deirdre caught on to something. Maybe she was doing a bit of detective work of her own. And someone made it his business to shut her up before she could make things warm for him.'

'I think that's going rather far,' Brierly said, 'but I must say your daughter did seem to find herself in strange company.' Perhaps the talk about Slinger had kindled his interest. Anna knew that he was sympathetic with Jackson's remark about a leopard and its spots. He had the unforgiving nature of a policeman.

'What do we do next, then?' Jackson asked, accepting unconsciously that the tide had turned.

'Well, since Miss Lee has had the foresight to keep her options open on Mr Slinger, I think she should follow up there as she has proposed. Quite what we stand to gain from it I don't know, but I don't see why she shouldn't.'

'Is there any chance I could have some help on it?' Anna said, hoping to increase her advantage.

'Of course she should,' Mrs Jackson said suddenly. 'If you two men are right about him, this Mr Slinger might be dangerous.'

'I didn't mean that,' Anna said quickly. 'It's just that he ought to be watched, and it's more than I can do alone. Also Slinger knows me, so I can't hang around him without good reason. I want to see if there's a connection between him and the laboratory Francis Neary worked at, and I'll need some help if that's to be established.'

'I do see that any link there would put a new complexion on the case,' Brierly admitted, 'but it is an expensive business keeping someone under observation round the clock.' He looked meaningfully at Jackson.

'That's all right by me. No expense spared. I've said that all along. I'd never forgive myself if we lost this battle for want of a horseshoe nail.'

Brierly had something more substantial in mind than horeshoe nails, and the two men drew together to discuss the budget. Mrs Jackson pulled her chair closer to Anna's.

'This young man, Simon,' she began, tapping the report with her lacquered fingernail, as if Simon were actually in there. 'He works in a laboratory too, doesn't he?'

Anna confirmed that he did.

'I hope he's not involved with anything bad,' Mrs Jackson said. 'He sounds like such a nice lad.'

'I think he is absolutely sound, Mrs Jackson.'

'Do you think he cared for Deirdre?' Mrs Jackson said.

'Yes, I'm sure he did,' Anna said cautiously.

'I'm glad about that. I was hoping you'd find someone who might have given her a little happiness. I would hate to think she was always as discontented as she seemed when we saw her. Do you think they were engaged?'

'No,' Anna said, puzzled, 'he didn't give me that impression at all.'

'Only when I went through her things I found an old-fashioned engagement ring. I know most of her jewellery. Thomas and I gave some to her for various birthdays; Thomas always said it was a good investment; but we always gave her modern things. I brought it with me in case you could find something out from it.'

She took a small soft leather ring-case from her handbag, and put it in Anna's hand as if it were a crystal ball from which they were supposed to read the past. Inside was a little pearl and turquoise ring. The jewels were set in gold claws, and it looked Georgian. It had 'always' inscribed in the band, but the word had been worn thin.

'It's quite pretty, isn't it? But I shouldn't think it's worth much. My grandmother had one just like it.'

'I don't know much about antique rings,' Anna said doubtfully, 'but I'll ask around.'

'I think we might ask Miss Doyle for a pot of tea,' Brierly said, his business concluded.

When Beryl came in with the tea, he waited until she had poured it and then said, 'Who do we have available this weekend? I want a watch put on a house in Harrow.'

'I'll have to see, sir,' Beryl said, casting a disbelieving look at Anna, 'but I think Mr Schiller's free.'

'Good. Would you see that he gets a copy of this report and has a meeting with Miss Lee as soon as possible?'

CHAPTER 18

· · · · · · · · · ·

ANNA drove hopefully down to Stamford Bridge. So far, Friday had been better than expected. She found the address Tina had given her without much trouble. It was in a newly prosperous street, south of Fulham Road and running parallel to it, made up mostly of tall semi-detached Victorian houses. Anna pulled up by one of them. A card next to one of the four doorbells read simply: Flat 3, Vida and Voitek Bratny. It was handwritten in green ink, and the i's were dotted with circles.

Behind the door someone was playing something bluesy on a piano.

A thin, dark girl let her into an airy front room that looked as if it had recently undergone a face-lift. The clean white paint smelled fresh. Bright Mexican rugs were scattered on a newly stripped pine floor that had not yet been darkened by light, and greenery ebbed and flowed from every available surface.

A bearded man dwarfing the Bechstein threw an amiable grin in her direction without missing a beat.

By the light of the window Vida Bratny turned out to

be neither thin nor a girl. She was in her late twenties or early thirties, but small-boned so as to appear fragile and immature. It was the cloud of dark curly hair, seeming to hover around her head, that made her face look tiny and gamine.

'Did you forward a letter to Deirdre Jackson a few days ago?' Anna began, unable to think of a more imaginative opening.

'Yes, I did,' Vida said. 'What's happened to Dee, anyway? I wrote her when I got back from the States early in December. You'd have thought she'd be in touch by now.'

She had a breathless childlike voice, too. Anna couldn't make out whether she was an American who had spent a lot of time in England or the other way round. It would have been an inappropriate question, so she said, 'I'm afraid I've got some bad news for you.' And told Vida what had happened to Deirdre.

'You must be joking!' Vida said, sounding shocked and distressed. 'I don't believe it!'

She went over to the piano as if she was having difficulty finding it. The big man stopped playing and made room for her on the stool. She didn't sit down, but stood very close to him. He put an arm round her waist.

She moved away after a moment's silence, and the big man began to play again, softly this time. To Anna's uneducated ears it sounded like a Chopin *étude*, but she couldn't be sure.

'Dee and I shared this place once,' Vida said quietly. 'It was a bit of a dump in those days, though, before the developers came in and tarted up the whole street. She would have liked it now.'

'How long did you share for?' Anna asked.

'About eighteen months, I guess. I didn't think it would work out at first. But it did, in an odd sort of way.' Vida stared out of the window.

'There was a whole family living in that house opposite, I remember. Five small boys, all under ten. It was a mess, that house, all bikes and go-carts and over-flowing trash-cans, but very lively. It's completely different now. Dee didn't like small boys.'

She sounded more sentimental than bereaved now. She turned back into the room, saying: 'She was a funny girl, you know, very up-tight and inhibited. She nearly drove me crazy to begin with. I'm not like that at all, you see. I get everything out in the open, walk round it a couple of times and see what I've got. That's me. But she used to bottle up every little grievance and go round tight-lipped.' Vida sighed and shook her head as if this was not what she wanted to remember.

'She's a lot younger than me, so I couldn't understand why she wasn't out with kids her own age setting off fireworks. It took me some time to realize she was intimidated by city people. She was a country girl, you see, and she thought they'd think she was just a hayseed. She came to London to find a bit of glamour and some action, and when she got here, she was afraid she couldn't cut it.'

'How did you meet?' Anna asked. It seemed an unlikely alliance. That they had kept in touch afterwards indicated something unusual in Deirdre's compartmentalized life.

'She worked for a photographer friend of mine,' Vida told her. 'I went to see him one day for some new pictures. He was out somewhere, and Dee and I got talking. She was living in a bedsit at that time and was pretty miserable with it. Whereas I had just taken this place on and was wondering how I'd manage the rent on my own. That was before I got off the ground and started making some decent bread.'

She smiled and went on reminiscently, 'I was working in a shop then, and singing in pubs at night. It was a lot of sweat and didn't give much back. So I was glad to split the costs of the flat with her. She was good for me in other ways, too. I mean, I was always very scatty about money, never knew how much I had or what I owed. Actually, if you must know, I was afraid of money much in the same way she was afraid of people.'

She said this as if she really thought fear of finance

was a virtue; artistic people were supposed to be other-worldly.

'Dee showed me how to balance a cheque-book and keep records so I always knew where the balloons went,' she went on. 'And she made me open all the buff mail when it came. I wasn't all that grateful at first. It was a pain, dealing with all that crud, but it did make things easier in the long run. You would have wondered who was the older one sometimes.'

Vida grimaced at the memory. She was punctuating her story by moving restlessly around the room, sitting down only to rise a few seconds later. She was supple and springy in her movements, as if she was demonstrating that there was nothing repressed or inhibited about her.

'It's a funny way to remember her,' Vida said, pausing for a moment by the window. It was growing dark now, and snow was falling steadily. 'Dee Jackson, who filled out a tidy stub and kept the accounts straight! What an epitaph!'

'This photographer,' Anna prompted. 'Was that Dmitrios Bruce?'

'That's right. Do you know him?' Vida said. 'Mitri and me go way back. I did some modelling for him ages ago . . . in the days before I got wise to how demeaning it is for a woman to exploit her body that way.'

She said this quite seriously, but illustrated the words with a comical posture, one hip stuck out like a gawky colt.

'Nowadays I employ him, rather than the other way round. He does all my publicity stills for me. Actually, he used to do them for nothing when I was broke, back in the dark ages. He's very successful now, you know. But so busy. He works his assistants into the ground. He's always flying off somewhere to do all the real juicy stuff, leaving them home with the grind.'

She remembered belatedly that she was supposed to be talking about Dee, so she said: 'Poor old Dee. She got Tuesdays off to go to the Tech, but otherwise she spent nearly twelve hours a day either in the studio or the dark-room. Sweated labour, I used to call it. Then there was night school. No wonder the poor girl was so fed up when I first met her.'

'What did she do at night school?' Anna asked.

'Acting classes,' Vida told her, with a minute curl of her perfect mouth. 'Some phoney little place up in Notting Hill Gate. They did a lot of Brecht. You know, mime and improvisation, lots of theory and no technique. Poor Dee.'

'Was she any good?' Anna asked curiously.

'Not at all.' Vida said with mild superciliousness. 'She was too stiff, had no spontaneity, if you see what I mean. Actually, it always amazed me she bothered at all. She was too private and secretive; too sort of tucked up. But then we all fantasize, don't we? Perhaps she had Aquarius rising?'

She sat down opposite Anna, crossing her slender legs with a natural abandonment that Dee might have envied.

'In the end she knew she wasn't getting anywhere, so she gave it up. She could never let go of herself. That's what I mean. She hardly drank at all and she never smoked. I used to smoke now and then when I could afford it, like just to unwind, I mean. But Dee didn't seem to want to unwind. Like she was afraid if she relaxed too much she'd fall apart. You know what?'' Vida leaned forward confidingly. 'She once told me about this weird dream she had where she started undressing in front of a mirror. And she couldn't stop, although she knew she was doing something bad. And then, as she took off the last garment and got down to bare skin, whoof, she vanished!'

'Poor Dee,' Anna said sadly, wondering how profound a dream like that might be.

'I know,' Vida continued. 'It sort of sums her up, doesn't it? I mean, she was always locking the bathroom door and wearing pyjamas in bed. Actually, I think I used to embarrass her before we got used to each other. I guess I don't know what it's like to be modest.'

'When did she get interested in films?' Anna asked, using the pause to change the subject before she had to hear just how immodest Vida was. She recognized 'Last Date' as Voitek's present tune.

'Films?' Vida was saying. 'She'd always been interested in those as long as I've known her. Actually, she could've made something of that. I mean it's more or less the same as photography, isn't it? But like I said, she was a weird chick. Even with all that technical know-how, she still went to the movies like some people read novels. She'd've never made a great director or anything like that.' Again, Vida could not suppress a hint of disdain. 'But she'd've been a damn good editor or something. She could have put all her orderliness and attention to detail to creative use. But maybe she didn't want to relate all that hard graft in the darkroom to her beloved movies. It's a shame, because that's what she wanted most of all, to be involved in movies. Mitri ruined her for that, if you ask me. He's got a lot to answer for, one way or another.'

'How do you mean?' Anna asked, with a sense of foreboding.

'Didn't you know?' Vida said, leaning forward again like someone dying to tell a long-kept secret. 'Dee was crazy about Dmitrios Bruce.'

'No, I didn't know,' Anna said neutrally, avoiding Vida's eyes.

'Well, I suppose she wasn't exactly publishing it at the time,' the small breathless voice went on insistently. 'He was a married man and all that. It began as a sort of crush she had on him, but after a while he started to take her more seriously. I blame myself a bit for that, but how was I to know it was Mitri she was blowing so hot for? You know, when we first met, she was a bit of a plain Jane. Nothing wrong with her, of course, but her clothes were so square. She didn't know how to make the most of herself. I just brought her out a little, that's all. I mean, she was tall, right? Well, it's nice for a woman to be tall. But she stooped. Self-conscious, you see? So I just sort of showed her how to dress and present herself.'

Vida leaned sideways, her own clothes gracefully accentuating the lines of her body.

'It's all a confidence trick, really,' Vida went on. 'I told her that. Anyway, that's when Mitri got interested. And poor old Dee blossomed. It was awful really.'

She stood up again and said energetically: 'You know, if I have a rule for love affairs, it's only play with equals. I mean, he was nearly twice her age, experienced, successful, and married. It had to be a disaster.'

'What happened?' Anna really didn't have to ask.

'Apart from playing in the wrong league?' Vida was almost gossiping now. 'Well, Mitri is the kind of guy who . . . well, actually, he's a very attractive man, sort of a cross between Anthony Quinn and Cary Grant, if you can imagine an animal like that. In fact . . .' She came and sat next to Anna on the sofa. 'In fact, I had a little fling with him myself once. What I mean is, Mitri's the kind of guy everyone wants to have a little scene with, but no one ought to take seriously. You know?'

'I suppose so,' Anna said distastefully. Everyone made mistakes, she thought.

Vida took this as endorsement, and said: 'Well, Mitri has this talent for making a girl feel attractive and wanted, and I suppose the poor kid had never felt that way before. So instead of thinking, well, that's great, I've tried my wings, now let's really have some fun, she decides he's got to be the only one. It couldn't have been worse for her. Just when she might have had the confidence to make friends and have a ball, she stayed home and waited for the phone to ring. She even hoped he'd marry her, for Christ's sake! That was plain dumb, and I told her so.'

'Did he ever talk about marriage?' Anna asked.

'I suppose he might have,' Vida admitted. 'To do him credit, he was going through a sticky patch just then. But it's all part of his spiel anyway. He says what he thinks a girl wants to hear. The trouble is, he's uncannily accurate about it. Actually,' she said, conspiratorially edging closer to Anna, 'if you must know, his wife was pregnant for the first time. It was a mistake, but she refused to have an abortion. All the same, she was giving him a hard time for knocking her up. Normally she's a very understanding lady. Well, she has to be, doesn't she?'

'Oh, hell,' Anna said. Vida was far too close to her. Besides, she was surprised to find herself quite angry with Deirdre. It all seemed so seedy seen at this distance. Up till now, the Deirdre she had been trying to know had seemed more capable of seeing through things like that, better able to protect herself.

'I suppose Dmitrios dropped her when the baby was born,' she said.

'And how!' Vida replied. 'Well, not all at once. At first he seemed keener than ever. He even stayed the night here, several times, which wasn't normal for him. Dee really thought she was winning, but actually I thought it was because the baby kept him awake at night, and he needed somewhere quiet to sleep. Anyway, the baby was a boy, and Mitri was really proud of him underneath. It did something for his ego. So poor Dee never stood a chance in the long run, and in the end nothing could unzip him from hearth and home any more.'

She yawned and stretched langorously. Watching her, Anna wondered if she really understood Deirdre's feelings. She did not look as if she had been ignominiously dropped many times in her life.

'I did warn her,' Vida went on. 'But she took it really hard, all the same. She seemed to shrivel up and die, sort of. Cut herself off from everyone. Even me.' She sounded surprised.

'Of course, you wouldn't expect her to go on working for Mitri, but she left the flat too. She really overreacted; just walked out one day with all her bags. I felt really bad about it. I could just about manage the rent myself by then, so it didn't really matter. But all the same . . . it took me ages to find her again.'

'When you did,' Anna asked, 'how was she then?'

'Well, she'd certainly toughened up double quick,' Vida said with approval. 'You could see that was one mistake she wasn't going to make again. But she was sort of back in her shell. She wouldn't tell me much. I could see she still needed me though, you know, to advise her. Anyway, last time I saw her she said she was dating some guy, so she must have got some of her oomph back. And I got the feeling she had made damn sure she had the whip hand this time. She wasn't going to be anyone's patsy ever again. Well, what's life for, if not learning from your mistakes?'

'It depends what you learn, though, doesn't it?' Anna said, thinking that Dee might have taken the wrong lesson from her experience.

'Well, she had to get tough,' Vida said. 'It's better than getting clobbered every time round the course.'

'Oh, come on!' said Anna, feeling that Vida was morally half-daft. 'Those aren't the only options.'

Vida offered coffee, but Anna refused as gracefully as she could.

'It's too bad you have to rush off like this,' Vida said at the door. 'It's really nice to talk to an intelligent woman for a change. You don't happen to be a Libran by any chance? No? Because I am.'

Anna left in a state of concealed irritability.

'Well, maybe it isn't irretrievable, after all,' Selwyn said, absently munching the slice of toast Anna had just buttered. She put some more bread under the grill. 'What are you up to now?'

'Scrambling eggs,' Anna said crossly. She had not yet recovered from her ill-humour. 'Anyway, it's not Vida I'm interested in, it's Deirdre. I've had Vida up to the hairline.'

'No, I mean what are you doing this weekend?'

'Working.'

'That's all you ever do these days,' he grumbled. 'What's the matter with you, Leo? Can't you find some nice young man to take you out?'

'And what's more, I'm fed up with nice young men, and I don't need one to take me out.'

'You never did tell me what happened to Steve. He just disappeared one day and never came back. He was a nice young man, and a good conversationalist.'

'Look, Selwyn,' Anna snapped, 'do you want to eat with me, or are you content to fiddle with toast while the eggs burn?'

'I'm not hungry,' Selwyn said as he finished the second piece of toast. Anna cut a third slice and took the eggs off the heat before they went solid.

CHAPTER 19

. . . .

'IT'S *Gauntlet* they're showing tonight,' Simon said as he got into the Triumph. It was snowing quite hard, and the snow was beginning to stick to the road. 'See what I mean? What does an obscure little film society want with a Clint Eastwood season? Most of them are quite satisfied with German Expressionism or French Nouvelle Vague or that sort of thing.'

'Give me Clint Eastwood any day,' Anna said driving carefully. 'Pretence without pretension. A journey through the doorways of enchantment. Who wants ciné bloody vérité on a night like this?'

'Have you had a bad day?' Simon asked sympathetically. 'You look very nice, I must say. This is the first time I've seen you in a skirt.'

'I dressed up for a session with the boss and Dee's parents. Oh, damn it to hell!' She had suddenly realized that she had forgotten to ask Vida about the ring with 'Always' inscribed on it.

'What's the matter?'

'Nothing much, I just remembered something I

should have done.' She could not very well tell Simon about Deirdre and Dmitrios Bruce.

'No. It hasn't been a very brilliant day so far. I'm a bit tired and I've been missing chances. What I need is a good night's sleep.'

'I suppose I forgot this is just work for you.'

'I'm sorry, Si. That was very graceless of me.' She chalked herself up another black mark. 'It must be that I'm nervous about tomorrow. Although I shouldn't be. I'm very thoroughly prepared for it, thanks to you.'

'No, it's me that should be sorry. I had a bit of a bum day, too.' But he sounded mollified. 'It was just that this felt like the beginning of the weekend to me, and I forgot you were still on a case.'

He hadn't asked about Deirdre's parents. Maybe it was a bad sign.

'What do you do when you're not working?' he asked instead.

'Oh. Lie in, read, go to the football, meet friends.' Anna negotiated a crossroad by running down through the gearbox and avoiding the brakes. 'Are we nearly there?'

'Yes. Turn right by the postbox. Do you play squash?'

'Sometimes. Where now?'

'Second left. Then it's halfway up the road on the right. Only you look as if you might be rather good.'

'Nope. Just for fun and exercise. Is this it?'

'Yes. Perhaps we could have a game sometime.'

'Mmm,' Anna said vaguely. 'I hope this snow doesn't get much worse.'

They went into what looked like a gymnasium. It was one of those temporary open-plan buildings the council had urgently put up in hundreds and then neglected to replace. It was dark, as the film had already started. They found two moulded plastic chairs free at the back and sat down.

An hour and fifty minutes passed quickly. It was the kind of unbelievable film which Anna enjoyed every minute of while it was on, yet could find nothing admirable about afterwards.

'Smashing,' Anna said when it was over.

'Yes, well . . .' murmured Simon, more judiciously, looking round the empty hall.

For whatever reason, the choice of movie or the icy weather, there were only seven other people in the audience. A fat lady in an old Persian lambswool coat offered coffee from the kitchenette at the back of the hall, but everyone declined and hurried away into the snow. Anna checked quickly, but Sarah Margolin was nowhere to be seen. Leonard was rewinding the film and hadn't noticed her yet. She nudged Simon. 'Do me a favour, will you. Go and have some coffee and keep the fat lady happy. I want to have a few private words with Mr Margolin.'

'That's blood you're asking,' he said aggrievedly.

'I'll rescue you when I'm finished.'

He set off reluctantly. Margolin looked even more stooped and hag-ridden than he had been on Tuesday. When he saw her approaching, something in him seemed to shrink even further.

'Aren't you . . . ? Are you following me about?'

'Hello, Mr Margolin,' Anna said amiably. 'Nice movie, wasn't it?'

'You're not a member, are you?' he asked, recovering himself. 'We could do with more members. Especially on a night like this. The snow keeps people away.' He looked around myopically.

'How many members do you have?'

Chairs had been set out for about forty people.

'I don't know really,' Margolin said, 'Sarah takes care of that side of things. In fact, I wouldn't really care if I was the only one to see the films. That's the nice thing about running a society like this. You choose the films you want to see.'

'But this one was only released last year, wasn't it?'

'A lot of people like Clint Eastwood. We do have a committee, you know. We try to cater to a lot of different tastes.'

Anna wondered where the committee was. Or if its only other member was the fat lady currently giving Simon a hard time over the Nescafé.

'Were you actually thinking of joining?'

'I don't know,' she said, glancing at Margolin in a obviously oblique way. 'I wouldn't like to trigger a repeat of the reception your wife gave me on Tuesday.'

'You did upset her rather badly. Did you come to apologize?' This was not so much a challenge as an obscure attempt at flirtation. Anna, who had caused it, was nevertheless slightly shocked.

'What for?' she said. 'It upset me too. She just blew up in my face for no reason other than my asking her about Deirdre Jackson.'

'Why did you do that, anyway?' The transition from warmth to wariness came easily to Len Margolin.

'Because her membership here was one of the only things I knew about Deirdre. I thought I might find someone through it who knew her well. She left no clue as to her private life. Her mother, I think, really wants to know if she was happy.'

'Happy!' Margolin snorted. 'What would any of us leave to show we were happy?'

'Well, that's mothers for you. Of a certain kind, I mean,' Anna qualified hastily. 'A diary maybe, an address book full of warm-sounding names, an engagement ring. I don't know what Mrs Jackson expected.'

'Well, she didn't have an engagement ring as far as I remember. I don't think she was the marrying kind, if you ask me. Her ambitions didn't seem to run to personal relationships, not in the ordinary sense.'

Anna noticed that he quickly checked her own left hand. If she wanted information out of him, it might have to be a deal with herself as collateral.

'She wasn't always that cold?' she said speculatively.

'I don't think it was exactly passion I was getting at.' The film flicked off the take-up spool with a snap and a whirr. Margolin stopped the projector. The hall seemed suddenly very quiet.

'No, it's more the way she used relationships to bolster her confidence, to increase her standing with herself.'

His voice seemed too loud, and he lowered it halfway through the sentence.

'Ah. Well, I suppose she was very young,' Anna said carefully.

'That's what made it all the more surprising.'

She was quite certain by now that he had a personal grievance in the matter, and wondered how much further she would have to pursue him.

He went on, 'One would have expected more softness, more naiveté. Less of the eye on the main chance.'

He put the film into a can marked CW. Still cautious, Anna said, 'Well, I suppose it's no crime to be ambitious.'

'That rather depends,' Margolin said ambiguously, 'Is that Simon Lester waiting for you now?'

'I came as his guest.'

'Oh, well, I have to take this back to the West End, anyway.' He looked at his watch. 'But it would have been nice to continue this conversation in more comfortable surroundings. It's all conjecture, of course.'

'Perhaps I could come with you. Simon can take my car.' She didn't even know if Simon could drive. 'You could drop me off on the way back. You have been saying some very perceptive things about Deirdre. It seems a pity to stop now.'

'Doesn't it?' He touched the back of her hand with his index finger in an oddly ineffectual gesture. His hand was warm and slightly damp. 'But I'm afraid it just isn't possible. Sarah will be waiting for me, and she does rather count the minutes, you see.'

'That must be a little difficult sometimes.' She turned quickly to see if Simon was still occupied, thus releasing her hand without seeming to want to.

'You do understand, don't you?' he said anxiously. 'I tell you what, though. It's not something I tell many people, but there is a place. Look, I'll write down the address. I go there for an hour or two over the weekend occasionally, just to get a little peace and quiet, you know. It can be terrible living with someone who is mentally not quite stable.'

'I do see. The constant responsibility must be rather wearing.' The dark horse was definitely pulling out on the stand side and making a run for the post.

'Just so,' Margolin handed her a scrap of paper, which she put in her pocket without looking at it, joining him in the implied conspiracy. 'One needs a little space to catch one's breath, so to speak. I wouldn't want this to go any further, though. Any secret kept from Sarah would be taken as a total betrayal. She wouldn't understand, of course, but any refreshment one gets is really entirely in her interest.'

'Well, of course,' Anna said.

'Anyway, I'll be there between five and six tomorrow afternoon, if you feel I can be of any further assistance.'

'Well, that's very kind of you. I don't want to keep you now, if you're in a hurry.'

'Quite, quite so.' Margolin buttoned up his greatcoat. 'Till tomorrow, then,' he said, and left without waiting for a reply, calling goodnight to Mrs Paget as he went. Anna went to the door and watched him wipe snow off the windscreen of a shabby Austin Maxi. Stretched over the bonnet he had the appearance of a spider with some legs missing. He was right, she thought, he did not look like a compulsive womanizer.

'I hope you got what you wanted.' Simon had been unexpectedly silent for the first few minutes of the journey. 'What did you do to poor old Len? He looked quite steamy behind his horn-rims.'

Anna looked at him quickly. The moonlight reflecting off the snow had bleached the small amount of colour from his face. His voice was light, but he was looking rigidly out of the window.

'Nothing at all,' she said. 'How much does it cost to join the society, by the way?'

'Why, are you thinking of joining?'

'No. Just some more small change for the fact fund.'

'Oh, well, it's five pounds for membership. You get a ticket which lets you see six films for that. Then, if you want to see six more, you buy another membership card. Do you like Len?'

'Not much. Why?'

'Only you seemed to be getting on like a house on fire.'

'I wouldn't say that. It's just not in my interests to antagonize him.'

'And how far do you go, not to antagonize him, I mean?' His voice was still light but flat. The question took her by surprise.

'Oh, come on, Si. I want information. That's all,' she said. 'You have to get what you can, where you can, how you can.'

'I seem to have heard that somewhere before,' he said.

'Where?'

He looked at her at last. 'Well, that's what Dee used to say when she went chatting someone up, if they had something to offer, that is.'

The shot found its target, and it did seem fair criticism. In the end she said, 'Yes, I see what you mean. There isn't much difference, is there? I don't know how you'd go about it, but, if I asked him straight out what I wanted to know, I wouldn't get any answers at all.'

'Well, isn't that his privilege, not to give any answers, if he doesn't want to?'

'Yes, it is. But what if Dee actually was killed, isn't it both my job and my privilege to find out what happened to her?'

'Possibly. Yes, it should be someone's job. But doesn't it matter how you go about it? Even if she was killed and you think that Len had something to do with it, you don't have to practically seduce him to find out, do you?'

'I'm not sure how to answer you. The Jacksons are very unhappy people, and I've taken on some responsibility for them. They don't want to stay ignorant, and nor do I. As to my ethics. I'm as straight as I'm allowed to be. And if that's not good enough for you, it's hard luck. It's not good enough for me either.' Anna ran down the car window. She felt hot and stifled.

'One other thing,' she went on, 'and it has nothing to do with ethics or truth or any of that. It's just job satisfaction. I work for a man whose usual idea of a suitable job for me is boutique inventories. This case gives me a chance to do something a bit more interesting. I want to see it through. And, funnily enough, sometime in the past week, I've come to mind what happened to Dee Jackson.'

He said nothing for a while. The car was too cold now, so Anna rolled the window back up. There was hardly any traffic about, and what there was crawled like cautious grubs along the white ribbons of roads.

Simon broke the silence by saying, 'Yes, I accept what you're saying, if what you mean is that truth is a cause that must be served. That's a bit pompous, but you know what I mean. What bothers me is that you also seem to have the attitude that the end justifies the means. I know I'm just a simple guy and I don't have any experience in your line of work, but isn't privacy an important consideration too?'

'Yes, it is. But I have to use my own judgement about it. It's not much of an excuse, but I have spent several years learning about this profession and I have developed a certain instinct for lies or evasions. Sometimes it's all I have to rely on. But when I first met Len Margolin, for instance, I knew he was not what he was pretending to be. If you're looking for something, you tend to look in dark corners. Len Margolin is a dark corner.'

'Okay. It sounds all very fine when you talk about it.' Simon sounded tired and depressed. 'But it didn't look too good when you were doing it. You looked almost as if you were flirting with Len.'

Anna was beginning to feel tired and depressed, too. She said, 'Well, that shouldn't concern you. It won't hurt him, and it won't hurt me either.'

'Something else I'm being childish about?'

With great relief she pulled up outside his flat. Simon made no move to get out of the car. So she said, 'Yes, I think so. That isn't important. But you've said a lot of things that are. They aren't thoughts that are comfortable. I'm never very fond of talking about my job in that way, because self-doubt is such an awful inhibitor.'

'You seem to have all the answers, though.'

'They weren't meant to be answers. They were only justifications. All I mean is, I do the best I can within some severe limitations.' And then, because she was really tired, she added, 'Take it or leave it.'

'Oh hell!' he said. 'You know I'll take it, if only because I like you.'

Anna almost said, 'More fool you, then,' but stopped herself in time. An argument was one thing late at night, but a quarrel was definitely another.

'Look, we're both tired,' she said in the end. 'Let's just pack it in for now, eh?'

'Of course,' he said. 'This is silly, and I'm sorry. But will you let me know how you get on in Stanmore tomorrow?'

CHAPTER 20

THE jangling of the phone woke Anna out of a deep sleep.

'They're all tucked up for the night, safe and sound,' Bernie said when the pips had stopped. 'It's not the weather for snooping round downstairs windows, though.'

'What a bloody awful night for you,' Anna said, trying to wake up properly.

'Not the cold, dummy, the footprints,' he said in his kindly way. 'There's about eight inches of snow. No, I'm all right. I've got the van and all the wife's dozens of hot-water-bottles and Thermos flasks. I'll be turning in myself, now they've got their heads down. No, I just wanted to check something out with you. Himself took a little drive around ten-thirty.'

'Big yellow Scimitar?'

'That's the job. Anyway, everything else being grave-yard round here, I thought I'd toddle off after him on the Norton.'

Brierly Security owned and maintained two Commer vans for surveillance. They were useful only if the mark was stationary. On a job like this one Bernie often carried his motor-bike in the back for quick and discreet forays. It was a good method, giving him more manœuvrability and less in the way of ostentation than a car. Anna had her doubts about using it in the snow.

'Where did he go?'

'He went up the West End, round Vigo Street way and fetched up at the back of the Royal Academy. You know the new museum they've got there?'

'Yes.'

'Well, there. It's very quiet there at night. So he waits for ten minutes, and a tall geezer in horn-rims turns up to meet him. Now, from your notes he answers quite neatly to your thumbnail of Leonard Margolin. Do you know what he drives?'

'A P-registration Austin Maxi. Dark green. I couldn't see the number, but it has a left brake-light with the glass thumped out.'

'Good girl. Looks like it's chummie, then. He got into my boy's motor and they had a bit of a natter. He had a big square box or case when he got in and sweet FA when he got out. So he left the box with my boy.'

'That's it?'

'That's it. Five minutes from hi to bye. Interesting?'

'Very. Thanks a lot, Bernie. I suppose you didn't get much of a gander at the box?'

'Not on your life. I was in Bond Street, window-shopping.'

'Never mind . . .'

'Wait a bit, that's not all. They my boy goes back, Marylebone Road, Westway, and I'm just thinking he's off home when he takes the M4 turning instead. He gets on the M4 and goes to the Heston Service area where he fills up with 4-star. Then he pulls out by the air-pump, but he doesn't do much with his tyres. Couple of minutes later an old post office van pulls up beside him, and he passes the same box through the window. The van takes off and my boy goes home.

'I think now I should have followed the box. Well, I

would have done if Mr Brierly hadn't insisted I shouldn't
let chummie out of my sight.'

'No, quite,' Anna said, wishing Brierly didn't give
the kind of explicit instructions that sometimes left no
room for imagination. 'What about the driver of the van?
Any luck there?'

'Sorry. I didn't get a proper look at him. Big, but
nothing else. I'll give you the van number, though.
Ready?' He gave her the number.

'Ring any bells?' he asked.

'Not a tinkle. Sorry. But thanks for ringing, Bernie,
thanks a lot.'

'No trouble. I thought you'd be interested. Get some
sleep now.'

'You too.' Anna looked at the clock. It was two-thirty.
She went back to bed.

CHAPTER 21

. . . .

IT was the kind of morning when people sensible enough to wear bed-socks refused to take them off. Anna drank coffee and looked at a steel-grey sky, inhospitable even to pigeons. The cold air seemed like an impenetrable barrier. It was a day for sheepskin, mittens, baked potatoes and postponed football matches.

Anna watched the postman toiling over the impacted snow of the unswept pavement and wondered at the sheer heroics that brought the milk and mail on a morning when everyone else gave up and stayed by the fire. She went downstairs, collecting two letters for herself and leaving the others outside the Prices' door. No one was stirring behind it.

Back upstairs she poured more coffee and read the mail. The phone bill didn't take too long. She would be able to claim some of that as expenses, but not enough. The second was from her sister exiled happily in some Kentish executive belt. It contained news of young Kenneth, the usual seasonal moans and a complaint from their mother that Anna hadn't visited since before Christmas.

One of Kenneth's latest drawings had been enclosed, an extraordinary three-legged bolster beside a house four times smaller. The drawing was labelled 'MY DOG.' Kenneth did not have a dog, but he wanted one. She propped the drawing on the mantelpiece under the Hockney print and consigned the letter to the wastepaper basket. The phone rang.

'Sleep well?'

'Morning, Bernie. Better than you, I bet. What's new?'

'One small item.' Bernie was as phlegmatic as ever. He did not sound as if he had spent the night freezing in a van. 'Sonny boy in the GPO van paid our friend a visit half an hour ago. Delivered something round the back and steamed off again. Didn't get invited in for kedgeree and devilled kidneys.'

'Same box?'

'Same size, same shape. Anyway, I'm off home now. Johnny just turned up. He says he'll most likely be in the caff opposite the dead-end, so not to worry if you don't see the Commer. You're due up here at ten-thirty, aren't you?'

'Yes. I'll be leaving shortly.' Anna looked at her watch. It was nine o'clock.

'Well, you drive carefully, then. Leave plenty of time. It's kamikaze on the roads round here.'

'Okay. Thanks, Bernie.'

'See you soon.' Bernie rang off.

Anna parked the Triumph near the end of the cul-de-sac. She let herself into the front garden. The Slingers had not swept the snow off their front path, and by now there were plenty of footprints. Only one set, however, led round the back. On an impulse she followed these, stepping inside them so as not to make fresh tracks. The early-morning visitor had been a tall man, and she had to stretch her legs quite considerably. The prints led around a garage which abutted on to the house, to the back door. This was unlocked. Anna opened it quietly and looked in. The kitchen on this side of the house did not seem to be used for anything except as a lobby to the garage. The only kitchen equipment to be seen was an electric kettle on one of the empty formica units, flanked by a box of teabags, a jar of coffee and another of powdered milk.

She dried her feet thoroughly on the mat. She tried the door to the garage, but it was locked, so she went over to the door leading into the hall and silently opened it. She stood for a few seconds absorbing the sounds of the house. Someone was moving around upstairs to the loud accompaniment of Radio One, which made it difficult to place anything else. Deeper in the hall she could hear voices and different music. Slinger's office door was ajar. She moved closer. In the confusion of noises, she listened to a familiar voice saying ' . . . nag, nag, nag . . .' At the same time, whoever was upstairs came to the top of the staircase. Anna slid quickly into the bar kitchen, closing the door silently behind her. Then with equal speed she let herself out of the back door and went back the way she had come.

The wind blowing off the playing fields behind the house pushed her as she went, forcing her collar up on one side and whipping her hair around her face. She joined the path and approached the front door the orthodox way.

Mrs Slinger let her in. She had a transistor radio slung over her shoulder like a bag, and was wearing a bright golden dress which made her blonde hair look colourless.

'Hello, you're early,' she said, making no attempt to turn the volume down. They were standing in the hall where Anna had been only a couple of minutes before. The office door was now shut tight.

'I know. Sorry,' Anna said, 'it's the weather. I started off early in case of accidents on the way. But nothing happened. I have a phobia about being late, you see.'

'Well, that makes a change, at least. Some of Freddie's people think they can turn up any time.'

She showed Anna into the sitting room on the other side of the house. It looked as if it had been unused since she had last waited there on Wednesday, giving off the same odour of a modern furniture showroom.

'How are the butterflies?'

'Moths,' Anna corrected her pedantically. 'No great breakthrough, I'm afraid. We just have to accept that it's going to be a matter of waiting patiently.'

'It must be fascinating,' Mrs Slinger said unconvincingly. 'Would you like a cup of coffee while you're waiting?'

'How kind. I'd love one,' Anna said. Mrs Slinger went out, closing the door firmly behind her. Anna made no effort to eavesdrop this time. She sat in one of the plastic armchairs and breathed deeply, trying to calm the nervous flutter of her pulse. Illegal entry was not a relaxing occupation.

She had finished her coffee and was perfectly serene when Mr Slinger made his appearance ten minutes later.

'Well, well, well, it's a bit on the parky side,' he said, rubbing his hands. 'Good job you're on time. It may take you a while to get to Stanmore in this snow. How's everything in the butterfly business?'

'Moths,' Anna said automatically, 'nothing spectacular yet, but we live in hope.'

'Well, let's get you started, then.' He led the way through to the empty kitchen and unlocked the door into the garage. It was fitted out neatly with shelves for the projectors and racks for the many film-cans and spare reels.

'Where did you park your car, by the way?' he asked as he passed a projector out to her. She saw from the way he made her wait in the kitchen that employees were not encouraged to pick out equipment for themselves.

'Just before the turning area.'

'Well, next time,' he said, choosing a large spool, 'park as close to the house as you can, or in one of the two driveways. We don't want the neighbours getting narky.'

'Is that a problem?' Anna asked. 'This being a residential area, I suppose.'

'Nothing we can't handle by keeping them sweet. After all, most of them have kids and those kids have parties. Throw in a free film show and you'd be surprised what they won't put up with.'

Anna hefted the projector to the front door.

'Think you can handle it all right?' Slinger said.

She lifted the case off. The projector looked straight-forward enough.

'I don't foresee any problems,' she lied primly. 'It looks like the sort of thing I'm accustomed to.'

'Okay. Now, what you do is, switch off after half an hour, so the little bleeders can stuff themselves with more jelly. There's a nice long bit of leader spliced in between the end of *Road Runner* and the start of *Woody Woodpecker*. You just have to switch on again when they're ready. Okay?'

'Fine. What happens if the film breaks?'

'It shouldn't, but if it does just thread up as quick as possible and don't panic. They won't notice a thing. Now, I'll just get you the address.'

He went into the office. Anna stood at the doorway, watching. There was a projector in there, too, and a screen hanging permanently on one wall with an editing bench underneath. The rest was normal office furniture, a glass-topped desk, a swivel chair and filing cabinets. He took an appointment diary from one of the desk drawers and tore a sheet from his scratch pad. Then, placing the single sheet on the glass, he copied out an address.

'It's the bride's mother you want to see.' He gave her the paper. 'A Mrs Taplow. She'll show you where she wants you to operate. Just make sure she's chosen a room with decent curtains that close all the way. But the most important thing is to get her to pay up. She promised cash over the phone, but it's amazing what people forget at the last moment. So jog her memory, will you?'

'Okay,' Anna said, 'Cash it is.'

'That's a girl,' Slinger said, switching on his sudden grin. 'Makes book-keeping that much quicker. Cash for me and the same for you when you get back, right?'

The Taplow house was big and friendly, and alive with caterers. Anna was early, so she could set up the screen, thread the projector and check the focus before the wedding party arrived. She was thankful not to have anyone breathing down her neck as she wrestled with unfamiliar equipment.

Mrs Taplow, when she introduced herself, was a large, generous lady all aquiver with nerves and green ostrich feathers.

'I'm so glad you're here,' she said breathlessly. 'Never, never get married in January, my dear. You've no idea what problems we've had today. Would you mind terribly if I paid you now? I know it's not quite the thing, only I might be the smallest bit squiffy when you want to leave.'

She gave Anna an envelope. It was heavy and sealed. There was no need to ask if it contained cash. The rest of the morning passed just as painlessly. Primed with a couple of glasses of champagne and a plateful of vol-au-vents, she showed her cartoons without any embarrassment whatsoever. The children appeared to be more drunk and disorderly than the adults, but, as someone was kind enough to furnish the projectionist with more champagne halfway through, Anna did not mind at all. In fact, several of the adult guests filtered into the children's room and seemed to appreciate the nonsense as much as they did. It was that kind of reception.

'Been at the bubbly?' Slinger said, taking note of her pink cheeks and bright eyes when she got back to Harrow. 'Well, I told you there were perks to this business.'

'They were kind enough to offer me a glass or three,' Anna replied with dignity, 'I hope you don't mind.'

'You are a one,' he laughed. 'Course I don't mind so long as Mrs T. came across with the necessary before you got too cross-eyed to ask for it.'

Anna handed him the fat envelope.

'No harm done, then,' he said, weighing it judiciously. 'Just remember not to get so paralytic you can't focus. We don't want complaints.'

'Mind how you drive,' he called after her as she went down the path to her car whistling 'Ain't Misbehavin.' Halfway home she remembered Slinger had omitted to pay her. It was indeed amazing what people forgot at the last moment.

CHAPTER 22

* * * * * * * * *

THE phone was ringing as Anna unlocked her door. She answered, balancing the box of groceries on one hip. After the pips there was a silence broken only by heavy breathing. Then a husky voice said, 'Are you wearing rubber-soled shoes?'

'Leave off, Johnny,' Anna said, 'or I'll tell your Mum.'

'I saw you go in,' Johnny said. 'Twice, no, three times. Wasn't that a bit hairy? B. and E. five minutes from when you're expected. You could have blown everything.'

'It's nice to know you were watching so carefully. Anyway, I didn't B. I just E'd.'

'Well, I hope it was worth it. You had my old ticker going double time, I can tell you. Listen, Bernie said you want to know about a square box with straps on.'

'Yes. Did you see it?'

'After you left, the second time. He opens his garage door, the one on the right, and takes off in a yellow Scimitar.'

'With the box?'

'I didn't see it then. He must be able to get into this garage from inside the house. But he went to the Export Cargo office at Heathrow, and took your box in there. I was standing off, so I didn't see if he actually filled anything in. But after a while he comes out again and takes the box into the cargo shed. Then he came out empty-handed.'

'No way to figure out where the box was going?'

'Short of holding his pen and taking dictation, no.'

'Well, never mind. What next?'

'He goes home, that's all. But he's a busy little bee. There's been people coming and going all afternoon.'

'Doing what?'

'Same as you. Collecting films and screens and things and driving off into the sunset.'

'Any sign of an old GPO van?'

'Bernie left standing instructions about that. But no, not a whisper. Okay?'

'Yes, Johnny, fine. Thanks a lot for ringing.'

He hung up. Anna sighed and put her shopping away in the kitchen. Then she took another deep breath and phoned Simon.

'Hello. How did you get on?' he asked. She needn't have worried. He sounded rested and carefree today.

'Piece of cake. Thank you very much,' she said. 'No problems.'

'Well, good, great. Listen, Anna, I'm sorry about last night. I don't know what got into me.'

'Not to worry. Perhaps I laid too much on you all at once. It's best to keep things simple.'

'Right. That's what I thought. Look, there's a court free at Westbourne Grove at five o'clock. Would you like a game?'

Anna quickly weighed up the pros and cons of meeting him again and then cautiously accepted.

She put the kettle on and made a cup of tea. Then she called Brierly Security's night line. A disembodied voice said, 'Martin Brierly is not now available. Please leave your message after the tone.'

'Anna Lee here,' she said, thinking fast, and, as

usual, feeling foolish when forced to talk to a machine. 'A link has been established between the subject and Leonard Margolin. There's been no contact between the subject and the laboratory yet. But I think I know what's going on. There should be some explanatory information available this evening. I'd like to speak to you as soon as possible.'

She rang off and drank her tea by the fire. Then she put her squash racket and tennis shoes in a bag and went out again.

At Kensington Public Library she found a book called *Films On Offer 1978*. Listed in it were films available in 16mm. *Gauntlet* was distributed by Columbia Warner and would cost a film society thirty pounds to hire. Anna compared this with other prices. Then she sat at one of the tables and did some rough sums based on what she had seen the night before. Even if all the seats were filled for most films, she reckoned that Seven Sisters Film Society must financially be a dead duck. Of course, that might not be unusual. She had never heard that film societies were supposed to make a fortune. All she had learned was that new colour films usually cost a lot more to rent than old ones in black and white. It was interesting, but not much more.

Simon was ready, and bouncing up and down to get his circulation moving, when she arrived at Westbourne Grove.

'It's court 3,' he said, 'not that it matters. There's no one else around. I'll warm up the ball while you change.'

It was freezing, and the ladies' changing-room was deserted. A notice informed members that the courts would not be heated owing to non-delivery of fuel, but a limited supply of hot water was available for showers after the game. Members were requested in the interest of public spirit not to linger over their ablutions. Members, it seemed, had responded by staying away altogether.

Anna changed hurriedly and found court 3.

'I think . . . ,' Simon served, 'that the more rallies we can get in, the better. It's really too chilly to spend all our time picking dead balls out of the corner.'

'Suits me,' Anna said, retrieving a long shot from the back of the court. 'I prefer playing with people than against them, anyway.'

They played without scoring for about ten minutes. The ball was slow to warm up, and the pace quickened only gradually. Finally they played properly.

'You're pretty quick,' Simon said as they took a breather. He was two games to one up.

'Speed,' Anna panted, 'is no substitute for accuracy.' Her game was rather rusty.

'It must be a change from brainwork, anyway.'

'Not that I've been especially brilliant at that recently, either.' She wiped the sweat from her face. 'Speaking of which, how difficult is it to copy films?'

'Is this a busman's holiday, or what?' he asked ruefully.

'Well, I was thinking about what you said a few nights ago about copyrights, and I wondered how easy it would be to copy a film you had no right to.'

'I suppose the biggest difficulty would be finding someone prepared to take the risk and do it for you.'

'And if you had a tame lab technician?' Anna was beginning to shiver again. 'Is it your service?'

'No, yours. Well, it all depends on the quality you want. If you aren't too fussy, you can make a poor quality duplicate without too much trouble. Good shot!'

The ball had flashed off the wall at a very shallow angle, leaving him floundering on the wrong side of the court.

'What would you need?' Anna served again and lost the point.

'All you have to have is the film you want to duplicate, print stock, access to a printing machine, and the baths.'

Simon took the next two points.

'Two-one,' he said. 'It's called slash duping. It's a one-step process where you do without a negative. The picture will be rather muddy, and the sound a bit fuzzy, but it's the quickest and cheapest way I know.'

Anna regained the service after a long rally.

'Slash duping? How long does it take to do?'

'Two-all. That depends on the length of the film and the speed of the machines you use.'

'Three-two. But roughly? A day, a week?'

'Bad luck.' Simon won the serve back. 'No, nothing like that. You should be able to make a dupe of a ninety-minute feature which is what, three thousand feet, in a couple of hours easily.'

'Three-all. Is that all? I thought it took ages.'

'Like I said, that's only for poor quality. It can take ages to get the sound and picture just right.'

'Four-three?'

It was a long game, which Simon won narrowly.

'It's always the same,' Anna complained, 'I'm just getting my eye in when my wind goes.'

Anna showered quickly and washed her hair. The hair-dryer accepted her coin and then refused to part with any hot air. She shook her head like a wet dog and went out to find Simon waiting in the lobby. Water dripped down the back of her neck.

'Home,' he said. 'This place is like a morgue, only twice as cold.'

She drove him back to Maida Vale.

'Do you want to come in for coffee?'

'Not really. I should get back. I'm expecting a call.'

'Only I wondered,' Simon said slowly, 'if you'd for-gotten Dee in all the excitement about Slinger.'

'No.' Anna had been wondering the same thing about Simon.

'Have you found any more people who knew her?'

'Yes.'

'People I don't know about?'

'Probably.'

'Will you tell me about them?'

'Probably.'

'Now?'

'No. When it's all over.'

'Why? Because the Jacksons are paying for the infor-mation and I'm not?'

'That would be my boss's attitude, yes. And I suppose I could get fired for what he'd call a breach of security. He guarantees confidentiality to his clients, you see.'

'What about you?'

'I think that if they have the right to know, then so do you or anyone who was concerned about Dee.'

'Then you will tell me?'

'If you'll let me do it in my own way. Anything I know about Dee right now is gossip and hearsay. I don't want to tell you anything that hasn't been verified. It would only give a false impression.'

'Okay. I see what you mean.' He rubbed his face with his forefinger. 'I'm sorry I attacked your ethics last night.'

'That's okay. Sometimes I'm not wild about them either.'

'Well, I wouldn't want to get you fired, anyway.'

'At least we agree on that,' Anna said drily.

Beryl phoned at seven-thirty. By then Anna knew quite positively she had a cold on the way. Her head and throat ached, and she felt shivery.

'I called you at five. But you weren't in.' It was typical of Beryl to begin a conversation with criticism.

'Did Mr Brierly get my message?'

'That's why I'm calling. He's spending the weekend in Berkshire.' It might have been Windsor Castle, given the hushed and respectful tone Beryl adopted.

'Can I get in touch?'

'How important is it? You know he doesn't appreciate disturbances when he's in Berkshire.'

'Proof of a crime, I think.'

'Conclusive?'

'Mmm. Should I report it?' Anna wanted to keep the chat as short as possible. She blamed Beryl for her cold.

'Oh.' Although assuming the position at God's right hand, Beryl was neither authorized nor equipped to take decisions of this kind. Anna was calling her bluff, and Beryl knew it.

'I will try to apprise the Commander of the situation,' she said stiffly. 'Meanwhile, only report if asked, and if you don't hear from me, come in first thing Monday.'

'Okay.'

'And don't make waves.' Beryl was getting the boot in while she could. She could not be wrong on an instruction so close to Brierly's heart.

'All right,' Anna said. '*Piano, piano* it is.'

'What?'

'Softly, softly in Italian.'

'Are you trying to be funny?' said Beryl.

CHAPTER 23

ANNA slept for twelve hours solid and spent what was left of Sunday morning watering the plants and washing clothes. Nobody rang. There was no further news of square boxes or old GPO vans. The sun did not shine, but there was no snow either, just a hard grey coldness that seeped through the windows and kept her close to the fire. It looked as if it was going to be a typically flat Sunday. Anna fought off the misery of sore throat and throbbing sinuses with lemon and honey tea. When that did not work, she left out the tea and added whisky and aspirin. The resulting grogginess did not help the subtleties of *Portrait of a Lady*. She had almost given up on it when Selwyn came bouncing in, rosy from the cold, or his lunch-time sabbatical at the pub.

'You're looking a bit peaky, young Leo,' he said. 'You should have come out for a noggin. It's not like you to mope.'

'I'm not moping,' Anna told him. 'I'm just keeping my viruses at home where they won't kill anyone else.'

'Very civilized, I'm sure. Is that whisky?'

'Help yourself.'

'I shouldn't.' Selwyn poured himself a generous three inches. 'Bea has roast pork all ready and grunting. Oh, I almost forgot. There are two gents downstairs wanting to see you. I said I'd ask. I met them on my way in.'

'Oh, who?' Anna wasn't expecting anyone.

'I forgot to ask,' Selwyn said helpfully. 'One has flat feet and the other one's a spiv. Shall I tell them to come up?'

'I can hardly wait.' Anna grinned. 'It sounds like my lucky day.'

'I thought the computer only sent them one at a time,' Selwyn said on his way out. 'Actually, neither of them looks your type. Thump on the floor if they give you any trouble. I'll send Bea up.'

Selwyn was having a remarkably perceptive day. Constable Collinwood did indeed have flat feet. The other man was a little older, perhaps thirty-seven or so, but he looked slimmer and fitter, as if he would be at home in a gymnasium or a swimming pool. His lean brown face looked misplaced in an English January. He stood still by the open door. Collinwood came in without any invitation.

'Nice little place,' he said, looking round. He wandered through the room as if he was in the insect house at London Zoo, examining books and furniture as he went, with painstaking inattention. He went into the bedroom area.

'Live here on your own?' he said.

'The bathroom's on your right, if that's what you're looking for,' Anna said, 'and my granny's in the airing cupboard on the top shelf above the towels. Why don't you ask her?'

'Touchy,' he said as if to an invisible friend at his shoulder.

'On the other hand,' Anna went on as if she hadn't heard him, 'you could come and introduce your friend like a normal civilized person. Or did bad manners come with the pointed hat? Nosiness doesn't have to be a fulltime occupation, you know.'

'Oh, yes.' Collinwood came back to the fire. 'This

here is Alan J. Luca. He wanted to meet you,' Collinwood added, as if this made Alan J. Luca unique.

'How do you do?' Anna said politely.

'Call me Alan. Please forgive us intruding on you like this. It really wasn't my idea.'

'He's from America,' Collinwood said, as if this explained everything. He sat himself down in the chair Anna had just vacated, raising one buttock slightly to rescue the flattened paperback from under his broad rear.

'You're not one of those Women's Libbers, are you?' he said, gazing suspiciously at the bent cover.

'Ah, actually I'm from the MPAA FSO,' Alan interrupted hurriedly, as if he wanted to disassociate himself from Collinwood's ignorance. Anna stared at him in silence.

'Perhaps you never heard of it?' he said, looking flustered.

'Perhaps you'll tell me what it is. Then I'll tell you if I've heard of it.'

'It's the Motion Picture Association of America Film Security Office. I'm sorry. Someone was supposed to have phoned you this morning.'

'You're quite right,' she said resignedly, 'I've never heard of it. But I'm sure you'll tell me all about it. How about some coffee in the meantime? Or would you prefer tea?' she asked Collinwood.

'Coffee will do.' Collinwood glanced meaningfully at the half-bottle of Black and White on the mantelpiece. Anna ignored him and retreated to the kitchen. She filled the kettle and put it on the stove. Then she went back to the living-room.

'Just who was supposed to have phoned me?' she asked the two men impartially.

Alan J. Luca said, 'Your office, I think.'

Collinwood said, 'Dunno,' at the same time.

She went to the phone and dialled.

'Martin Brierly is not now available . . .' the answering machine repeated its perpetual message. When it stopped, Anna said, 'Anna Lee. I have two visitors, PC Collinwood and Alan J. Luca, who claim I was supposed to have received instructions. Would someone get back to me quickly, please.'

She replaced the receiver. Collinwood looked as if he was about to say something, so she went hastily back to the kitchen, threw some coffee beans into the grinder, and switched it on. It was an antiquated Moulinex, and very noisy. Anna kept it going until the kettle had boiled. Fastidiously, she filtered the coffee. It was the slowest method she could think of. Then she laid a tray with mugs, milk and sugar and carried it carefully out of the kitchen.

'Real coffee!' Alan J. Luca murmured. 'I haven't had much of that lately.'

Unasked, Collinwood adulterated his with a slug of Black and White.

They made a nice contrast, sitting on either side of the fire. Collinwood, it seemed, had been held together by his uniform. Out of it, he sprawled untidily in Anna's arm-chair in an assortment of ill-matched colours and textures. Luca, on the other hand, was neat in his dark blue suit. His shoes were mirrors, and he showed just the right amount of cuff. He looked as if he had been dressed by a computer, while Collinwood might have been assembled by a child for the Fifth of November.

Anna pulled up a third chair and sat down.

'Okay. To what do I owe the pleasure?' she said in her best imitation of a county hostess.

'Look, I'm just supposed to introduce you two,' Collinwood said, 'but if you ask me, there's something going on between my chief and your governor. Maybe, there's more to what you're doing than meets the eye. I was just told to bring him here. Seeing as I know you. It was a matter of tact.'

'Your strongest suit.'

'Don't get shirty. People like you and me are always pig-in-the-middle. We just do the work. The brass share the honours. Like the old song says, "It's the rich what gets the gravy" '.

' "And the poor what gets the blame",' Anna finished for him, 'that's just what I'm afraid of.'

'I don't see how any blame could attach.' Luca looked mystified. 'Perhaps I should explain why I'm here.'

'You might as well,' said Collinwood, 'you won't get a dicky-bird out of her till that phone rings.'

'I don't know what's eating you, Mr Collinwood,' Luca said. 'She doesn't even know what we want yet.'

'Well, don't hold your breath.' Collinwood stretched his legs and folded his arms. 'I've got better things to do with my time off.'

'As I said,' Luca turned to Anna, 'I'm an agent with the MPAA Film Security Office. It's an LA-based organization, set up to combat film piracy. In the past few years we have estimated that the major studios have lost over a hundred million dollars to pirates through illegal sales of their films. We are working very closely with the FBI in an attempt to enforce the copyright laws.'

'In England?' Anna asked politely.

'I should add that I'm only here in an investigatory capacity and that we have established offices in capitals throughout the world. But we do have the co-operation of Interpol and Scotland Yard. London and Paris are particularly important, because these cities still have connections with old colonial networks in Africa, say, or India or the Caribbean Islands.'

'You mean that the countries you've just mentioned provide a market for illegal copies of films?'

'Uh-huh,' Luca said.

'Why them in particular?' Anna asked.

'Well, they have looser copyright laws, and practically no enforcement. Also, sometimes the major companies don't find it worth their while to distribute to them.'

'But if they did, then surely there would be no market for illegal films? If there was no market, there would be no pirates.'

'It's economics,' Luca said. 'It might cost, say, ten thousand dollars for a studio to distribute a film to a little African country where they could only return seven thousand dollars. It wouldn't make sense.'

'But if someone else can get an illegal copy of the

same film cheaply, then that someone would clear the seven thousand?'

'That's right. Those are the people we want to stop.'

'Well,' Anna said, 'it still seems a bit cock-eyed to me. The studios must be spending millions to save themselves thousands, and meanwhile your little African countries don't get to see all the films we enjoy.'

'What did I tell you?' Collinwood said, with his eyes shut. 'She's probably a communist at heart.'

'It can work the other way round, too.' Luca ignored him. 'A local distributor who could buy the rights to a certain film might prefer a pirated copy because it's cheaper.'

'Well, maybe the big studios should have more reasonable expectations of what they can hope to return from Third World countries,' Anna said thoughtfully. 'Some of them are pretty poor. You can't expect everyone to pay the equivalent of two quid for a seat in the stalls just to keep the box-office receipts in line with what Hollywood thinks is a worthwhile profit.'

'Well, I guess that's up to Hollywood,' Luca said, not unreasonably. 'I'm only here because I was told you had a line on an operation in this country.'

'Now, you're talking,' drawled Collinwood, 'I was wondering when you'd stop answering her questions and start asking yours.'

The telephone rang. Anna answered it.

'Hello, love,' Bernie said. 'There's been a bit of a balls-up. I'm at Ken. High now.'

'What's up?'

'Nothing to make you put on brown trousers,' Bernie said placidly. 'It's just Beryl had someone drive into her on her way back from church this morning so she's at St Thomas's having her neck put in a sling.'

'That bad?'

'No, not really. They're only strapping up her knee. Don't worry. Anyway, I gather you've got company.'

'That's right, and someone was supposed to have warned me.'

'Beryl would have if she hadn't been making bus and

lorry sarnies at the time. She phoned Mr Brierly from
casualty, and he phoned me. Why one of them couldn't
phone you, I don't know. But then, I'm simple-minded.
The trouble is, they want to know what you've got before
telling you to tell someone else.'

'Then why send the company round now? They could
have left it till Monday. It's a bit late now.'

'That's what I said. Anyway, Mr B. says not to toss
them out. That'd be bad for PR. Shall I quote? He said
you must use your own discretion and try not to prejudice
the prior claims of this office.'

'What the hell's that supposed to mean?'

'Calm down. Probably it means give them the skinny
but keep the kudos for His Nibs. You don't have the kind
of evidence they can nick, do you?'

'No.'

'All right, so keep it foggy if you can.'

'Okay, Bernie.'

'I'm sorry I couldn't do better than that.'

'It's not your fault,' Anna said, 'but it'll probably end
up being mine.'

Anna hung up and went back to her chair.

'More coffee, anyone?' she said, pouring herself
some.

'Was that your liaison officer?' Luca held his cup out.

'Not exactly,' Anna said pouring. 'She was in a motor accident this morning, which is why I wasn't expecting
you.'

Collinwood snorted. 'Look, I've told John Wayne
here about Francis Neary, and I've told him what my chief
told me about you filling us in. If you've got anything
hard, you should have turned it in anyway.'

'That's just it. I haven't.'

'I'd like to know what you've got, even so,' Luca
said.

'Well, I'm really working on something completely
different,' Anna said, 'and I stumbled on this by chance.
A man called Frederick Slinger runs a projection service
in Harrow. I can't prove it, but I think he is making illegal

copies of films hired legitimately by a film society in North London, and shipping them abroad.'

'How do you know?' Luca asked. 'What were the steps, I mean?'

'I went to interview the secretary of the film society on Friday night. The film they were showing that night was *Gauntlet*. I saw him rewind the film and box it up at roughly ten-thirty p.m. About half an hour later a box of the same description was passed to Frederick Slinger in the West End. He passed it on to an unknown man at a service station on the M4. Next morning the same unknown, or someone driving the same van, delivered a similar box to Frederick Slinger. When I was at Slinger's house later that morning, I overheard a piece of soundtrack which I knew to be from *Gauntlet*. Later, Slinger was seen to leave a box at the Export Cargo Office at Heathrow Airport. That's all.'

'Not what you'd call an unbroken trail,' Collinwood said.

'Exactly,' Anna said cheerfully.

'How do you know it was the same film, then?' Collinwood was not being very bright.

'I'm not saying it's the same piece of celluloid,' Anna said patiently. 'I think that the one Slinger passed on at Heston was the original and the one he received on Saturday morning was a copy. The original would have been returned to Columbia Warner.'

'Are you sure that what you heard was from *Gauntlet*?' Luca asked.

'Positive,' Anna said.

'Could have been a coincidence,' Collinwood said.

'Quite so,' Anna said just as definitely. Luca looked at her, puzzled. If he had expected her to defend her own case he was being disappointed.

'This man Slinger,' he said, changing tack. 'He's the careless type, then?'

'The reverse, I'd have thought,' Anna said warily.

'Then you know him well?'

'Not at all. I've only met him twice.' She saw Collinwood grin suddenly.

'Then how come he lets a total stranger hear evidence of illegal material?' Luca asked doubtfully. Collinwood laughed. It wasn't a pleasant laugh.

'The bleeding bathroom window!' he said triumphantly. 'They're all tarred with the same brush.'

Luca looked from one to the other, nonplussed. Collinwood was still grinning wolfishly. Anna sipped her coffee decorously and said nothing.

In the end Collinwood said, 'I'd change the subject, if I were you. When little Miss Marple here heard what she heard, she hadn't been invited in for tea and toast like a normal law-abiding citizen. She wouldn't want to tell you about it with me hanging on her every word.'

'I'm sorry,' Luca said in confusion, as if he had been guilty of a breach of manners. No one helped him, and there was silence for about half a minute. Then he cleared his throat and said, 'Then I suppose you have no idea what volume this Slinger might be dealing in?'

Anna said, 'No.'

Luca asked, 'Who do you think is doing this copying for Slinger?'

Anna looked at Collinwood, who appeared to be snoozing.

'I think it might be someone at Colour Cine Services. But I was told to lay off that side of things after Francis Neary killed himself. My boss said the police were turning that one over.'

Luca said, 'What about that, Mr Collinwood?'

Collinwood stirred at last. Unhurriedly, he took a packet of Embassy from his pocket and lit one. Anna fetched him an ashtray, but not quickly enough to prevent him dropping the spent match into his coffee-cup.

'Co-operation seems to be the name of the game,' he said at last. 'I suppose our betters know what they're doing, but I wish they'd let me in on the secret. We haven't finished our investigation of Neary yet, but the gist of it so far is that he came over here in '75. He was the eldest of a family or four. The father was knocked off in a pub bombing in Antrim in '74 and apart from our lad the family's been on the SS ever since. He's worked for Colour

Cine for roughly two years. No trouble there. He sent his Mum money, sometimes. But you couldn't say he was supporting her, or anyone, unless it was a couple of bookies in Wembley. He couldn't stay away from three-legged geegees, it seems. But then, who can? It's dumbos like him keeping Ladbrokes in business everywhere. Nothing serious, he wasn't in hock or behind with the rent, but what with the beer and the ponies he only just kept himself this side of the breadline. He didn't have woman trouble either, unless it was famine.'

Collinwood paused to drag on his cigarette.

'How long had he been on the night shift?' Anna asked.

'Yeah, that did account for a change. He went on to the one-to-nine about eight months ago. It meant some extra money coming in.'

'Enough to account for the hundred-quid suit and cassette recorder?'

'You want to watch that nose of yours,' Collinwood said sourly. 'It might get caught in a keyhole one day. He could have afforded them. If he'd saved. Or if he'd had a decent win. We know he didn't save. Don't know about the other.'

'Who are the other regulars on the one-to-nine?' Anna asked, undeterred.

'Don't push. I'm getting to it.' Collinwood felt in his coat for his notebook.

'There's Raymond Brough and James Eady. Addresses supplied, if you want them. We haven't talked to them yet. No reason to, apart from these suspicions. But anyway, you aren't the only one been told to use the soft pedal. You haven't got a drop of beer, by any chance? I had to give up my Sunday pint to come here.'

'There's some Stella Artois in the fridge,' Anna said, getting up.

'That'll do.' Collinwood followed her to the kitchen door.

Anna gave him a glass. Luca didn't want any. His belly was far too flat to belong to a beer-drinker.

Collinwood took his drink back to his chair and disposed of half of it in a single suck.

'Well, like I was saying, those three, Brough, Eady, and Neary when he was still with us, represent the scrag-end of the lab's workforce. The brown-coat brigade. Semi-to unskilled. What they do is finish off for the previous shift. They deal with any material that's still in the machines and they clear up and change the chemicals, and generally make sure it's all spick and span for the morning shift. They don't have a supervisor or anything like that.' He took another swig of his drink.

'That's about it. They none of them have any form, apart from Neary. But you know about that. And there's been no half-inching as Colour Cine knows about. According to the stockman there, every little thing is accounted for.'

Collinwood drained his glass. 'Those names mean anything to you?'

'Not a thing,' Anna said. 'On the other hand, there's a registration number that might mean something to you. Whoever picked up the box and delivered again was driving an old post office van. You might know it.'

She read the number from her own notebook. Collinwood solemnly wrote it in his. He flipped back a few pages.

'Not so's you'd notice. But someone could take a gander in the car-park one of these nights. Is that the lot, then?'

'I think so,' Anna said. Both she and Collinwood looked at Luca.

'Well,' he said judiciously, 'I think you might have found the kind of set-up that interests us, potentially.'

'Oh, jolly good,' said Collinwood.

'I expect the boss class'll keep you informed,' Anna said. 'They're passing this one between them like Edwards to Bennett to Gravell.'

'You've got a point there,' Collinwood put in, quite amiably for a change. 'It's just us suckers in the scrum who don't get told. Well, if that's everything, I'll be on my bike. I'll drop you back at the Hilton.'

Luca looked as if he was going to say something, but got up and shook hands with Anna instead.

'Don't leave the country,' Collinwood said, almost jovial now he was on his way out. 'If you fall over any evidence of the admissible variety, I mean, don't forget where it ought to go.'

When they had gone, Anna washed some rice and put a pork chop under the grill. She was just washing the mushrooms when the doorbell rang. She turned the grill off and went downstairs to open the door.

The collar of his trenchcoat was turned up, and the shoulders were sparkling with melting sleet.

'Sorry to interrupt you again so soon,' Luca said, 'but I seem to need the subtitles and I thought it might be easier without my escort. Can I come in?'

'I'm just making lunch,' Anna said as they went upstairs. 'Do you want some or have you eaten already?'

'That'd be great.'

Anna took another chop from the fridge.

'Mustard and cardamoms?'

'Yeah. You know, I've only been over here a couple of months, but it strikes me that this is the first time anyone's offered a meal on the spur of the moment. I've had tea by the gallon, but no food.'

'It's probably more a question of diffidence than generosity,' Anna said, stirring the rice. 'We'd prefer to be criticized for our inhospitality than for the quality of our cooking. You know, the old competition between sins of omission and sins of commission. In England omission wins every time.'

'But you're the sins of commission type,' Luca said, leaning against the sink with his arms folded.

'As far as cooking goes,' Anna garnished the other side of the chops and wondered if she had chosen the wrong metaphor.

'That's really why I came back. It seems to me that with you British it's what you leave out that counts.'

'Well,' Anna said, beginning to grate some large carrots, 'one has to economize somewhere. But, speaking for myself, if I left anything out, it wasn't to be subtle. It was because of Mr Collinwood.'

She turned the rice out into a bowl and put it into the oven to dry.

'He impressed me as being pretty hostile. Who was he sore at?'

'He seemed quite impartial. Last time I saw him, he was friendly enough. Perhaps he thinks I left something out, too.'

She cut some cucumber sticks and put them with the grated carrots.

'I thought your firm got on pretty well with the police,' Luca said. 'At least, that's what Mr Brierly was telling me.'

'We do,' Anna said, squeezing a lemon, 'or, at least, he does. But it doesn't always follow that you want them to know exactly what you know when you know it. The law's the law, of course, but Joe Fuzz has big feet. And you have to be awfully certain you know where he's going to put them.'

She dripped some olive oil slowly into the lemon juice and stirred it.

'Also, we are supposed to be private investigators, although Mr Brierly doesn't attach much importance to the word. You want some of this on that?'

'Sure.' He watched Anna sprinkle the mixture on the carrots and cucumber. 'I thought your British policemen were supposed to be just wonderful,' he said idly.

'On street level they are, as you say, wonderful. Make no mistake, they're fantastic.' She went through to the living-room and pulled out the leaf of the table by the window. Going back for dishes and cutlery, she said, 'I don't know, it's just that, if there's a pinch to be made in this case, I'd want to know it was justified. I don't see myself as a police informer first and foremost.'

She set the table.

'Well, such as it is, it's ready. What do you want to drink?'

Luca drank milk. He ate precisely and efficiently, cutting his food into geometrical shapes of identical size. He

felt exiled in England, he told her. Eighteen months ago
he had been working happily in MGM's law office. Contracts, he said, were his meat and potatoes; organizing
words with pietistic accuracy. Then the MPAA had ex-
panded and called for keen legal minds, and he had been
transferred to the Film Security Office. He had been sent
to England to help in the London Office, where the weather
was unimaginably bad and his training was of no use to
him. The man he was supposed to be working for had
taken a putative business trip to South Africa—his only
acquaintance in London. He had comforted himself by
buying a sun-ray lamp.

'Where do you fit into the Slinger case?' Anna asked.
'I mean, what will you actually do?'

She was beginning to warm to him slightly. He told
his story wryly and with humour. His eyes were as dark
as Pontefract cakes, and he sported a lopsided white smile.

'You've got me there,' he said. 'I'm supposed to col-
late, advise, and then report. In fact, in this country the
MPAA FSO is toothless. What the hell, I'm a contract
lawyer. I should be back in the States writing contracts.'

He fell silent. They had been talking steadily for almost two hours, partly because there was a lot to be said
and partly out of the awkward pressure on strangers to
leave no long gaps in conversation. In the lull Anna suddenly felt uneasy. It was a price she often paid for the
luxury of spontaneous hospitality. Generosity wasn't an
easy thing to undo, and Luca showed no signs of wanting
to leave. At this rate lunch would turn into dinner, and
then what? He looked warm, well-fed and nicely settled.
Logically, if the conversation were to progress, it would
have to become more personal. Anna was not feeling pro-
gressive. Therefore she would have to invent a reason for
turning him out into the snow.

She looked at her watch. She never felt it was a good
start, but it always seemed to work. 'Oh, Christ, look at
the time,' she said despicably.

'It's bloody cowardly, you are,' Selwyn said later, when
it was dark. They were drinking tea and eating crumpets

downstairs. 'The poor fellow probably thought he'd found a home.'

'He had,' Anna said, 'only it was mine.'

'Well, it's time you shared it with someone,' Selwyn persisted. 'You'll end up a raddled old spinster at this rate.'

'Don't be so rude,' Bea put in. 'If you ask me, she's better off without. I should know.'

'What's got into you, Selwyn?' Anna said. 'You never used to take such an interest in my social life.'

'That was when you had one. I'm afraid you'll lose your bloom if you carry on like this.'

'Well, there's nothing like a man to make a girl lose her bloom,' Bea said acidly.

'There's nothing like a man, full stop.' Selwyn stretched complacently.

CHAPTER 24

• • • • • • • • • •

AT eight-fifteen on a silently frozen morning, Anna was
drinking orange juice by the kitchen sink, looking
down to the road. Radio One was playing 'Me and You
and a Dog Named Boo.' Breakfasting on caffeine, vitamin
C and nostalgia was becoming a habit.

She saw a car draw up outside the house. It was Bernie's sand-coloured Hillman. Surprised, Anna ran downstairs and opened the door before Bernie had a chance to
ring the bell.

'You should eat a proper breakfast,' he said, looking
round in vain for signs of bacon and eggs. He drank his
coffee standing in the time-honoured policeman's pose,
weight nicely centred over spread feet, swaying impercep-
tibly.

'I thought you might like a lift to work,' he went on,
'and a word in your ear now might save a spot of bother
later on.'

'That's nice of you, Bernie. What's the bother?'

'Well, don't lose your rag, but as you know, Beryl's

a bit under the weather and Mr B. thinks you can fill in
for her for a couple of days.'

'Oh, no!' Anna said furiously, 'oh no, no, no. You
must be joking.'

'The exact words,' Bernie continued calmly, 'were,
"I believe Miss Lee can type, so we shouldn't be too
badly inconvenienced." '

'What a frigging nerve!' She was seriously annoyed
now. 'I call that value-added chutzpah. Well, sod him,
then. I'm going sick. If he wants a bleeding typist, it won't
be me.'

'Don't get all aeriated yet. Forewarned is forearmed,
so use your noddle. Phil Maitland and Tim Baker can both
type too, you know. They both started Army life in the
Signals.'

'They keep rather quiet about it,' Anna grumbled.

'So what you want,' Bernie went on patiently, 'is a
couple of urgent appointments for the morning. Then you
finger Tim and Phil. I'll bet you we'll either have a temp
or a fair roster by lunch-time.'

'You're a prince, Bernie. Have some more coffee.'
She went to the phone and rang first Arthur Craven of
Celluloid Cellar, and then Dmitrios Bruce, making ap-
pointments for ten o'clock and eleven.

After a fifteen-minute interview in which Anna, ready
primed, had reported on progress so far, and, without
pause for breath or interruption, had gone on to outline
her plans for the morning, Mr Brierly called an *ad hoc*
conference. Faced with a near mutiny he submitted and
agreed to employ a temp until Beryl was fit enough to
resume her place at the centre of his web. Tim was to
stand guard over the switchboard until the temp arrived.

'Most inexpedient,' Brierly said, pale with annoyance. 'Perhaps someone will tell me where I can locate a
discreet temporary employee. We'll be advertising in
newspapers next.'

'You played a nifty one-two there,' Tim groused as
Anna passed the office on her way out. 'I'd lay odds the
old man had you lined up for this perch.'

'I took legal advice,' Anna said cheerily, starting downstairs.

'Bloody Bernie!' Tim said vengefully.

Freezing rain was driving from west to east up the High Street. She crossed to the north side of the road and caught a number 9 to Piccadilly.

The spotty boy at the counter of Celluloid Cellar had been replaced by a lank-haired girl who was reading *Watership Down*. She reluctantly showed a sliver of pale face between the dull flanges of hair that hung on either side of her nose.

'Can I help you?' she enquired, in a manner that said she hoped she wouldn't have to.

'Mr Craven's expecting me. I know the way.'

She went through behind the counter and knocked on the office door. Arthur Craven seemed very pleased to see her, as if a face he recognized was automatically a friendly one. His office was still a dismal shambles, the only difference being that there was more dust on the dust.

'How have you been getting along?' he asked, shifting a pile of papers from the spare chair. It looked like the same pile he had moved from the same chair the previous Tuesday.

'Did you go and see Reggie Lottman and Dmitrios Bruce? Very decent fellows, both of them.'

'I saw Mr Lottman,' Anna told him. 'He was very helpful. Mr Bruce has been in Nairobi, but I have an appointment with him today.'

'Good. Good. That's capital.' He rubbed his hands, as if any success Anna might have was also his by proxy. 'I hope you've been able to shed some light on poor Deirdre's past. Her parents must find that a great comfort.'

'Well, I don't know about that,' Anna said, 'but I'm doing what I can.'

'Of course you are, and it can't be easy. It's a sad reflection on the times that a girl like that can pass on and leave her parents in such ignorance. It makes me quite glad I don't have a daughter. I know I'd be worried sick all the time.'

Arthur Craven's face took on a suitably anxious expression.

'Anyway, what can I do for you today?'

'Well,' Anna said slowly, 'maybe nothing, but when Deirdre left you, she went to work for a man called Frederick Slinger.'

'Freddie Slinger?' Craven said, surprised. 'Film Services? How very odd. I wonder why no one told me.'

'You know him, then?'

'Old Freddie? I should say I do. He's a regular customer here. But I wonder why Deirdre would want to work for him. If she wanted to get on in the business, she'd have done much better to stay here or work for someone like Reggie. He could have really taught her the trade. I mean, anyone can learn to run a projector, anyone at all.'

'I know,' Anna said ruefully. 'It didn't seem much of a step forward to me, either. Anyhow, this must have been where they got to know each other.'

'I don't know about that, either,' he said doubtfully. 'In fact, I can't recall them ever meeting.'

'But if he's a regular customer, wouldn't she have served him behind the counter?'

'No, she wouldn't. The fact is that I always deal with him personally. He comes straight into this office. I wouldn't let any of those doolallies handle a customer like Freddie. I mean, he and one or two others represent eighty per cent of the business. I wish there were more like him. Anyway, he's a chap who always comes in late, about six-ish, just before I'm closing up. Every other Friday, regular as clockwork.'

'And your staff would have left by then?'

'Usually. They skive off at about five. I'm lucky if I get an eight-hour day out of them, especially just before the weekend. You'd think Friday ended at high noon. Of course, Deirdre was the conscientious type. But if she stayed late it was probably in the darkroom. No, she might have seen him once or twice, but I'm positive they didn't know each other.'

'Well, that's curious,' she said thoughtfully.

'It is,' Craven agreed, 'but then Freddie's a curious

man. A bit foxy, if you ask me. I wouldn't put it past him
to pinch my brightest worker and keep buttoned about it.'

'Why do you think he's foxy?'

'Well, I'm not knocking him,' Craven began hastily,
'because he's a good customer. The best, in fact. But most
people think he just runs a projection service, while actually he's got quite a nice little line in exporting films to
the USA. You've got to see the funny side; selling American films back to the Americans. That's what I mean,
foxy. Freddie could sell sphinxes to the Egyptians. I
wouldn't be surprised if he did, too.'

'Oh, it's all perfectly legal,' he added, seeing Anna
staring incredulously. 'All the films are in the public domain now. In the US, that is.'

'What do you mean, "in the public domain?" ' Anna
asked, wondering if her whole case was going up in smoke.

'Well, in the US films are registered with the Library
of Congress, which protects the copyright for twenty-eight
years. If they aren't then registered, anyone can use them
for whatever they want. Only in the States, though. In
most other countries you have to wait fifty years. Anyway,
Freddie has a lovely little list of films that haven't been
reregistered, including a couple of old Charlie Chaplins
that the collectors go a bundle on.'

'Twenty-eight years,' Anna said, curiously relieved.
'So what does he buy from you?'

'Oh, colour printing stock to copy these films on to.
I give him a special rate for quantity, and, of course, with
VAT exemption for export it couldn't be cheaper.'

'He must be doing rather well,' Anna said.

'I should say!' Craven smiled in satisfaction. 'I mean
sixteen thousand feet every fourteen days or so means he's
selling his films at the rate of about three or four a week.
No flies on our Freddie.'

Anna couldn't argue with that. Instead she said, 'But
surely Charlie Chaplin films are in black and white. What's
the colour stock for?'

'You can still print black and white on colour stock,'
Craven told her. 'It isn't as sharp, but it's cheaper than
buying a little of this and a little of that. He's probably

selling mainly colour films. Anyway, I get a special rate from the makers, Fuji, just for him.'

'Why only him?' Anna asked. 'Isn't that what you normally sell?'

'Dear me, no,' Craven sighed. 'I can see you don't know too much about this business. The bulk of my trade is in camera negative stock. Sorry, that is the stuff you put in a camera. The laboratories who print the film you see on the screen always supply the print stock themselves. But Freddie doesn't use a lab. He's a do-it-yourself merchant. Anyway, I don't know why I'm boring you with all the technical details. It won't help you much with Deirdre.'

'Maybe she got interested in him because of the invoices,' Anna suggested. 'You said she sorted your office out for you.'

'I doubt it. Like I said, I deal with him personally. The sales records aren't kept in the same place as the counter invoices either, so Deirdre wouldn't have seen them.'

Craven tapped the desk drawer in front of him. 'There's a special book for Fuji in here, but she wouldn't have been interested.'

Privately, Anna disagreed, but she said, 'So it'll have to remain a mystery, then.'

'It's certainly very peculiar.' Craven scratched his head, disturbing a dormant layer of dandruff. 'But if I have any ideas about it, I'll let you know. When are you seeing Dmitrios?'

'At eleven,' Anna said, looking at her watch. It was twenty to. 'I ought to be going. I've probably disturbed you enough as it is.'

'Not at all, it's been a pleasure,' Craven got up and held out his hand. 'Drop in any time. And give my best to old Dmitrios. I'm sure you'll get along with him.'

CHAPTER 25

* * * * * * * * * *

ANNA caught a Bakerloo line train and got out at Baker Street with only a minute or so to spare.

Dmitrios Bruce had his studio on the second floor of a building in Chiltern Street. The front office was decorated with hanging ferns and leather and steel Bauhaus chairs. It was painted a dusty pink. A receptionist, who had eyes made up to look like shiners, and hair artfully arranged like a kinky thatched roof, asked Anna to wait. Mr Bruce was in conference. Anna sat down and found a position where the dangling flora didn't either tickle her nose or knock her hat over her eyes.

Sitting opposite was a row of four girls who looked like models. Each had a portfolio case, and they were all groomed into a nonchalant, grubby perfection. All four of them affected an expression of scowling poutishness. Anna concluded that it was no longer fashionable to be caught smiling. They sat silent and very still, with eyes vacant as empty parking spaces.

Anna was afflicted by a bout of sudden boredom. The

view through the glass doors behind the receptionist's desk showed that active life was still going on somewhere in the studio, but in the outer office the atmosphere was one of completely suspended animation. She yawned and leaned back. Her hat automatically tilted forward over her eyes, so she shut them, folded her arms and crossed her ankles like a dozing cowboy. People came and went. She heard them. Nothing disturbed the immobility of the reception room for half an hour. Then a buzzer sounded on the receptionist's desk.

'You can go through now, Miss Lee,' the receptionist said. 'It's the second door on the right.'

Dmitrios Bruce was a tall man with crinkly hair greying self-consciously over the ears. His was the kind of face that might have sold pipe tobacco if it hadn't been spoiled by a soft, dissipated mouth and a yellow tinge to the whites of his eyes. Ten years ago he had probably been a very striking man. But his face looked as if it had rotted when it should have matured. His office was oak-panelled throughout, and examples of his own photographs hung everywhere. The style of the pictures seemed to indicate that he had emerged as one of the photographic *wunderkinder* of the middle Sixties. His work looked extremely competent, but, looking around, Anna decided that innovation was not his forte. He seemed to be sensitive to every nuance of style, but the styles were always someone else's.

'Well, hello,' he said, employing the warm, tough handclasp that lasted three seconds too long, and the interested steady gaze which failed to convince Anna that he saw anything at all.

Anna sat in a green leather armchair, facing Dmitrios over a massive reproduction desk.

He touched a switch on the intercom at his elbow and said, 'Christy, darling? Where's the fucking coffee?'

Anna said, 'I've been talking to Arthur Craven, and he suggested that I come and see you.'

'How is poor old Arty? I haven't seen him for years.'

'He's okay,' Anna said. 'He sends his best.'

'Better than his worst, eh? Ha Ha. I shouldn't laugh,

but he's become an old woman since his wife died. You know, that shop of his was such a good idea, a real little money-spinner, but lately he's lost all his drive. It's rather depressing.'

'I really don't know him that well,' Anna said unresponsively, 'but he thought you could tell me something about Deirdre Jackson.'

'Well, well, little Dee Jackson,' he interrupted before she could go on. 'You really are a voice from the past, aren't you?'

'Yes. But Dee was killed in an accident in December and . . .'

'Killed? Good Heavens. How very tragic.' He tried to be broken-hearted, but only succeeded in looking petulant.

'Yes, and her parents have asked me to look up everyone I can find who knew her to try and get some idea of what her life was like.'

'I see. Well, what can I say, except she was one of the most efficient assistants I ever had? She fitted in very well here and made lots of friends. I was sorry to let her go.'

Anna stared at him in silence.

'You know, you really do have tiger's eyes. You make me feel quite nervous, looking at me like that.' He seemed to be the kind of man who became uncomfortable if someone did not warm to him instantly. Anna continued to watch him coldly.

'Er, well, she was taking a course in Technical Photography at Paddington. A mate of mine who teaches there thought she'd make an ideal assistant. She impressed me as being bright and hard-working, so I gave her a job. You can tell her parents she was a competent, intelligent kid. She would have done very well if she hadn't left.'

Anna said, 'Perhaps I should have added that I've also been talking to Vida Bratny.'

'Ah.' Dmitrios ran a finger round the neck of his white sweater. 'Perhaps you should have!'

He hit the switch on the intercom again and snapped,

'Sweetheart, would you kindly get off your backside and bring the coffee. Two cups.'

They waited. But Anna waited more effectively. Dmitrios seemed to find something condemning in the silence.

'How is Vida these days? I really should look her up. She's a lovely kid, but she does rather foam at the mouth.'

A blonde girl who walked as if she was on stilts came in without knocking and deposited two cups unceremoniously on the desk.

Some of the coffee had remained in the cups, but not much. Dmitrios made quite a production of pouring what was in the saucers back into them and mopping the desktop with a paper handkerchief. Anna didn't touch her cup. Dmitrios was a blatherer when nervous, she thought. He dropped two sweeteners into his drink, and pulled at the flesh under his jaw as if he could finger away the incipient double-chin. The silence defeated him again.

'Look,' he said, 'it wasn't that serious. Never mind what Vida says. She wasn't that important. I'm a family man. I don't go around making irresponsible promises. I can't help what Dee thought.'

'What about the ring?' Anna said, gently speculative.

'Oh, that damned thing. I'd almost forgotten it.'

She said nothing.

'Look, Deirdre was just a country mouse when she came here. I hardly noticed her at first. But then she sort of threw herself at me. What could I do? I was kind of sorry for the poor kid. So I took her out once or twice. Where's the harm?'

Anna didn't answer him.

'Listen, she was like a little lost dog that adores you for a kind word and a pat, and I must admit I got quite fond of her after a time. It does something for a man, being looked at like that. How was I to know that bloody ring would become a totem? I couldn't believe they were still making them that parochial down on the farm. I blame Vida, you know. It was Vida that smartened Dee up and gave her a veneer of sophistication. It's a dangerous thing when underneath it all you leave the clodbuster mentally intact.'

She watched him contemptuously while he fiddled uncomfortably with his teaspoon and tried to smile charmingly.

'I suppose you think I'm a bit of a sod, seducing a poor young girl like that. But it wasn't that way at all. It never is. After all, if your Liberation movement has taught us anything, it's that women are just as capable of initiating affairs as men.'

'Oh, is that what the women's movement was all about?' Anna said softly. 'I didn't know.'

'Oh, come on,' he said. 'You're quite a beautiful girl yourself. You know what I'm talking about. You've been around.'

He tried to make her answer his smile.

When she did not respond, he said, 'Look, it's not as if she didn't get her own back. Because she did. In spades. Quite a little chiseller she turned out to be in the end.

'She swiped my private address book and some pictures I'd taken, and threatened to show my wife all the gory details. How do you square that with innocence betrayed? I had to give her money—goddamn it—and a first-class cruise ticket to get them all back. Is that what you're going to tell her parents about their poor hard-done-by little daughter? Because, if you're going to tell them anything, you might as well get the full story.'

'I don't suppose I'll tell them that,' Anna said, getting up.

'Then why have you been wasting my time, asking me all these questions?' Dmitrios said angrily.

'Think back,' Anna said, walking to the door. 'I hardly asked you a damned thing.'

'Well, you've got no right to judge anyone, no right at all,' he almost stammered in annoyance.

'I'm not making a judgement,' she said, opening the door, 'unless it's that you're so wet that the colours run.'

She went out and closed the door quietly behind her. Anna stopped at the Farm Bar on her way back to Baker Street station. Her head was throbbing, her throat ached, and she was shivering again. Adrenaline was a fine thing for keeping cold symptoms at bay, but it didn't last. It was early for lunch, but that meant that she could eat without having her elbow jogged. She chose a thick egg mayonnaise sandwich and a glass of apple juice, and took them to a seat by the window.

While she ate, she considered what to do next. It seemed that she had come to the difficult bit. There were no new people to see; or rather, those she wanted to see, Brough and Eady, had been put off limits. She would not be able to go on using the guise she had been keeping for Slinger, because any time now he could walk into Celluloid Cellar and Arthur Craven would innocently topple her story. She could not tackle him directly because he would warn the men at the lab. That left Len Margolin. If she wanted to unsettle Margolin enough to be useful, she should do it now. On the other hand, if he tipped Slinger off too quickly, Slinger would simply shut up shop and not be seen within a mile of any incriminating evidence. It would happen anyway when Slinger talked to Craven, but that would not be until Friday. Whereas Margolin would spill immediately. She knew he hadn't done that on Friday night, because if he had Slinger would have tumbled to her on Saturday morning. That could mean two things. Either Margolin did not know of Deirdre's connection with Slinger, or he did not know what happened to his films once he passed them on, and therefore did not consider Anna's questions any more important than a possible source of domestic embarrassment. The last seemed most likely. Slinger would never give himself away to any more people than was absolutely necessary.

In one way, now that Slinger and his gang of two had emerged as a possible collar, she should be free to pursue Deirdre's ghost wherever it led. But it led directly to Slinger, Brough and Eady. She cursed Brierly's sycophantic attitude to the police. They would watch and wait and finally make a pinch for film piracy. Meanwhile, Deirdre's death would get lost in the demolition.

She was aware that her thinking was despondent because she was not feeling well. That worried her, too. She had reached an age when she could not stay up all night and then attack the next day confidently. It was an age when fatigue and illness counted. Not a lot, but just enough to be significant. These days she did not shrug a cold off in a day; it hung around and nagged for three or four. And these days, too, she had to work at being fit and supple. They were no longer gifts she could take for granted. Like an athlete sensitive to any change in performance, she knew that she was physically past her natural peak and that her condition now had to be maintained by careful endeavour.

Bernie was right. It was a time for regular meals and sleep. The thought was depressing.

She left the restaurant and walked north to Marylebone Road. As she went, the winter sun suddenly wrenched free of its cloud bindings and shone bravely for a few minutes. The green dome of the Planetarium roof briefly looked airy and weightless. Anna's spirits rose, too. It wasn't the virus or age—what she needed was a little sunshine.

In the station she found a free phone-box and dialled Len Margolin's home number. The phone rang for a long time. Just as she was about to give up, someone at the other end lifted the receiver. When the pips stopped, she heard a childish voice say, 'Hello, Hello. There's no one here.'

What had they called the little girl? She said. 'Hello, is that Mandy?'

'Yes,' the uncertain little voice replied. 'Who are you?'

'Anna. Is your mother there?'

'My mummy isn't feeling very well. She's lying in her bed.'

'Oh, what a pity,' Anna said, feeling secretly relieved.

'No, it's all right.' Mandy was growing more confident. 'She lies in her bed a lot. I haven't got anything to do.'

'Then it's a good thing I phoned. You can talk to me. Is your father in?'

'No, my daddy goes away every day after his breakfast.'

'Where does he go?'

'To his school. I go to my school, too. But I come back for my lunch.'

'Do you know what your daddy's school is called?'

'It's called Saint Angus's. Do you want to know something?'

'Yes.'

'My school is called Seven Sisters Nursery School.'

'That's a long name.'

'Yes. What's your school called?'

'I don't go to school any more.'

'Never mind,' Mandy said comfortingly. 'I've got to go now. My mummy is calling.'

There was no school called Saint Angus in the telephone book. There was a Saint Agnes, however. Anna rang the number. A secretary told her that Mr Margolin was taking fourth form prep that afternoon and wouldn't be free until four-thirty. Anna said she would get in touch later.

She caught the Circle Line back to Kensington High Street, wondering why children insisted so on the possessive: my mummy, her bed, his breakfast. They seemed to derive some obscure satisfaction from it, and she couldn't remember what it was.

CHAPTER 26

• • • • • • • • • •

BY four-thirty she was in Saint Agnes's car park, waiting patiently beside Len's Austin Maxi.

The school lurked behind a high blank wall that backed on to Lisson Grove. It was a Victorian red-brick affair with an extraordinary exoskeletal structure of black fire-escapes propping it up like scaffolding. The playground was five tarmacadamed netball courts with faint markings for summer tennis. Not a joyous place, Anna thought, fighting down the feelings of repression and inferiority that such schools invariably brought her.

It was nearly dark when she saw Len coming down the front steps, hands in his pockets, shoulders hunched in his pale Burberry coat. He wore a brown knitted hat with a pompom on it, which made him look more ineffectual than ever.

'What on earth are you doing here?' he said, looking round quickly. 'Are you mad? If one of my colleagues saw us and told Sarah, there'd be hell to pay.'

'I wanted to talk to you.'

'Well, get in the car and we'll go somewhere quiet.'

He unlocked the car hurriedly and then got in. 'If you wanted to see me, why didn't you come to that address I gave you over the weekend?'

'Perhaps that was a little too quiet,' Anna said.

'I don't know what you mean.' Margolin was flushed with irritation. 'I thought we had an understanding.'

Anna didn't reply, so he said: 'Well, where do you want to go?'

'Paddington station.'

'What on earth for? Look, I haven't got time to mess around. I've got to be home by half past five.'

But he turned the car towards the station and a few minutes later parked outside it.

'What's all this about?' He had composed himself better by then.

Anna felt it was time to take the stopper out, so she said: 'Did Deirdre Jackson have the bite on you?'

He jerked his head up as if someone had hit him. 'What are you talking about? Blackmail? Why would she blackmail me?'

'You know why. And how. If you had an affair with her, or even if you didn't but only showed you wanted to, it'd be enough with a wife like yours. You're very vulnerable, you know.'

'Don't be absurd,' he said pompously. 'I would never give anyone any cause to blackmail me.'

'No?' Anna said mildly, 'What about the films you slip Freddie Slinger after all your film society shows?'

'Good God, how do you know about that?' He turned to face her. He was pale now, and angry, but he didn't look particularly worried. 'Look, who are you? And what are you trying to do to me?'

'You know who I am. And I'm doing what I said I was doing when we first met. What I didn't tell you was that I work for a firm of private enquiry agents.'

'Did my wife employ you?' He was worried now.

'Don't be absurd,' Anna said in her turn. 'Deirdre's parents did.'

'Then you won't tell my wife?' He was pitifully rattled.

'Tell her what? I'm in the asking business.'

'Well, all right, then.' He relaxed slightly. 'But, as you said, with a wife like Sarah I'm always vulnerable.'

'I don't know why you're so worried about Sarah. If I were you, I'd be worried about the law.'

'What do you mean, the law? She was over sixteen, wasn't she?'

'What? No, you still don't get it, do you? It's the films that could get you into trouble, not Deirdre.'

'The films? How? Freddie takes them back the next morning.'

'But in the meantime he copies them and sells the copies abroad. You didn't think he was just another film buff, did you.'

'Fred does that? You must be joking!' Margolin bit something back. Anna thought he might have been about to call Slinger a sneak. There was something of the schoolboy surviving in the teacher.

'It's true,' she said. 'Freddie Slinger is running a bootleg film caper. And you are part of it.'

'Look, you've got to believe me, I knew nothing whatsoever about this.'

'All the same,' she studiously ignored the pleading expression on his face, 'you handed him the material and you accepted back-handers from him.'

'No! That's a rotten way of putting it. Fred is—was—a friend.'

'Well, how would you put it, then?'

'We had a mutually beneficial arrangement. That's all.'

'What sort of an arrangement?'

'I can hardly go into the details now.' He was terribly unsettled.

'You don't have to now,' Anna said soothingly.

'You mean, I will later?' Panic rearing up again.

'Well, I expect there will be some interest in how a family man can keep a secret *pied-à-terre* on a teacher's pay.'

'It's Fred's flat! I mean, I hold the lease but he pays for it. Look, this is going to ruin me. It isn't fair!' The last protest of a weak man. Anna thought. 'Why don't you tell me about it,' she said gently. 'It may not be as bad as it looks.'

The penny had dropped. Accustomed to thinking of himself as one of the few responsible members of society, Margolin was shocked and humiliated to find himself in a position where he would be considered by society to be no better than a delinquent. He told her all about it.

He had first met Slinger five years ago. The Art and English Department had jointly put on a series of Arts Council films for an A-level course. Slinger had provided the films. At the time Margolin was keen to set up a film society at the school for the sixth-formers, but he was stumped for money. He was desperately in need of an activity separate from both school and home. Mandy had just been born, and Sarah, suffering badly from post-natal depression, was suffocating him. He asked Slinger's advice.

Slinger loved films himself, he told Margolin. But he rarely got the time to go to the cinema. He would help Margolin organize his society. All he wanted in return was to have some say in what films were shown and the chance to see them afterwards. Of course, Slinger's taste in films tended towards the modern and gaudy. But that was natural, wasn't it? Slinger wasn't a refined intellectual like Margolin. So the Seven Sisters Film Society was organized.

It was never a great success, but Margolin enjoyed it. He liked meeting the people who came and having coffee with them afterwards. He liked being president. He felt he had lost contact with the world because of his marriage; Sarah had always been a little jealous and difficult; he had lost friendships and hadn't been able to remake them. So he liked being at the centre of a little social group again.

Sarah, meanwhile, was becoming more and more of a problem. Pregnancy had disturbed her. She thought she had become obscenely fat and ugly. Mandy's birth tipped her over the edge, and soon she stopped eating altogether. She became seriously ill, and Margolin could not cope. So Sarah went to hospital and a friend took care of Mandy.

When she was released, supposedly cured, the film society was well under way. At first she fought it tooth and nail. She could not bear any activity of his that did not directly concern her.

Then, without warning, she had changed her tactics. She came to the shows and started to organize the membership. That nearly finished Margolin off. She was wrecking his social group from the inside. She was by turns aloof and hysterically confiding. She sabotaged his conversations and made fun of him in front of his new acquaintances.

He decided to give it all up, leave Sarah and find another job; just disappear and start again. But he was not a man of action. Cutbacks in education had decimated positions in the teaching profession. It would be hard for him to find another job. Everything he owned was mortgaged.

Again he turned to Slinger for advice, and Slinger advised Margolin not to leave Sarah.

'You'll end up a pauper if you do,' Margolin remembered him saying. 'A woman like that will take the shoes from your feet and have your socks for afters. No, old son. You hang on to what you've got. Believe me—I know!'

Margolin did believe him. Sarah could be wickedly vindictive.

'I've been doing a bit of thinking along those lines myself,' Slinger had said ambiguously, 'and I think I know of something that will fill the bill for both of us. Same deal, mind. You scratch my back and I'll scratch yours. Just you keep *cave* for a while, and I'll come up with something.'

He had come up with a flat between Praed Street and Sussex Gardens.

'Think of yourself as a holding company,' Slinger had said when Margolin protested about the lease. 'I just happen to have a spot of the old how's y' father going spare. And I don't want anyone to know about it, see? What better than a bit of property to draw in the slack? But for reasons I expect you can guess, I don't want to have my name associated with this place.'

Margolin thought he could guess. Margolin used the flat mainly at weekends. Slinger had a room, which he kept locked, and their visits never coincided. Margolin felt he was a free man again.

'This locked room,' Anna interrupted. 'Have you ever looked inside it?'

'Of course not,' Margolin said huffily, 'what do you take me for?' Then he blushed.

'Perhaps you should have,' Anna continued, 'for your own safety.'

'You mean he might have stolen property there?' he asked, scared again. 'Of course! I own the lease. Jesus Christ, we must go round there at once!'

'Take it easy,' Anna said. 'There's no need to panic about it yet. Tell me about Deirdre. Did she ever go to the flat?'

Margolin said that Simon had brought her to a party especially to meet him. He had introduced her to Slinger himself.

'Was that the first time they met?' Anna asked, 'or did you get any impression that they knew each other from somewhere before?'

'I don't think so,' he said. 'I really didn't notice. I noticed her, of course. It's odd, really, she wasn't beautiful, you know. But she was very impressive. She was talking about how she had gone to Portugal on a photographic assignment and had stayed on because she loved the country so. And how she had met an old man, a travelling projectionist, and they had gone round from village to village showing old movies. And how when he fell ill, she had gone on her own to keep the business going for him till he got better. It was right up Fred's street, of course. They got on like a house on fire. I didn't talk to her much that night, because she and Fred went into a huddle.'

Anna was struck by an almost resentful expression on his face. The line of his mouth drooped as if he was tasting something bad. She realized suddenly that Margolin was jealous of Slinger, and probably had been ever since he had first asked for his help.

'But I remember thinking how confident she was,'

Margolin said. 'I mean, she was so young, but she had the courage to get up and go abroad and live there. She seemed to have the sun in her eyes and the wind in her hair. And I was thinking of my life, doing everything by bells in the classroom and being questioned at home by Sarah. Every moment and every penny accounted for. What a contrast.'

He paused for a moment. Anna was thinking of Deirdre, trapped in a darkroom on the second floor of a studio in Chiltern Street, waiting by the phone in Fulham, sorting out the accounts for an incompetent employer in Soho. She had done a good job that night. Her time in drama classes had not been entirely wasted.

After a while, Margolin said: 'I suppose I should have known she was trouble, the way she left poor old Simon floundering at the party.'

He stopped again. Anna waited for him in silence. The car was an island. Outside, traffic moved sluggishly. Taxis pulled up, debouching hurrying passengers into the station.

'I expect that's why she liked having Simon around,' he continued. 'He was loyal, patient, and uncritical. He was never a challenge to her, and she towed him around like a trophy. I suppose he was constant proof that she was superior. I was stupid really.' He stirred uncomfortably on the car seat.

'I shouldn't have gone anywhere near her. But you know, having that flat had gone to my head. I had taken girls there before, I admit that. But no one like her. She was very provoking, well brought up, accustomed to the good things of life. Sometimes you were sure she was interested, and at other times she acted as if she'd never met you before. I never knew where I was with her. When I got to know her better, I realized that she was very un-educated. Not dumb, of course, she was very smart; what I mean is, she was uncultured. I thought I could open her eyes to a thing or two, like poetry or literature.'

He just wanted an excuse, Anna thought sadly. She said: 'Did she go to the flat?'

'Twice with me. Then, she wouldn't come any more.

But she wanted the key. I suspected she wanted to take someone else there. It was very humiliating.'

'Did you give it to her?'

'I had to in the end. I told her the place really belonged to Fred, but she didn't care. She came round to the school a couple of times in broad daylight. I was afraid she'd go to Sarah, you see.'

'Did you tell Fred any of this?'

'Well, you see, there was always a chance that Dee had something going with Fred, too.'

'So you didn't tell him?'

He squirmed in his seat again.

'No, I didn't. I didn't want him thinking that I would pinch one of his girls after all he'd done for me. And God knows I felt enough of a fool as it was. When I heard she was dead, heaven help me, all I felt was relief. I was off the hook, you see.'

'Who told you?'

'Fred did. She was working for him, you know.'

'And how did Fred find out?'

'Well, the police must have told him, of course.'

They were silent for a few minutes. Margolin took off his glasses and wiped the lenses, staring blindly ahead of him. Then he said: 'What am I going to do? What on earth am I going to do?'

He looked exposed and ashamed without his glasses. Anna turned away. He was utterly dependent now.

'Come with me,' Anna said opening the car door. 'I'm going to phone my boss. I think you should go and talk to him. If he hears your story, and you're willing to co-operate, he may help you make a deal with the police. He may even know a good solicitor. Meanwhile, you should phone Sarah and tell her you won't be home for a while, or you'll be in worse lumber.'

'Oh, my God, Sarah!' Margolin said despairingly. But he got out of the car and followed her into the station.

They made their calls in phone booths without doors, competing with the jumbled cacophony of station noises and PA announcements.

'Listen,' Anna said as they walked past platform 1

on the way out to the car. 'Mr Brierly has a detective-superintendent with him now. It's connected to Slinger's business. And they are both very keen to see you. I don't know if you feel ready to talk to the police yet.'

'I think I should,' Margolin said, very anxious to become respectable again. 'After all, I had no idea what Fred was doing until you told me.'

'Well, I should warn you that ignorance is no defence,' Anna told him.

'But if I go of my own free will and tell them everything, surely that will count in my favour?'

'All the same,' she said dubiously. 'It would be safer to talk to a solicitor first, and perhaps take one along with you.'

'But that looks like an admission of guilt,' he protested.

'No, it doesn't,' she tried to persuade him, 'you're entitled to some advice and protection. You need it.'

'No,' he said stubbornly. 'It wouldn't look good if I saw a solicitor first. After all, I've only just learned the facts, and all I'm doing is coming forward as any good citizen should.'

'Okay,' Anna said. 'It's up to you. But a lawyer could save you a lot of grief.'

'I know what I'm doing.' Margolin unlocked the car. 'I say, would you mind driving? I don't know the way, and besides, I'm feeling a bit shaky.'

CHAPTER 27

* * * * * * * * * *

ANNA walked quickly north up Abbotsbury Road, cosily lit houses to the left, silent, cold park to the right. Hard snow was still packed in the gutter and close to the wall, but the pavement was clear.

She felt slightly guilty about Len Margolin. He had gone into Brierly's office so eagerly, like a penitent to a priest, as if unaware that the two men waiting for him were not in the absolution trade. Anna had introduced him to Brierly. Brierly had introduced him to Detective-Superintendent Woking. No one introduced Anna. She stood to one side, like the plain bridesmaid in a photograph. Margolin shook hands enthusiastically, pathetically pleased to show himself a professional man among professional men: a man whose innocence had been taken advantage of, but who was ready to be understood.

Brierly and Woking understood him to be a fool. That she was sure of. She had only stayed long enough to help him with his story, but they had listened to that sympathetically enough. Now that he had nothing to hide, Margolin was disarmingly frank, almost boyish. Also, he had the happy knack of seeming to defer constantly, as if they were the dominant males and he knew his place a little further down the pecking order. It was a stance that invited bullying, but Margolin knew the hierarchy. For, where Brierly and Woking bullied, they were also tempted to protect afterwards. She thought he would fare well enough.

She sneezed and walked briskly on, blowing her nose and shaking her head. Blocked sinuses were beginning to affect her hearing.

She left the stillness of Abbotsbury Road for Holland Park Avenue. She crossed it and went on into the no-man's-land that is neither Shepherds Bush nor Notting Hill Gate, hurrying towards a hot bath and a cup of tea—it was seven o'clock, and her ambitions did not yet reach any further than that.

She let herself in through the front door and turned on the light. The Prices were watching television. The flat rumble of horses' hooves and sporadic gunfire invaded the quiet of the hallway. Selwyn loved a good Western, but then, he also loved a bad one. Wearily, she climbed the stairs. Halfway up, unaccountably, the light went out. She went on up. There was a spare bulb somewhere in the kitchen; just one more thing to do before giving up on Monday.

She had reached the landing before she noticed the extra-cold draught from the skylight. As she put out her hand to feel for the lock of the flat's door she felt it move slightly under her hand. Stepping back, she unconsciously clenched her key-ring in her left hand so that the keys stood out stiffly between her fingers. Whoever was behind the door had turned off the hall light. She was just reaching out to turn it on again when the door flew open, and a man erupted; she just had time to brace her back against the newel at the top of the stairs. She bent her left knee up, and took the impact of him on her left foot. Hot, beery breath bruised her cheek, and then she kicked out as hard as she could. Breath exploded audibly, and she could dimly see a large figure hunched over, only about four feet away.

Anna had only twice before been in a fight, and on

both occasions had suffered more injury than she had inflicted. The sensible course of action was therefore to run like hell—but she had not hurt her assailant badly enough to provide sufficient time to get away. She had only taken two steps down the stairs when she was caught by the right arm, just under the shoulder, and wrenched back onto the landing. As she was forced round towards him she submitted to the pull, and at the same time swung her left fist to meet the side of his head. It smashed, keys and all, into his right ear. The grip on her arm relaxed momentarily, but did not release. Trying to capitalize on a very small advantage, she swung again and trod sideways on to his instep with as much force as she could muster. This time he protected his head with his arm and shoulder. In theory she should have been able to hurt his feet quite considerably, but in fact his shoes were more substantial than hers, and besides, she was not heavy enough. He responded by lifting her off the ground and throwing her against the wall. He was big, but not very fast. She should have had time to roll and avoid the subsequent kick, but the seven-foot landing did not provide enough space. Although she moved enough for the first one to land no more dangerously than on the thigh, the second caught her hard in the ribs. She tried to protect her guts and tried to shield her head, but a man with big feet can do a lot of damage in a short time. He was saying something now, repeating it over and over again. It sounded like: 'Mind your own fucking business.'

Then the light went on, and the kicking stopped suddenly. Bea screamed something and Selwyn shouted: 'What's going on up there?' She heard the stranger run down the stairs. The whole house shook as he fled down and Selwyn rushed up. They met in the middle. Selwyn did the wise thing and flattened himself against the wall in order to allow the charge to proceed. He also stuck out a foot, inadequately clad in an ancient bedroom slipper. The intruder obligingly fell head-first down the remainder of the stairs.

'Phone the police!' Selwyn yelled.

'Phone them yourself,' Bea replied, running up the stairs. 'Anna's hurt.'

'I can't,' Selwyn howled, 'I'm sitting on this bastard's head.'

'Oh, Jesus,' Bea said, 'Anna, are you all right? Anna!' Anna gingerly tried to unfold herself. 'It's okay,' she muttered. Everything felt wrong or missing.

'Oh God,' Bea said, 'Well, don't move. You just sit there a minute.' She scampered down the stairs.

'Damn it, woman!' Selwyn roared. 'Phone the bloody coppers, will you? I can't sit here all night.'

'Well, don't then,' Bea retorted. 'Can't you see he's knocked out cold? And what's more, I think he's broken his leg. It looks awfully funny to me.'

Selwyn came to the top of the stairs and knelt down by Anna. He tried to straighten her out. 'Can't you move, old dear?' She struggled up into a sitting position.

'Oh dear, oh dear,' Selwyn said, and then shouted: 'Bea, phone the ambulance, too.'

Anna tried to say: 'Don't be silly,' but it came out as: 'Von't be filly.'

'Oh, Anna!' wailed Bea, coming up again. 'What's happened to your teeth?'

Anna didn't know. There seemed to be a gap a mile wide somewhere, but that was a minor problem compared with the pain in her ribs and arms.

'I'll call the ambulance,' Bea said, hurrying away again. 'The police are coming. Selwyn, you should do something with a wet flannel, I think. Should I put the kettle on?'

Selwyn got a towel from Anna's bedroom, but since she was crouched, immovable, in a foetal ball, he could only apply it to the back of her neck.

'Selwyn!' Bea called from the bottom of the stairs. 'The ambulances are on strike or something.' She was almost in tears. 'What are we going to do?'

'Wait for the police and then get a taxi!'

'Selwyn,' Anna said, her voice all muffled. She found it just bearable if she sat very still with her knees drawn up and her head buried between them.

'Sh!' Selwyn said. 'Don't try to talk yet.'

'Police—' Anna whispered.

'They're coming, old dear. Don't worry.'

'Who is he?'

'Never mind who he is now,' Selwyn said, 'You stay quiet.'

'Find out who he is. 'S important.'

'For God's sake—' But he went down, and Anna could dimly hear a commotion from below. Her ears were ringing and everything was muddled.

'The sod woke up,' Selwyn panted when he came up again. 'But don't worry, I've tied him to the banisters with a pair of tights. His name is Raymond Brough. I've got his driving licence.'

'Ah!' Anna tried to concentrate. 'Must talk to the police.'

'Don't be silly, Anna.' Bea had appeared from somewhere. 'I've got a taxi. We're taking you to hospital.'

'No. Tell them he killed Dee.'

'Did he, by Christ?' Selwyn asked, much struck.

'Don't know,' Anna mumbled, 'but tell them anyway.'

'Anna, this isn't the time.' Bea was trying to soothe. 'It'll be all right, but now we've got to get you to a doctor.'

'No. Must phone Brierly.'

'Don't be an ass, Anna,' Selwyn said, 'come on, we're going to try to get you downstairs.'

But the police arrived and Bea went down to let them in. There was a confab for a few minutes, which Selwyn couldn't resist joining.

'I'll bleeding sue him,' she heard Brough's voice raised for the first time. 'He broke my fucking leg.'

A sergeant came upstairs and looked around, taking note of the open skylight and the forced door to Anna's flat.

'Can you talk yet, Miss?' he asked, going down on one knee.

'No she bloody well can't,' Selwyn said from behind him. 'Can't you see she's in no condition?'

'What happened, Miss?' The sergeant pretended Selwyn did not exist. 'Broke in, did he? And you disturbed him?'

'Yes,' Anna tried to speak clearly, 'but he killed Dee Jackson.'

'What did she say?' the sergeant asked Selwyn.

'She said what's 'is name down there killed a girl called Deirdre Jackson. She's a private investigator.'

'Is she, now?' The sergeant stared at Anna. 'Who does she work for, do you know?'

'Brierly Security. She wants someone to phone them.'

'I've heard of them. Well, maybe I will phone in a minute.'

'Now,' Anna mumbled, 'while Superintendent Woking's there.'

'He's in Woking, you say?' The sergeant sounded puzzled.

'No,' Anna said desperately. 'Selwyn?'

'What is it, old thing?' Selwyn sat down beside her.

'Brierly's got Superintendent Woking with him now. It's all connected.'

'Brierly's at the Kensington High Street Office.' Selwyn used his imagination. 'There's a Superintendent Woking with him. They're all working on the same case.'

'Ah. Has she got a phone in that flat?'

'He's phoning,' Selwyn told Anna.

'Can we take her to hospital now?' he asked when the sergeant came back.

'Just a minute, if you don't mind, sir. Her boss wants a word with her. Can you talk to your boss, love? Oh blimey, well, never mind.' The sergeant caught a glimpse of Anna's face for the first time. 'Can't you wipe some of that blood off?' he asked Selwyn. He went back to Anna's flat. Selwyn made a few tentative passes with the damp towel.

The sergeant returned. 'Well, well, things are hotting up,' he said. 'Has anyone been in her flat, except the uninvited guest, I mean? Only it's been turned over something chronic.'

'Oh, no!' Bea cried, joining them. 'Now, that's really cruel.'

'Bloody women,' muttered Selwyn. 'What is it, then?' He bent over Anna, who was trying to say something.

'What's she saying now?' asked the sergeant, who had by now recognized Selwyn as the official interpreter.

'She said something like "Book him for attempted, then we might get somewhere on Deirdre." '

'Did she, now?' said the sergeant. 'Well, I think you might get her seen to now. Why don't you go round the other side, Mr Price, and we'll see if we can't get her downstairs. Ups-a-daisy!'

Anna unhelpfully passed out.

She woke up in the middle of the night. A stretcher, she thought, how silly. They make you feel even worse when they won't let you walk. But she wasn't on a stretcher any more. She was in bed. But where? She tried to sit up and found she couldn't move. The painkillers had numbed her mind as well as her body. Suddenly she felt frightened and confused. She called out.

'What is it, dear?' A swishing noise, a round black face and a strong smell of peppermint materialized at the side of the bed.

'There's a hole in my mouth.' She hadn't meant to say that.

'Want a drink of water, dear? Here, take two of these.'

A glass of water touched her lips. It was lovely and cold.

'They've tied me up.' Hadn't they?

'Sleep now, dear. You'll feel better in the morning.'

Someone patted her shoulder. She went back to sleep.

CHAPTER 28

· · · · · · · · · · ·

SHE slept through the morning and most of the afternoon. Selwyn came at six with a tiny bunch of freesias hidden shamefully in his donkey-jacket. 'Bea's hopping mad,' he said. 'They wouldn't let her tidy up your flat till now. She sent you this.'

His coat also concealed a plastic bowl. He brought it out, looking surreptitiously round like a dope dealer. When he took the lid off, she found it contained homemade yogurt and honey. He searched his pockets and discovered a plastic spoon.

'She said you'd probably like it better than hospital food, but I can always lob it if you don't want it.'

'No, it's lovely,' Anna said, eating cautiously. 'She's a darling. Tell her not to bother with the flat.'

She picked at speech as if it was distasteful food. She had found that she could talk with stiff lips without disturbing the stitches. But the broken and missing teeth made her lisp distressingly.

'Can't stop her, can I?' Selwyn said grudgingly. 'I've only got cold pork for my supper. She took the day off, too. Actually, it's been quite exciting,' he went on more enthusiastically. 'There've been plain-clothes men round all day. Upstairs, downstairs and in my lady's chamber. And Chaterjee came, too. He's promised to fix the sky-light at last. About time too. That's how that bastard came in, you know. Round the back through the derelict at number seventy-six, up the fire escape, and Bob's your uncle.'

'What about Brough?'

'They wouldn't tell us a thing.' He was offended. 'It's not as if Bea doesn't pay her taxes. And after all, it was me that caught him. You'd think they'd show a little more gratitude. Have you had enough?' He put the lid back on the bowl. 'I hope they're cutting your food up for you. It's going to be a bit of a nuisance till that arm mends.'

'I don't know, I haven't felt much like eating till now.'

'No, I don't suppose you have.' He got up to leave, suddenly embarrassed, and looking as out of place among the starched sheets as a dustbin in a ballroom.

'You are a bloody fool, though,' he said, hovering at the end of the bed. 'Why on earth didn't you scream or something? I'd have been up like a shot.'

'There wasn't time.' Anna closed her eyes. She didn't want to tell him that she hadn't yelled precisely because Bea or Selwyn would have come, and they might have been hurt, too. Selwyn had been lucky this time. His penchant for schoolboy heroics hadn't done him any harm, but she thought he would have done much better to open the front door and let Raymond Brough run out, rather than risk a brawl in which either Bea or he might have been injured.

She watched him leave—his stride bouncy, a contrast to the diffident shuffle that had propelled him in—grateful to the impulse that had brought him. Selwyn hated visiting the sick. He was not easy with sympathy or condescension. What he needed were opponents; people he could respect but fight. No one could oppose the halt and lame.

She heard nothing from the office until Bernie arrived at five the next afternoon.

'Lots of news,' he said, sitting astride an inadequate

hospital chair and folding his arms across the back of it. 'If you're up to hearing it all. I'd've come yesterday, but when we phoned they said you were still a touch non compos. Actually, we had a devil of a job stopping the old man trundling over with a wreath. You know, maundy money, tribute to his wounded troops, etcetera.'

'Good God,' Anna said, surprised, 'what a hideous idea.'

'Nothing personal mind,' Bernie grinned, 'just living the legend of the great leader.'

'Bernie?'

'Yeah?'

'Can you get me out of here? They're driving me conkers, and they say I can't leave till they've taken the stitches out.'

Bernie looked at her seriously. 'How many ribs was it?'

'Only three.'

'No internals?'

'Not that I know of. Please, Bernie. They won't listen to me.'

He regarded her steadily for a minute. Then he said, 'Take it easy for a minute, I'll go and find someone to talk to.'

He disappeared for about twenty minutes. When he came back he was smiling cheerfully. 'No sweat. You're sprung. I'm picking you up tomorrow morning after the doc's done his rounds. How are you feeling really?'

'Shitty. But that's mostly being in this place. You're supposed to feel shitty here.'

'What are you going to do when you get out?'

'Find a cheap dentist.'

'You're insured, you know,' Bernie said.

'For teeth, too?'

'Some of us read our policies. For any injury in the course of duty. In fact, I know a very good dentist. He can do you a proper crown and bridge job. You won't know the difference.'

'Quickly?'

'Temporaries the day you go in. Permanents a few

weeks later. I can ring him in the morning if you like, make an appointment.'

'Would you, Bernie? I feel better already.'

'I've brought you some clothes,' Bea said disapprovingly when she turned up at seven. 'Mr Schiller rang up and told me you'd be needing them. I told him you should stay in bed and be looked after, but he wouldn't listen. He said it'd do you good to get up and fend for yourself.'

'He's right, Bea,' Anna said. 'I'm just wallowing in here. It's so depressing.'

'Well, suit yourself,' Bea sniffed, 'it's such a pity about your nice coat, though. They slit the sleeve to get your arm out. They should have gone up the seam instead of cutting the fabric. You'll never mend it now. I've brought your biggest shirt and woolly and my old cape, so you should be able to manage that plaster cast.'

'That's very sweet of you, Bea.' Anna couldn't think of anything else to say. Bea rummaged in her basket and brought out the plastic bowl.

'I've brought you a nice banana custard. Can you manage the spoon if I hold the bowl?'

'Go and have a wash,' Selwyn said, 'you look all grey and sweaty.'

'I'll put the kettle on,' Bernie said.

Anna went into the bedroom and splashed water around. She did not think grey was the most accurate description as she faced the mirror above the basin. Lurid colours stained the swollen flesh around brow, cheek-bones and jaw. A bleeding Turner sunset, she thought, looking away, repelled.

The flat had never looked so tidy. Bea's strong and sentimental hand ruled it even in her absence. Everything was squared off and at right angles, but a new bunch of flowers rioted on the table by the window, and a potted violet bloomed coyly by the bedside.

'The electric blanket's been on since breakfast,' Selwyn informed her. 'And there's a clean nightie somewhere.'

'Do me a favour,' Anna said, sitting down carefully. 'I only just got up.'

'It's all right by me,' Selwyn said happily, pleased with the hint of resurrected retaliation.

Bernie handed out mugs of tea. He could make even a mixture of Ceylon and Earl Grey look and taste like NAAFI fare.

'That's more like it!' Anna said, sipping guardedly and relaxing into familiar surroundings.

'Well, I expect you'd like me to start with Brough, wouldn't you?' Bernie started, easing his big frame comfortably back into the armchair. 'That part being closest to your hearts.'

'Rough stuff Brough, apprehended by the avenging poet,' Selwyn said modestly.

'Yes, and it was a good job you did, too, as things turned out. If he'd run loose we might all have had to pack up and go home. I shouldn't make a habit of it, though. Not unless you're well insured. They aren't always cretinous pissy-arsed berks like our Raymond.'

'The trouble with you professionals,' Selwyn said with massive dignity, 'is that you can't forgive the man in the street doing your job for you.'

Bernie looked from Selwyn to Anna and back again, making up his mind about something.

Then he said: 'Oh, I don't mean that, Mr Price, but he was drunk and a fool or he wouldn't have been here in the first place. Look, I'm going to keep this short, Anna, I'm supposed to be in Church Street right now. Let's just say that Brough, Eady and Slinger are all answering questions now. Once it started it was a bit of a chain reaction. Slinger was the last domino, and he toppled Tuesday morning. So there's nothing to do any more. We're finished and out of it.'

'Wait a minute,' Selwyn said, 'Anna said Brough killed Deirdre. I thought I'd nabbed a murderer.'

'Yes, that wasn't a bad idea, at the time, considering the mess she was in. It looks as if Deirdre did die at the lab. But if you don't mind I'll fill you in later. Nobody's been charged yet, they're still talking their heads off. But since I don't know for certain what's been decided I'll leave it at that. Come on, Mr Price,' he said, cutting off Selwyn's faceful of questions. 'Shall we leave her to get a bit of shut-eye? She's got a lot of mending to do.'

Selwyn reluctantly followed Bernie to the door. Like any man who spent his days mainly occupied with solitary and imaginative work, he cherished his few skirmishes with life, and overestimated his own part in the action. He had never been badly hurt, so he couldn't understand the physical weakness that resulted, and the reductions it made in the mind. But he watched Bernie take the phone off the hook as he passed it, and stood by as he opened a tin of beef broth in the kitchen, without protesting. Experience was dictating Bernie's small actions, and Selwyn respected experience, especially if it was not his own.

'Now, you keep people out of here, don't let anyone bother her for a while,' Bernie said. Anna heard them clatter downstairs.

She undressed and put on the huge viyella nightgown Bea had left under the pillow. It took twenty minutes. Then she took two pain-killers and crawled into bed. The euphoria of being home again had drained away too quickly, leaving her exhausted and wretched.

CHAPTER 29

MR Vernon was a handsome man. Anna would have preferred him homely. It was embarrassing to display a split lip and kicked teeth to such a good-looking man. They were halfway through a three-hour appointment, so there was still plenty of time for things to get worse. But, she reflected, as the only relationship she could sustain with a dentist was one of humble submission in the best of circumstances, her bizarre appearance would not make much difference.

'So you're a detective,' Mr Vernon had said. 'That must be an extremely interesting occupation. Interesting enough to compensate for this sort of accident, I mean?'

Anna had been taught never to speak with her mouth full, so a sour remark about the accidental nature of the damage went unsaid.

'You're quite lucky, really,' he said at another time, over the whine of the drill. 'As far as I can see, you never had particularly straight front teeth to begin with. So we can iron out a few of the wrinkles as we go.'

Anna felt that before the attack her front teeth had

been nicely unremarkable, neither perfect nor crooked, and she would have given a lot to have them back again in place of the cosmetic equivalents Mr Vernon was about to provide.

He was presently grinding down the two broken ones on either side of the gap to provide solid pegs over which he would eventually fix a porcelain and gold bridge. Her mouth was stiff with local anaesthetic, but there were enough sensitive spots left on her teeth to make her wince and curse Raymond Brough. According to Bernie, Brough had only given very confused reasons for breaking into her flat. Sometimes he said he had wanted to find out if Anna had any evidence to incriminate him, and at others he said he blamed her for Francis Neary's suicide and had wanted to trash her place over by way of revenge. Either way, he was probably regretting the drunken impulse almost as much as she was. He was still in hospital, flat on his back, with his right leg in traction, having been charged with breaking and entering, criminal damage and grievous bodily harm.

'What would you like to hear now?' Mr Vernon said. He liked to play tapes while he was working, perhaps with the excuse that music relaxed his patients, but more obviously for his own enjoyment. It was apparent that he liked opera best. He had been singing along with Joan Sutherland for the last half-hour, and making a better job of it than she did, to Anna's ears at least, who preferred a baritone to a soprano nine times out of ten.

'Bach,' Anna replied quickly, partly because she was usually only allowed enough time for a monosyllabic response, and partly because as far as she could remember Bach hadn't written any opera.

'I don't think we've got any Bach. Open wide.' He placed something large in her mouth and told her to bite. 'How about a little Wagner?'

The first few bars of *Tannhäuser*, far from being relaxing, added to the general sum of Anna's discomfort. At another time Mr Vernon's idiosyncrasies might have appealed to her. After all, it was unusual to find a dentist who hummed and sang so happily while carrying out grisly excavations into pulp cavities. But at the moment Anna was irritated and discomforted by practically anything. For the past week she had been in an alarming mood which fluctuated between depression and discontent. It was as if she had a broken personality as well as an arm and three ribs. She couldn't find anything to read, or anything she wanted to listen to, and when she looked at her books and records, searching for something to divert herself with, she couldn't remember what she had bought them for in the first place. Everything seemed to have been chosen by someone else, someone who didn't know her any more. Only the Triumph works manual exerted its old influence, but she found she couldn't even concentrate on exploded diagrams for long.

'I suppose you'll want to get away when the arm's mended and we've finished this treatment. Have a proper holiday,' Mr Vernon said. And then between whistling and grinding he told her about Sharm el Sheikh in winter, and how he had recently discovered in himself a passion for underwater botany.

'It's quite wonderful,' he said, 'very restful and green, with the sun filtering through the water. Everything moves constantly. It's not unlike being in the middle of a forest on a windy day, only much quieter, and far more mysterious. And the sun would do you a power of good.'

It must have been a recent trip he was describing. His forearms, emerging from the short-sleeved white dental smock he wore, were copper-brown, and furred with bleached golden hair.

Anna wasn't sure if she wanted to go away yet, although the thought of sunshine and sea-water was strongly seductive. She was caught in two minds about nearly everything. It was true that she wanted to go to a strange place among strangers, though. In London she felt too available. She was too easy to find. Raymond Brough had found her without any trouble at all. Bernie said that when Brough had been searched the police had found a letter from Francis Neary in his pocket. It was a pathetic letter, he told her, full of guilt and recriminations, of how they had all sinned and would be punished. Neary seemed to favour divine punishment over earthly justice, but unfortunately he had not been specific about what he would be punished for. He had mentioned Anna's name while warning Brough that the pigeons were coming home to roost. The barman at the Royal Oak had passed on her telephone number, and the telephone directory had completed the trail. Anna couldn't remember having given her card out at the Royal Oak, but maybe the barman had got it from Collinwood. It didn't matter much how Brough had come by the information. What concerned her was that he had found her so easily.

'I think,' Mr Vernon said, 'that we're just about ready to try the temporaries.'

The sound of the drill and smell of burnt tooth-enamel ceased, allowing *Tannhäuser* to blast out without competition.

'Open wide,' said Mr Vernon. 'Bite. Good.'

This part was not so bad. When he used the drill again, it was to shape the plastic and not to aggravate her tortured nerve-ends. He had been very quick and deft, but there had not been a dentist born who was quick and deft enough for Anna. He took another impression, and the false teeth came out in the wax, leaving her mouth cold and exposed again. Anna had a sudden and horrifying vision of him being struck by lightning or somehow being prevented from putting them back. They were such silly plastic things, but they meant a lot to Anna. He refitted them, this time using more cement.

'There you are,' he said, after fiddling and adjusting some more. 'That'll do till we have the Crown Jewels ready.'

He laughed genially at his own joke, and gave Anna a mirror. She smiled suspiciously at herself, and then grinned broadly. Silly plastic things they might be, but they were the difference between an ordinary smile and a black hole in her mouth.

'Just don't go mad with the toffee apples,' Mr Vernon said as he showed her out of his surgery. Anna felt as if she was halfway back into the human race.

* * *

She picked up a taxi in Sloane Square. A visit to the office would be necessary sooner or later, and it might as well be made now, while she was still feeling the effects of returned self-respect.

'Strewth!' the cabman said as she got in. 'That must have been some door you walked into. I haven't seen a pair of shiners like that since Dave Boy Green last year. What you been up to then, hammering the old man again?'

'Well, someone's old man, I suppose,' Anna said, trying the new teeth against the sibilants and finding them refreshingly adequate.

'It's disgusting what some villains'll do these days just for a handful of coppers,' he said comfortably. 'Time was when your average thief had a bit of savvy. Nowadays he'll use his boots soon as look at you. There's no class any more.'

'I don't know that thieving's ever classy,' Anna said. It was wonderful to be able to talk without feeling her lips puff flatulently in thin air.

'All I'm saying is that London had to be a better place to live in when even the villains had style,' the driver said, looking disgustedly at the Knightsbridge clutter. 'Look at it now. I ask you. It's all sand in your shoes and out for the easy bunce. No wonder there's no standards no more.'

'You can't blame foreigners for that.'

'Don't get me wrong,' the driver said. 'I'm not saying they ain't colourful. Me, I wouldn't give a monkey's who came here as long as they went home again after. But they don't, see? Makes you feel a tourist in your own home. Some of 'em spend money like there was no tomorrow and buy up property or what-not. And there's others just live on the state. I mean, what does it look like to a young bloke just married and can't get a council house?'

It sounded like a favourite grudge, a well-rehearsed routine that the driver liked to launch into at the slightest opportunity.

'It's what the young people see as worries me,' he went on. 'Other people getting what should be theirs by rights. And without lifting a finger. That's what gets me.

It's a wrong example. Makes 'em think they should have a bit of the cream, too, without having to work for it.

'Makes 'em want to take advantage,' he added elliptically. 'That's why there's so much crime around today.'

Anna didn't want to argue, although most of what he said offended her own creed of self-determinism. He was obviously well-practised in his own argument, and besides, taxi-drivers, she thought, were all too dogmatic. It was something about the nature of their jobs that led them to half-cocked theories. They saw too much out of the front window and too little of the people they were talking to behind them. She wondered how this one would have explained Deirdre in the light of what he had just been saying, and she was almost tempted to ask. After all, Deirdre was, in a sense, privileged. She had had brains, guts, an education, and money behind her. What had made her systematically try to take advantage of other people's weaknesses instead of her own strengths? That was the real mystery. There were excuses: she had felt rejected by her own family, and had been badly treated in her first serious affair, but no solid reasons for her extraordinary shift into blackmail had emerged. It seemed as if it had been part of a private evolution that had died with her. Nothing external remained, and Anna felt that she could only go a very little way towards understanding someone who was dead.

Nearly three weeks ago she had been asked to find out how Deirdre had died. That was more or less cleared up now. But it was part of Anna's general malaise that she almost didn't care. It was an unsatisfactory job that finished with the facts. Mr Jackson had wanted facts, and facts he had been given. It was immaterial that Anna was left frustrated. Perhaps she should try a different kind of work; the sort of work where she could ask her own questions and satisfy her own curiosity. She was tired of being limited by other people's demands. She felt she had a lot in common with the taxi-driver, in that she could only go where the fare-payer wanted.

She was tired when she paid off the cab at the corner of Allen Street. It seemed that even her moods were being dictated to her by physical weakness resulting from the job. Perhaps she would just go up to the office and resign. And then what? Sharm el Sheikh? And then?

'Did you bring your medical certificate?' was the first thing Beryl said when she emerged at the top of the stairs. 'Only I can't put you down for sick-leave till I get it.'

'Hello, Beryl,' Anna said extracting the certificate from her coat pocket. 'How are you feeling? How's the knee coming along?'

'Mustn't grumble.' Beryl pinned the certificate to another sheaf of papers. 'I must say, you still look rather poorly. You'd better sign this or you won't be able to claim for the dentist.'

Anna scrawled a signature on the proffered form. Her left hand was still stiff and swollen. She would have to remember not to hit anyone with a fistful of keys again. It might have nearly torn Brough's ear off, a fact she contemplated sometimes with vindictive pleasure, but it had been hardly worth doing in the circumstances.

'Are those the new teeth, then?' Beryl asked curiously. 'Oh, yes, I can see now. They're a bit whiter than your own.'

'Is Mr Brierly free,' Anna said crossly, 'or shall I come back another day?'

'No. He's got a few minutes before tea, and he's expecting you. Anyway, you'll probably want to stay indoors for a while, I mean, you can't be very happy going about in public looking like that.'

'Not very,' Anna said knocking on Brierly's door. 'People will keep making the most insulting remarks.'

Mr Brierly stood up when she came into the room. He even drew up a chair for her.

'Do sit down, Miss Lee. It's good of you to come, in the circumstances,' he said with unaccustomed courtliness. 'It's extraordinary how accident-prone the ladies in my employ have become all of a sudden. Still, I must say it's a great relief to have Miss Doyle back in harness. We were quite lost without her.'

He went back to his own side of the desk and sat down.

'Well, it has been a most unfortunate episode. Most unfortunate. But, as they say, it's an ill wind that blows nobody good. At least we were in a position to put pressure on that fool who attacked you. Without that we might never have learned what happened to the Jackson girl.'

'Is anyone being charged with that?' Anna asked. 'I haven't heard.'

'Not at the present,' Brierly said, 'and I doubt if they will be in the future. Both Eady and Brough blame that poor idiot who committed suicide, of course. And even if that was not the case, there were too many mitigating factors.'

'The way they tell it.'

'Well, quite. But she had no business to be at the laboratory, and a jury could be easily convinced that they thought they were scaring off a burglar. Anyway, the police have no evidence. They are much more interested in the film piracy business. It would appear to be a new one on them, in Q District at least.' He said the last with a superior smile, as if he was congratulating himself on teaching an old dog new tricks.

'Conspiracy to defraud distributors of their hiring fees.' He rolled the phrase around his mouth as if assessing the taste. It was a new one on him, too.

'Slinger, of course, has a modicum of native wit. Had he had more acumen in choosing his personnel . . . Well, as I say, a regrettable incident.'

He paused momentarily, glancing at Anna sideways.

'It is, of course, one of the reasons why one hesitates to employ women in this sort of work. They do seem less able to defend themselves when these stupid situations arise.' He wasn't looking at her now, preferring to gaze at the print of an egret behind her head.

'I wouldn't necessarily agree with that,' Anna said slowly. She was thinking of an incident quite recently when Phil had been put out of action by a kick in the groin while serving a bankruptcy notice.

'Nevertheless,' he went on, 'one finds oneself reluctant to put at risk an employee one feels to be physically vulnerable.'

Then she realized what was happening. Brierly wanted to give her the sack, but couldn't quite bring himself to do it.

'Normally,' Anna said firmly, 'there is very little risk.'

'But one should always anticipate the unexpected. And, as the director of this company, I feel responsible for your safety.'

'And so do I,' she responded sharply. 'The risks and responsibilities are my own affair, too.'

'Good of you to say so,' Brierly said, with a hint of disappointment in his voice.

Now, far from wanting to resign, Anna was perversely remembering how hard it had been to get a job with Brierly in the first place. All those months of floor-walking at Boots, meetings with store security associations, and dark little rooms where she had watched television monitors all day, threatened to return. A small firm like Brierly's at least offered some freedom and diversity.

Brierly continued: 'All the same, one does not like to have to think twice before sending an agent into the field.'

'I'm sure any good director feels that, whether the agent is a man or a woman,' Anna said, trying to inject a tone of both flattery and finality. She felt very weary.

'Well, quite so, quite so. Now, perhaps we can move on to another matter.' His voice changed now that he was on firmer ground. The threat receded.

'Naturally, I have already telephoned Mr Jackson and outlined the bare bones of our findings. He was very pleased to find his suspicions of foul play vindicated. Unfortunately, Mrs Jackson is proving more of a problem. She wanted to come to London to hear the whole story, as she put it. I managed to dissuade her temporarily.'

'Yes,' Anna said, 'she might find the whole story rather hurtful.'

'Quite so. Some of your revelations are a trifle embarrassing. But also, as case officer, it is really your responsibility to fill them in if they so require.'

'I suppose so,' Anna said resignedly.

'I shall, of course, rely on your tact and discretion. I did suggest to Mrs Jackson that you would report in full when you had recovered from your injuries. She was most sympathetic. However, she did indicate that the sooner she could, as it were, lay her daughter's ghost to rest, the sooner she would recover from her bereavement. I'm sure you can understand that.'

'Of course,' Anna agreed.

'Yes, I knew you would,' he went on, 'and in view of that, when Mrs Jackson suggested that you visit Wiltshire and report to her in person, I said it might be a very good idea. You can make the appointment to suit yourself. And I dare say that after a week or so's sick leave you might enjoy a day in the country.'

'Well, I'll certainly phone her,' Anna said tiredly. She felt she had been outmanoeuvred. Mr Brierly would do anything to prevent a distraught Mrs Jackson emoting in his office.

'Good. Then, I'll leave it in your hands.' Brierly got up. The interview was over. 'You will let Miss Doyle know when you intend to return to work? And'— he added belatedly—'if there is anything we can do?'

Anna promised that she would.

She found Bernie waiting for her in the passage outside, leaning against Beryl's counter making small talk.

'I heard you were in,' he said, 'so I thought I'd wait and see if you wanted a lift home.'

'Aren't you the lucky girl?' Beryl said huffily.

Bernie wagged a finger at her. 'You told me Mr Brierly was taking you to the station. You can't have all the men running after you.'

Beryl patted her hair with a strawberry-tipped hand, and said good night quite pleasantly.

'Do you know,' Anna said when they were in the car, 'the old bastard was within an inch of giving me the old heave-ho?'

'Was he, by God?' Bernie said. 'That would've been pretty poor form. Firing someone who had been injured in his service.'

'I think that's what held him back. But he did let me

know that he found the responsibility of employing women rather overwhelming,' she mimicked Brierly's voice, 'and that my resignation would not have been unacceptable.'

'He always was a silly old fart,' Bernie said with unexpected heat. 'Don't you take any notice.'

'I didn't,' Anna said, and fell silent. Bernie was normally very loyal to the firm he worked for, and sparing with his criticism even when it was merited. She didn't like to have been the cause of such an unaccustomed outburst.

After a while, he said, 'It's not as if he didn't get quite a few pats on the back out of all this. It may have been a mess from your point of view, but he's still smelling of roses where the authorities are concerned.'

'I didn't mean to moan,' she said cautiously. 'In fact, I thought it was a bit of a joke.'

'Well, it isn't,' Bernie said flatly, and drove the rest of the way without speaking again.

CHAPTER 30

· · · · · · · · · ·

ANNA let herself into the house and went quietly upstairs. It had been her first day out since coming home from hospital, and she was exhausted. It was only six-thirty, but she went straight to the bathroom, washed and got ready for bed. She was aching all over, and her gums were sore, so she took a couple of pain-killers, and stood in front of the bathroom mirror wondering whether she had the nerve to clean her teeth. Mr Vernon had assured her that they were very secure, but she didn't feel at all confident about them yet. In the end she brushed them very gently and rinsed her mouth with salt water. They felt all right. She smiled experimentally. They looked all right, too. It was true they were a shade whiter than her own teeth, but Mr Vernon had promised that the permanent set would be a perfect match.

She was about to get into bed when someone knocked on the door. She opened it and found Bea holding a large mug of hot chocolate.

'Oh dear,' Bea said, looking at the nightgown. 'I

heard you come in, and I thought you might like a hot drink.'

'That's very sweet of you,' Anna said politely, taking the mug and standing aside to let Bea pass. She would either have to pour the drink away, or if she couldn't do that she would have to drink it and be forced to clean her teeth again. Small things were becoming problematical.

Bea said, 'I've made sausages and mash; I thought you might like to come down.' She was oddly tentative.

'Well, that's very sweet of you,' Anna said again, 'but I am rather whacked out. I just wanted to go to bed.'

'Only there's a young man downstairs who's been waiting for you for over an hour now. I didn't think you'd mind, seeing as you went to the dentist today,' Bea said hesitantly.

'Oh, Bea!' Anna sighed. 'Who is it?'

'It's Simon. He's been round two or three times, and I just couldn't turn him away again. He's so nice and polite. I'm sure he won't stay more than a minute.'

'Oh well,' Anna said weakly. 'Never mind.'

She lit the gas-fire and wrapped herself in a woollen shawl, as her dressing-gown sleeve couldn't accommodate the plaster cast. Then she poured the hot chocolate down the kitchen sink and rinsed the mug.

Simon appeared in the doorway, carrying a tray.

'It's bangers and mash,' he said awkwardly. 'Mrs Price asked me to bring it up.'

'Oh, Christ,' Anna said. 'I can't. Do you want it?'

'I've already had some. She's a very generous lady, is Mrs Price.'

'Isn't she!' Anna said ungraciously. 'Well, could you put it in the fridge, then?'

She went and sat down, leaving him to juggle with the unwanted food. It was not a good beginning.

'I was awfully shocked to hear what happened,' he said formally, when he joined her a couple of minutes later.

'Well, it's very kind of you to come round.' Anna felt guilty. He did look very concerned, and he had put on his black cord suit and a fresh white shirt for the visit.

'I won't stay long.' He sat down. 'I just wanted to see how you were. I know you must be awfully tired.'

'No. I'm much better now.'

After an embarrassed pause, he said: 'Mr and Mrs Price have told me some of the news. But I don't suppose you want to talk about that now.'

'It's quite all right,' Anna said, feeling trapped by his tact.

'I mean, I know now that Dee was murdered by one of the technicians at CCS,' he said painfully, 'but I can't understand why. They were copying films illegally, I know. But even so, it's not the kind of crime you'd cover up for by murdering someone, is it?'

'I think murder is putting it a little strongly. I don't really know what happened, but I think they were only trying to frighten her off. Both Brough and Eady say Neary was responsible. They claim he thought he was scaring off an intruder, and she broke her neck by struggling. No one believes either of them, but there's no proof it happened any other way, and a blunder like that would seem somehow typical of them. I really don't think anyone intended to kill Dee.'

'That doesn't make it any easier to accept,' Simon said.

'No, it doesn't.'

'I mean, I'd almost rather it was intentional,' he continued sadly. 'It seems so undignified that she should be dead through dumb carelessness.'

Anna couldn't think of any reply to that.

'Don't you think, though, that it's more likely that the one who killed her was the same one who attacked you?'

'Well, maybe I'm biased.'

'But wouldn't it be in character?'

'It might be,' Anna said carefully.

'Well, can't you do anything about it?' Simon said, suddenly violent.

'Like what?' she said angrily. 'The only way you'd know for certain would be if he admitted it, or Eady grassed. What do you expect me to do—go down to the nick with a pair of electrodes and force a confession out of him?'

'You were the one who was so keen on the truth!'

'And you were the one who was so keen on ethical method,' Anna said unfairly. They stared at each other.

'I'm sorry,' he said, after a while. 'I didn't mean to go on like that. It's just seeing you like this, all bruised and ill. And the same man may have killed Dee, but the worst anyone can say about him is that he was stupid. It makes me so angry.'

'I know,' Anna said. 'I'm sorry, too.'

'You didn't think Freddie Slinger put him up to it?' he asked hopefully.

'Absolutely not,' she said firmly. 'That would be totally out of character.'

'Another thing I don't understand,' Simon said, after a short silence, 'is what Dee was doing at CCS anyway. Why did she get involved? If she thought there was something fishy going on, why didn't she go to the police?'

Anna had been dreading this question. The Jacksons would ask it, too, and she would have to find a truthful but not overtly hurtful way of answering. She considered trying a few specimen replies on Simon now, but she felt too weary.

In the end, she said: 'Look, Si, could we go into that some other time? I'm a bit flaked right now, and I can't concentrate properly.'

Simon jumped up immediately, looking aghast. 'I'm most awfully sorry,' he said. 'I didn't mean to overtire you.'

Anna felt guilty again in the face of this solicitude. He had helped her considerably in the past, and it seemed shabby to put him off with such a lame excuse.

'Look, tomorrow's Saturday,' he went on. 'There must be something I can bring you for the weekend.'

'No, it's okay. Thanks,' Anna said, 'but I ought to start doing my own shopping soon.'

'There must be something I can do,' he said anxiously. 'You must be finding things pretty difficult these days. I'd really like to help.'

'Well, perhaps there is something,' she said reluctantly. 'I ought to disconnect the car battery and bring it up here. And I can't do it with one hand.'

'Nothing easier,' he said contentedly. 'I'll see you tomorrow, then.'

When he had gone she turned the fire out and went to bed, thinking uneasy thoughts about him. He was too nice, too eager to please. She seemed to be constantly caught between using him and rejecting him, and she did not want to do either. It was hard to meet him on equal terms. She felt that bit by bit she had run up a debt to him that she could not pay off except by using him further. She did want the battery upstairs, but it wasn't crucial. She had manufactured a service for him to perform tomorrow in order to make up for pushing him out tonight. And he had accepted gratefully so that he could have an excuse for coming back. It was no way to run a friendship. Much as she liked him, she thought, she would have to choke him off entirely or stick to playing squash with him. That, at least, had been a game they had played with the same end in mind.

She tried to explain something of the problem to Selwyn in the morning, as he sat on the end of her bed drinking the cup of coffee Bea had sent him up with.

'You're just being cranky,' he said, bouncing slightly and crushing the quilt. 'If he wants to help, let him help. I don't see why you're being so scrupulous all of a sudden. Besides, I think he's quite keen on you, from the way he was talking last night.'

'There you are, then,' Anna exclaimed. 'That makes it doubly impossible.'

'What's wrong with him being keen?' Selwyn asked. 'He seemed a nice intelligent chap to me.'

'Since when did you find "nice" admirable?'

'Well, I gave him some of my poems to read while he was waiting and he was very complimentary about them, especially the "Ode to an Electron Microscope." Oh, well,' he said sheepishly, 'I suppose there is something a bit wet there, if you look hard enough.'

' "Electron Microscope" is a very nice poem, hardly wet at all.'

'Good God, girl!' Selwyn shouted. 'What are you talking about? Are you deliberately trying to misrepresent me?'

'Yes,' Anna said.

'Well, that's all right then,' he said. 'I thought you might be serious. Shall I bring you up another cup of coffee? Or was one enough?'

The phone rang while she was getting dressed.

'I'm glad to see you're answering your phone again,' Collinwood said. 'You must be on the mend. Too bad, your getting clobbered like that. How's it going?'

'Okay, thanks.'

'Only we don't have your statement yet. Are you up to it?'

'Yes,' Anna said. 'Whenever you like.'

'Right. I thought of sending Bisgood over early next week, does that suit?'

'Fine.'

'We just didn't want to interfere with your plans,' he said, with weighty courtesy.

'I don't have any plans,' she said. 'I'm on sick leave, so any time'll do.'

'Best time for a little trip abroad then, isn't it? A nice drop of sunshine in flaming bloody January? We wouldn't want boring little details like statements getting in the way of a Caribbean cruise.'

'I should be so lucky,' she said, wondering where Collinwood got his inflated notion of what she earned.

'No cruise? Well, that's what I'd do in your shoes. Never mind, two and half grand's a tidy sum, maybe you've got better things to do than frittering it all away in Barbados.'

'I don't know what you're rabbiting on about,' Anna said in exasperation.

'Pull the other one,' Collinwood said neutrally. 'Oh, and give your pal Alan J. my very kindest regards.'

He hung up, leaving Anna glaring wrathfully at the receiver.

Half an hour later, as if summoned, Bea came up with a tall bunch of pink and white carnations wrapped in cellophane.

'These were just delivered,' she said, unpinning the wrapping. A soft bomb of heavy scent exploded in the kitchen. 'Aren't they lovely?'

They reminded Anna too strongly of Beryl's favourite perfume. She opened the envelope which some overenthusiastic florist had skewered to a flower stem. They were from Alan Luca.

'You remember, Bea, the homesick American who wanted to stay to supper?'

'Oh, yes,' Bea said, reading shamelessly over her shoulder. 'Look at that now, he wants to take you out to dinner when you're better. Isn't that romantic?'

'Watch it, Bea. You're getting as bad as Selwyn.'

'Oh, I didn't mean that.' Bea looked shocked. 'But what with everyone coming round asking about you and these flowers and all, it's almost worth getting bashed up, isn't it?'

'Why don't you take the flowers?' Anna suddenly felt a little queasy. 'They're a bit too overpowering, and besides, I haven't got a tall vase.'

'Oh, I couldn't,' Bea said, looking at them admiringly. 'They're for you. And poor Mr Luca would be so offended.'

'Not if you don't tell him. Go on, you know you appreciate them more than I do.'

'Well, if you really don't want them,' Bea said, gathering them up tenderly. 'You are a funny one, Anna.'

CHAPTER 31

· · · · · · · · · ·

IT would have been a large and unremarkable house without the extensions. But the twin garages on one side and the granny-flat on the other, with their matching stone-faced arches, made it look off-balance. It was a mock Tudor building with a gabled second floor, probably put up in the Thirties, a comfortable house for a large family if it had been left alone. But a heavy hand had shaped the front garden, and cut down the rambling roses and the old trees, leaving an empty stretch of lawn islanded by a new yellow gravel drive. Mr Jackson's Range-Rover was parked outside the front door, steaming slightly in the cold air. Anna took a deep breath and pulled a wrought-iron handle marked 'Bell', setting up a loud clamour of chimes behind the door, joined almost instantly by the high-pitched barking of several dogs.

Mr Jackson opened the door, and three of the ugliest dogs Anna had ever seen spilled out on to the drive.

'Good heavens! They're Boston Terriers, aren't they?' she asked, amazed that anyone should give one of them house-room, let alone three.

'That's right,' Mr Jackson said, unsuccessfully trying to call them to heel. 'Pedigree. You wouldn't believe the price if I told you. I don't know,' he said gloomily, taking Anna's cape, 'give me a good Labrador any day. Still, these are a valuable investment, I will say that for them.'

They went into the living-room and the dogs claimed the sofa, lying like three piebald sausages, their flat faces resting on their paws, and their bulging toad-eyes swiveling vaguely.

Mrs Jackson wore a black dress and a mournful expression. She came forward to shake hands, realizing too late that Anna's right arm was in a sling.

'How silly of me,' Mrs Jackson said in her tight-throated voice. 'I was very sorry, no, we were very sorry about what happened. We blame ourselves in a way.'

'Speak for yourself,' Mr Jackson interrupted her. 'I'm sure Miss Lee knew what she was getting into when she took on this job.'

'Well, hardly, dear,' Mrs Jackson said. 'It didn't look as if anyone would get hurt at the outset.'

'Heaven help us!' he exclaimed impatiently. 'That's what we went to London for in the first place. I knew my daughter had met with foul play! That's what we set out to prove. And we proved it.'

'All the same, dear, we wouldn't have knowingly put her in danger.'

'That's what she gets paid for,' Jackson said firmly.

A fraught silence greeted this remark. Jackson reddened, and then rushed on: 'And what are the police going to do about it, after we've spent good money doing their work for them? Sweet FA, that's what they're going to do. Lazy sods. It takes a slip of a girl to show them how the world turns, and even then they can't be bothered to get their fingers out and finish the job off properly.'

He was working himself up into a rage. So Anna said, 'They really can't be blamed that much, Mr Jackson. After all, they didn't know Deirdre as you did, or have your instinct about her.'

'Well, they should have taken my word for it, then. I told them, I don't know how many times, my girl knew how to get out of a skid, and she wouldn't have been caught dead without her seatbelt.'

Another silence followed that one.

Anna said hurriedly, 'All the same, Mr Jackson, everything else was consistent with the accident verdict. If anything had looked funny to them, it would have been a different story. I mean, it looked like an accident because it was an accident. It was the most amazing stroke of luck for those three from the lab, although I don't suppose they thought so at the time. They couldn't have faked a spin-off like that in a thousand years. They're much too dozy. If the car had hit the post front-on instead of rear, things would have been far more obvious.'

'It all seems so senseless,' Mrs Jackson said, forestalling her husband, who looked as if he was about to jump in with both feet again. 'What did they think they were going to do?'

'I don't really know,' Anna said, 'I haven't talked to them. But I gather from what the police say, when they realized Deirdre was dead, they just wanted to get her and her car as far away from the lab as possible. They say they had no intention of hiding her body. But I don't know. There's an awful lot of wasteland around Cranford Lane. They both say that they wanted to report Deirdre's death, but Neary panicked and persuaded them not to.'

'You don't believe that, though?' Jackson said disdainfully.

'Not really. But then I don't think they knew what they wanted to do. It's ridiculous, isn't it? They couldn't have manufactured a better cover-up if they'd thought about it for a week. I expect they couldn't believe their luck when no one suspected anything.'

'Except me.'

'Except you.'

'And you, of course.' Mr Jackson generously shared the honours. 'I mean, you are the type to notice little things. Like the smell, for instance.'

'Don't give me too much credit,' Anna said. 'I didn't know anything for certain until Brough coughed. I thought it was likely she had been to the lab. The chemical smell is certainly very distinctive and lingering. The location of the accident was interesting, too. But anyway, even if she had been to the lab, it didn't follow that she was killed there.'

'You knew.' Mr Jackson nodded his head firmly. 'The night you got beaten up, you told the police that Brough had killed my daughter. Mr Brierly told me you did.'

'I was just trying it on. It was my last chance.'

'All the same,' Jackson said stubbornly, 'you're a smart girl. I'm sorry I didn't think so when we met first. But I'm saying so now. I think you did a good job.'

That had a welcome ring of finality about it, and Anna was hoping she would be able to get away without saying any more when Mrs Jackson said, 'You will stay for lunch, won't you? I've got coq-au-vin in the oven. You've come all this way, and I know there's a lot more you can tell us.'

This was obviously a contested point between husband and wife. They avoided each other's eyes. Mr Jackson said: 'You'll have to excuse me, then. I've work to do. I've got the information I paid for, and I'm not very interested in the rest, thank you very much. I wouldn't have pushed my nose into the girl's private life if she was alive, and I'm damned if I'll do it now she's dead.'

He left rather abruptly, patting Anna clumsily on the shoulder as he passed her. The coq-au-vin turned out to be a nicely ordinary chicken stew. While they ate she presented Mrs Jackson with a gently domesticated outline of Deirdre's career and private life. When she had finished, Mrs Jackson sat quietly for a while. Then she said: 'You don't think Deirdre was going to go to the police about Mr Slinger's shenanigans, do you?'

Anna stared at her with a spoonful of caramel custard half-way to her mouth.

'Oh, you don't have to worry. I won't say a word to Tom. It'd only upset him. But he never could see Deirdre as I saw her. She could be a little bugger. She was going to use the information to get something for herself, wasn't she?'

She calmly finished her own dessert. Anna fiddled

with her spoon. The whitewash she had been applying in kindness now looked like a cheap trick.

Mrs Jackson said, 'She was my daughter, and I wanted the best for her. But she could never accept things the way they were. She always thought the world was there for her benefit, that everyone owed her something for being born. She didn't know the effort you have to put in. Straight to the top of the heap, that's what she wanted.'

Her voice had changed now that she was talking naturally. Her throat had relaxed, allowing the rounded Wiltshire vowel-sounds full play. 'I always thought that the right man would sort her out. I hoped that nice young chap you told me about might have been the one to do it. But he wasn't, was he? She'd got too much into the habit of manipulating, hadn't she?'

Anna could only spread her hand in a helpless gesture. She had made all the wrong assumptions about Mrs Jackson, and she felt stupid.

'You've been very kind about her,' she went on. 'Don't think I don't appreciate what you were trying to do. She was my daughter, and I loved her, but I don't know that I liked her very much.'

'I'm sorry,' Anna said feebly. 'The awful thing was that she didn't have time to change. The one lesson she might have learned from killed her.'

'Don't you worry about it any more.' She leaned over and touched Anna's hand as if Anna was the one who needed comforting. 'There never is enough time for some folk. You finish your pudding and I'll drive you to the station.'

CHAPTER 32

THE early-afternoon sun momentarily brightened the black and white countryside, glinting gold and silver on the icy canal as the train passed, casting blue alpine shadows as it went.

Perhaps Mother really does know best after all, Anna thought. But her mood brightened with the sun, and she didn't believe it. All the same, motherhood did not necessarily preclude clear sight, and she hated finding herself guilty of presuming it did. She felt she had been disrespectful and narrow-minded about Mrs Jackson, basing her conclusions on trite preconception rather than on direct observation. It was the kind of mistake that made her toes curl. But, clear-sighted or not, Anna wondered what sort of mother Mrs Jackson had been. The two young sons had been away at school, but colour photographs of them, formally posed, and smiling impersonally, hung in the living room. Even so, it did not look like the kind of house children played in. Perhaps the dogs were allowed on the velour-covered sofa as a tribute to their value, but Anna was sure that small boys didn't bounce on it. She had seen a kidney-shaped swimming pool from the dining-room window, but there was no trace of swings or rubber tyres or bicycles.

There were many absences in the house. In fact, it looked more like a hotel than a home, so lacking was it in personal touches. Anna had felt the same deficiencies in Deirdre. What had happened to the postcards, the letters, the mementoes? She had been a photographer at one time, a collector of images. Where were the photographs? Whatever it was that had distinguished Deirdre from anyone else, she had not left any expression of it in the things she kept around her. And whatever drove the Jacksons from day to day was not revealed in their house. Anna wondered if this was because they were afraid of someone judging them by their personal possessions and finding them wanting.

With Deirdre it had seemed clearer. She had spent a lot of energy finding weaknesses in others that she could exploit. It could have been that she was just as interested in making sure that no one did the same to her. But now, after seeing the Jacksons' home, a place that told of nothing but its owners' economic status, she wondered if Deirdre's reticence was part of a broader insecurity.

Thinking of Deirdre's possessions, Anna was still doubtful about what had happened to her address book and the money. Everyone had an address book, surely. Even people as concerned with anonymity as Deirdre. It seemed most likely that Neary or one of the other two, fearing some reference to himself in it, had destroyed it. But this was one of the questions to which she had not found a satisfactory answer. Another one was why, if she had been so concerned with anonymity, had Deirdre wanted to become an actress? Had she been trying to crack some of her inhibitions, or was she merely looking for better protection?

Deirdre was still an enigma, but Anna suddenly felt she should draw a line under her and get on with the next thing.

CHAPTER 33

· · · · · · · · · · ·

'**TO** convalescence,' Luca said, raising his glass. Anna obediently raised hers in return.

'What are you going to do now?' he asked, attacking his steak with Pythagorean accuracy. Anna had chosen Boêuf Stroganoff to avoid the indignity of having her meat cut up for her.

'I don't know,' she said. 'Sick leave is wasted on the sick. What would you do?'

'I have three passions, but all of them require two arms and two legs.'

'What are they?' Anna asked, although she thought she could guess.

'Swimming, skiing, and tennis,' he replied, not disappointing her. 'What are yours?'

'Well, not exactly passions,' she said, 'but motor-rallying, swimming and squash will do at a pinch.'

'Ah well, that is a bit difficult. But you ought to go away anyway. I honestly don't know how you British even recover from your common cold in this climate. Why don't you take a cruise or something?'

'No, thanks,' Anna cried. 'That doesn't appeal at all. No, I think I'll save the holiday for when I can enjoy it actively. If I went away now, I wouldn't be able to take a trip in the summer.'

'Surely you could do both?' he said.

'No chance, I can only afford to go away once a year.'

Luca looked at her seriously for a minute, then he said: 'Look, forgive me for asking, but what about the five thousand bucks?'

That had a familiar ring to it, once she had roughly converted dollars into pounds.

She said: 'That's what Collinwood was on about, too. Do you mind telling me why I should have five thousand dollars to blow on a cruise? Because I can assure you I haven't.'

'You don't know?' He straightened his already perfectly perpendicular tie and refilled his glass. Anna shook her head.

'Oh, shoot!' he said, leaning back in his chair and losing interest in the meal. 'I thought that boss of yours was a slimy bastard, but I never thought he was quite as big a creep as this.'

Anna waited while he took a long drink of his wine. Then he said: 'The MPAA offers a five-thousand-dollar bounty to anyone providing information leading to film piracy arrests and convictions. You didn't know?'

'No.'

'Well, your Martin Brierly knew, for sure. I told him when I first saw him, and before I met you.'

'Did Collinwood know, too?'

'Sure he knew. I talked to the police, too. But they can't claim bounty.'

'Ah,' Anna said, grinning, 'well, that explains his change of attitude.'

'You don't seem too upset.'

'Well, you said arrest and conviction,' she said, getting on with her Stroganoff before it got cold. 'Nobody's convicted yet.'

'No,' he said flatly. 'The money's already through. When I heard you were in hospital I telexed and explained the situation. They wired the money right back, and I took the cheque over to your office myself.'

'Was it made out to me?'

'No, I wasn't sure at the time how to make it out. But your boss said he'd see you got it.'

'Were those his exact words? I bet they weren't.'

Luca thought for a minute. 'He said, "Let me assure you, I will do what is proper!" '

'There you are, then. That cheque has sunk without trace in the murky waters of Brierly Security.'

'Son of a bitch!' Luca said explosively. 'He knew that money was for you!'

'Yes, but look at it from his point of view. I do a fair day's work for a reasonably fair day's pay. He has all the responsibilities and overheads. Also, at one time or another nearly everyone in the office took a hand in keeping tabs on Slinger. Brierly wouldn't see it as individual effort.'

'But it was your case. You did all the thinking. You did most of the work. And you sure as hell got nailed for it.'

'Look, don't be so angry about it. Thank you very much for trying.' Luca did look furious. 'I am grateful, really, but honestly, I'm not sure I don't prefer it this way.'

'What are you talking about? You wouldn't have torn up a cheque for five grand, would you?'

'Probably not,' Anna said more thoughtfully. 'But it would have made me feel a bit like a scalp-hunter. I'm still not too convinced that what Slinger was doing was so awful in itself. After all, the films were going to little cinemas in Africa, and no one could call the major film studios the poor widows of America.'

'That's just sentimental. That's the Robin Hood syndrome you Brits never recovered from.'

'Okay,' Anna said, picking up her glass. 'What do you want to drink to now? Slimy Limeys or Robin Hood?'

'You're nuts,' Luca said, recovering some of his urbanity. 'Look, why don't you come and work for us? We may rob the poor to give to the rich, but at least we won't con you out of your blood-money.'

'Are you responsible for hiring?' Anna asked curiously.

'I could recommend you. In fact, my boss cabled me from Johannesburg yesterday. He'll be back next week. And we're looking for local talent to help us out.'

'Aren't we all?' said Anna.

ABOUT THE AUTHOR

Before becoming a novelist, Liza Cody trained as a painter and graphic artist at London's Royal Academy School of Art and worked for a time at Madame Tussaud's. Her first Anna Lee mystery, *Dupe*, won the John Creasey Memorial Award for Best First Crime Novel and was nominated for an Edgar Award. Her fifth Anna Lee novel, *Under Contract*, was shortlisted for a Golden Dagger Award for Best Crime Novel. Her most recent novel is *Backhand*, also featuring Anna Lee. She lives in Somerset, England.

AN ANNA LEE MYSTERY

Here are special preview chapters from *Backhand*, the new Anna Lee novel by Liza Cody, coming from Bantam Books in December. Look for it at your local bookseller.

BACKHAND

LIZA CODY

CHAPTER 1

・ ・ ・ ・ ・ ・ ・ ・ ・

A high-pitched wail split the silence. It pulsed through the room and made the dog howl. Anna turned the key and there was a sudden hush. The dog scampered to the door and whined to be let out.

Johnny said, 'This siren has at least three quarters of a mile range. As I've just demonstrated, if the electric supply is cut off it will operate on battery power.'

'Most impressive,' the big man said.

'The electronic sound has completely superseded the old bell,' Johnny went on. 'But we brought one along in case.'

'That won't be necessary.' The big man glanced at the stack of hardware in the middle of his carpet.

It was a large room, painted cream, with the mouldings picked out in white. Apart from the carpet and a few canvas chairs it was unfurnished. A woman with hair the colour of old gold sat attentively against the wall listening to Johnny's pitch. But Johnny addressed himself exclusively to the big man. Given a choice, Johnny always concentrated on the men.

'The system you select depends to a great extent on your own unique security requirements,' he was saying now. 'There is an enormous choice on the market, but Brierly Security has the expertise to ensure a wise decision. Shall I begin with the infrared?'

'How about tremblers?' the big man asked. 'Guy I know in Miami swears by them.'

Anna looked at the dog. It was still upset but no one had thought to let it out.

'Honey,' the woman said suddenly, 'why don't you and Mr Crocker talk tremblers. I'll acquaint Miss Lee with the layout.' She rose and stretched.

'We'll thrash out the technical details, Lara.' The big man smiled indulgently.

The woman's expression was sweet but a flash in the powder-blue eyes warned Anna that indulgence was not required. She got up and followed her out. The dog raced across the empty hall, its claws slipping on the polished boards.

'Technical details,' the woman said neutrally. 'What do you think?'

'Well, Mrs Shomacher . . .' Anna began.

'Mr Shomacher's my brother,' the woman cut in. 'I'm Lara Crowther. I know how the British are about Mr and Mrs, but if you don't mind, I'll be just plain Lara.'

'Anna,' Anna replied, thinking that Lara Crowther would have to neglect herself considerably if she wanted to be just plain anything. She was probably in her mid-fifties but nothing had been left to nature and it was only the ropy folds of skin under her chin that gave her away. Her golden tan did not speak of a summer spent in England.

'Why don't you take a look around on your own,' Lara said. 'I'll make us some coffee. Technical details. I know my brother. He's gismo crazy and if I read your colleague right . . .'

'He likes the hardware too,' Anna said, smiling. 'But he does know what he's doing.'

'Oh, I'm sure,' Lara said hastily. 'But you're on commission, right? So the more you sell, the more you make, right? Oh, don't get me wrong, I'm not saying you'd gyp Donald. I had your firm checked out before I rang.' Pale blue eyelids fluttered harmlessly over the baby-blue eyes. Anna grinned.

'I don't mind spending money on security,' Lara went on. 'But I don't want to be up to the eyes in state of the art technology. Do you get me?'

'Alternative security,' Anna said.

'Right.' Lara turned towards the kitchen.

'Do you plan to keep the dog in the house?' Anna asked.

'I didn't mean quite *that* alternative,' Lara said. 'I don't mind some gismos.'

'It's not that. It's just that animals loose in a house can trigger some alarms, and before I start I need to know what normal conditions would be.'

'See what I mean?' Lara showed a mouthful of gleaming white teeth. 'I'll bet Donald never thought of the dog.'

The big yellow Labrador was certainly no guard-dog. It followed Anna from room to room, and every time she stopped to make a note or take a measurement it presented her with a gift: a paperback in the bathroom, a sponge in a bedroom, a slipper in another bedroom. She was forced to accept these objects; otherwise the poor dog would prance in tighter and tighter circles looking more and more anxious. When she took one, however, he would lay back his ears, wag his tail and take on an expression of intense relief.

She arrived in the kitchen with her notebook in her mouth and her arms full of bric-a-brac.

'Put them on the table,' Lara said. 'I'll get rid of them when he isn't looking. I should have warned you. That dog's got his retriever instincts all balled up.'

If proof were needed of Mr Shomacher's interest in technology the kitchen was it. An operating theatre on the flight deck of a supersonic aircraft was how Anna described it later. It was not the sort of room to become the warm hub of family life. Lara Crowther had made coffee in a tall, stainless steel coffee pot and poured it into straight-sided white cups and sat down.

'Well?' she asked.

'Well,' Anna said. 'You're lucky in that the design of this house allows you to be as simple or as fancy as you like. You have three entrances: front, back and from the garage. They all connect with a single space—your entrance hall. So by covering that you can take care of a number of factors in one go. There aren't any major problems with upstairs because there are no abutting roofs or overhanging trees. There's the garage roof, of course, but no windows on that side.'

She stopped. There was no point going further until she had some idea of how the house would be used and what there was to protect.

'Yes?' Lara said, encouragingly.

'It's a question of what you want from security.'

'Sounds like a philosophical question.' Lara sipped her coffee and smiled. 'I know there's no such thing as total security. I've got an apartment in New York.'

'So you know that anyone determined enough can break in anywhere.'

'Right.'

'So, do you just want to discourage the casual opportunist,' Anna asked, 'or do you want to go a bit further?'

'A bit further,' Lara said firmly. 'Donald will want to go all the way. But only as a project, if you see what I mean. He isn't paranoid, he just wants what he thinks is the best . . . the latest.'

Anna regarded Lara over the rim of her cup. The next question, put crudely, would be, which of you signs the cheques? Anna, as a representative of Brierly Security, was not supposed to ask crude questions. Someone, Martin Brierly or Beryl Doyle, would already have made enquiries. They might even have received payment for the advisory service the firm offered: advice Anna did not want to give to the wrong person. She decided on an oblique approach.

'How long have you been over here, Lara?' she asked and smiled in a sociable way.

'Oh, I'm here on and off all the time,' Lara said. 'That's why I'm helping out now. I'm a buyer for a chain of fashion stores. They keep me travelling. Donald has only been here a few months. He's been staying in a company apartment in Kensington. Now it looks as if he'll be here for a couple of years at least, so his wife and family want to join him.'

'So he bought a family house,' Anna said. It was a big neo-Georgian house: five bedrooms, three bathrooms. 'Small children?' she asked.

'Growing and grown,' Lara said. 'Does that make a difference?'

'It can do,' Anna told her. 'There are a lot of considerations. For one thing, the harder you make it for thieves to get in, the harder it is to get out yourself. So if there was a fire . . .'

'Right,' Lara interrupted, grimacing. 'Small kids might make a difference. Like dogs.'

'Yes.'

'Well, I'm sure glad I talked to you,' Lara said. 'There's more to this than just the hardware.'

'Won't Mrs Shomacher want to be consulted?' Anna asked.

'No,' Lara said quickly. 'She'll want to decorate, buy furniture and all that, but she'll want the basic structural decisions to be made already. That's where I come in.' Lara paused. 'She isn't very . . .' She paused again. 'Anyway, I have to make sure that when Donald plumps for a security system it'll be something she can handle on her own.'

'He listens to you?' Anna thought about Donald Shomacher's enthusiasm for the most complicated pamphlets Johnny had shown him.

'Oh, yes.' Lara blinked guilelessly, and Anna believed her.

'Well then . . .' Anna got up. 'I'll have a look outside. I've already drawn a floor plan. But good security starts outside.'

Lara walked with her to the front door just as Donald Shomacher and Johnny came out of the drawing room.

'You going outside?' Mr Shomacher asked. 'Honey, there's the neatest device you ever saw with miniaturized heat-sensitive TV cameras and a console you can put in the hall. I figure if we mount one in front and one out back we can get maybe a hundred and eighty degree sweep . . .'

'That's nice,' Lara interrupted. 'But why don't we let these people get on with their survey before it rains again?'

CHAPTER 2

· · · · · · · · ·

ANNA took her shoes off in the car. Both she and Johnny were wearing sober business suits. Johnny loosened his tie and ran a hand through his crinkly hair. He was driving a nearly new Volvo Estate which gave them plenty of room for all the demonstration equipment.

'Hooray for Hollywood,' he said at length. 'Did you cop the size of that Jacuzzi in the master bedroom?'

They were leaving Barnes behind and crossing the river back towards Kensington.

'What're you going to do?' Anna asked. 'Wire it up with miniature TV cameras and a monitor over the master bed?'

Johnny grinned. 'The bloke's gadget-mad,' he said. 'Could've been a lovely little job if that bleeding sister of his hadn't stepped in and wrecked it. He didn't say the wife was a spam-head.'

'You should've asked.'

'Don't have to, do I?' Johnny said. 'Not with you there to do it for me.'

'Could've saved us a couple of hours.' Anna was irritated. It was not the first time Johnny had ignored the human element in his passion for electronics. A short while ago it had expressed itself in cheap watches, calculators and telephones. Now that Brierly Security, along with most of the security industry, had gone up-market he was in his element. He loved the toys. He loved his new car with its phone, its electric windows, the quadraphonic stereo he had installed himself. He knew everything about bugs, anti-bugging devices, and the whole technology of surveillance. It was only a pity, Anna thought sourly, he didn't have the opportunity to use it. He should have worked for one of the classy City firms. But although Johnny admired class he was not himself classy enough to fit in. Underneath it all he was still the ex–Signals Corps wide boy at heart, a little too ready to cut corners or do a deal. And Brierly Security, for all its expansion, was still a small firm nibbling away at the private end of the market.

Kensington High Street might have become flashier and trashier over the years, but Martin Brierly had not changed, nor had his personal assistant and office manager Beryl Doyle. An atmosphere of small-minded, tightfisted respectability still hung over the office.

Nowadays Anna had a room to herself, furnished with a desk, typewriter and swivel chair. But it was a narrow sliver of a room and the walls were glass from the waist up. It had a glass door too, so Beryl could see if Anna had taken her shoes off under the desk or left her tea mug on the floor. Beryl, of course, had her own office: a sentry box which stood guard over the supply room, the copier and the switchboard. Brierly Security now employed a receptionist who was also switchboard operator, but Beryl had a nose for private calls: an agent only called home in the gravest emergencies. No one liked to have Beryl monitoring the outside lines which she did if she suspected anyone of taking liberties with the company phone bill.

Anna laid her notebook open on the desk. She took paper from the drawer marked 'stationery' and some graph paper from the drawer marked 'plans'. It was time to write up the preliminary report on the Shomacher account. She could have done it with her eyes shut. To her right, behind the glass, she could see Johnny on the phone to the supplier. To her left was Tim's empty cubicle, and beyond that Phil's. Bernie, on the other side of the corridor, was writing up a court report. Sean was next to him, and Anna could see him pretending to work. Soon, when he thought it appropriate, he would get up and tap on Bernie's door, asking for advice or reassurance. Sean was a new addition to the team. He wanted to get on, and he had chosen Bernie to be his mentor. A wise choice, Anna thought.

But Bernie preferred to pick his own protégés: as he told Anna, over a quiet drink one rainy evening, he was getting too old to train a puppy—especially one whose interest in the job was solely commercial. 'He wants to make a career for himself,' Bernie complained. 'I don't think he's interested in anything but that. Promotion was too slow in the police, that's the only reason he's here. More money. Bugger him. I never could abide a climber.'

Anna yawned. The preliminary report would have to be on Mr Brierly's desk next morning. There was a new client to see at eleven, and a follow-up job in the afternoon. The new client was a Turkish shopkeeper who wanted a potential manager vetted, and the old one was another security job. All Anna had to do was check that the equipment was of the type she had recommended and that it worked.

She leafed through her desk diary. Every day, for a month ahead, a scribbled note told her where she should be and who she should be talking to. She yawned again. There were no gaps left open for surprises.

CHAPTER 3

* * * * * * * * * *

IN Holland Park the few remaining leaves were brown and brittle. Anna walked north to Holland Park Avenue wondering how many pick-up cricket games or soccer matches she had seen in the time she had been coming home this way. How many children grizzling because they had to go home for supper, how many pairs of lovers on benches, how many elderly ladies giving the squirrels their tea? They all ran together, like one very long walk. I should change my route, she thought, go the long way round. Anything for a change. But there were far worse ways to come and go than through one of London's parks, especially when it was dry and shafts of evening sun filtered through the trees.

At one time Anna had used the route for a run. But that wasn't possible any more. She could hardly think of a recent occasion when she had not been forced to turn up for work in respectable clothes and shoes. She couldn't arrive sweating and with her hair in a tangle. Clients expected tailored suits and shiny briefcases, and Beryl saw to it that clients got what they expected.

A couple of years ago a memo, initialled by Martin Brierly himself, had been circulated in the office. It detailed a Proper Dress Code and caused a lot of crude humour about cross dressing. But the code was adhered to, and overnight Brierly Security changed from quietly informal to rigidly smart. 'Might as well still be in bloody uniform,' Bernie grumbled, fingering his chafed neck. 'This is going to look right inconspicuous on obbo in Kilburn.'

That was in the early days. It had been a long time, Anna thought, since there had been anything as different as an observation in Kilburn. Walking through the park that evening in September she realised that her job had been reduced to that of a saleswoman. She represented, not so much a private detective agency, as the manufacturers of security equipment. She could be selling double-glazing or cosmetics for all the excitement she got out of the job now, or for all the judgement she put into it.

'A rep, a manky, boring rep,' she muttered to herself as she watched her shiny tan shoes emerge and disappear from under the hem of her linen skirt. 'That's what I am.'

She kicked a stone and sent an overweight pigeon scuttling into the bushes. The pigeon was too well fed and too accustomed to the idiocies of humans to take off and fly.

Anna looked at it glumly. 'You and me, kid,' she said, and walked on.

BANTAM DOUBLEDAY DELL
PRESENTS THE
WINNERS CLASSIC SWEEPSTAKES

Dear Bantam Doubleday Dell Reader,

We'd like to say "Thanks" for choosing our books. So we're giving you a chance to enter our Winners Classic Sweepstakes, where you can win a Grand Prize of $25,000.00, or one of over 1,000 other sensational prizes! All prizes are guaranteed to be awarded. Return the Official Entry Form at once! And when you're ready for another great reading experience, we hope you'll keep Bantam Doubleday Dell books at the top of your reading list!

OFFICIAL ENTRY FORM

Yes! Enter me in the Winners Classic Sweepstakes and guarantee my eligibility to be awarded any prize, including the $25,000.00 Grand Prize. Notify me at once if I am declared a winner.

NAME _____

ADDRESS _____ APT. # ____

CITY _____

STATE _____ ZIP _____

REGISTRATION NUMBER | 01995A |

Please mail to: AC-SBA
BANTAM DOUBLEDAY DELL DIRECT, INC.
WINNERS CLASSIC SWEEPSTAKES
PO Box 985, Hicksville, NY 11802-0985

OFFICIAL PRIZE LIST

GRAND PRIZE: *$25,000.00 CASH!*

FIRST PRIZE: FISHER HOME ENTERTAINMENT CENTER

Including complete integrated audio/video system with 130-watt amplifier, AM/FM stereo tuner, dual cassette deck, CD player, Surround Sound speakers and universal remote control unit.

SECOND PRIZE: TOSHIBA VCR *5 winners!*

Featuring full-function, high-quality 4-Head performance, with 8-event/365-day timer, wireless remote control, and more.

THIRD PRIZE: CONCORD 35MM CAMERA OUTFIT *35 winners!*

Featuring focus-free precision lens, built-in automatic film loading, advance and rewind.

FOURTH PRIZE: BOOK LIGHT *1,000 winners!*

A model of convenience, with a flexible neck that bends in any direction, and a steady clip that holds sure on any surface.

OFFICIAL RULES AND REGULATIONS